Revolt of the R…

Book 5 in the Sword of Cartimandua series

By

Griff Hosker

Published by Sword Books Ltd 2014

A CIP catalogue record for this title is available from the British Library.

Chapter 1

Lulach looked at the Roman fort of Coriosopitum. It was over five years since he had failed to capture and destroy this symbol of Roman power in the north of Britannia. It still rankled with him that he and his warband had been defeated south of Morbium and that defeat had begun at Coriosopitum where the garrison foiled his attempts to take and destroy it. In the past five years he, and his father King Calgathus, had built up his armies to their former strength attacking and harrying the Romans wherever possible. Lulach had urged his father to allow him to redeem himself for his former failure and rid the north of the blight that was Coriosopitum.

His men were hidden in the many wooded areas around the fort and the settlement of Corio. They had spent the night moving secretly into position. He would not assault the fort as he had attempted previously; he had a more cunning plan. He and his elite force were hidden in the settlement of Corio. During the night they had silently entered the houses and huts and murdered all the inhabitants. A gory and grisly task, especially when it came to killing children but he had reminded those few of his men who had qualms about such action that these people were Roman lovers and, as such, deserved the same treatment as Romans. The sentries on the walls had detected and heard nothing of the slaughter in the civilian settlement.

As dawn approached the raiders could hear the sounds of the fort coming to life: the guards were changing and the garrison preparing for another day on the frontier. Having watched for days they knew the familiar and well practised routine. Once the guards were changed the Porta Decumana would be opened and sentries stationed outside the walls to inspect the visitors who wished to enter or pass through the fort. Lulach had identified several regular visitors taking food and other goods to clients in the fort. Once the Porta Decumana had been secured the Porta

Praetorium would be opened and a larger number of sentries would march to their sentry points.

The gates nearest the settlement swung slowly and ponderously open, Lulach and five of his men wandered haphazardly towards the gate; their hoods and cowls protecting their identity and disguising their short saxes. The sentries had become complacent for most of them were a new auxiliary cohort brought from the south. They saw what they wanted to see; the same villagers with the same goods for they saw the northern tribes as being identical, they were all barbarians. Lulach and his men held their goods in front of them and, when the sentries inspected them, they were stabbed quickly and died without a sound. Time was of the essence and the six warriors raced for the open gate. Behind them the horde emerged from the settlement and raced along the road. The guards on the tower shouted the alarm when they saw the mass of men descending upon the gate but, before they could be closed the luckless sentries were savagely and ruthlessly slaughtered. The warband raced through the gates and the auxiliaries, just awakening to a new day, barely had time to register that there was an attack.

Lulach and his men did not pause in their stride as they raced towards the Porta Praetorium. Barely dressed and half asleep auxiliaries tried to stop the horde of ferocious warriors but the speed of the assault took them by surprise. Outside the unopened main gate the rest of the warband shot the sentries from the towers and by the time the gates had been opened the battle was already decided. In the open the cohort might have fought off a warband; on the walls of the fort, using their artillery they might have withstood the onslaught but fighting in tiny groups they were overwhelmed and slaughtered. The First Spear and his century held out the longest, fighting shield to shield around the Praetorium but Lulach remembered the devastation by the bolt throwers and the Romans suffered the final irony of being destroyed by their own weapons as the Caledonii climbed the towers and turned the hated ballistae on to the last stand of the auxiliaries.

"Strip the bodies of all that we can use and then burn this fort!"

Warriors eagerly seized the swords and javelins. Others stripped the bodies of the leather armour and daggers. Some took the shields but most left them where they were. Within the hour the fort was a burning pyre. The wooden fort on the eastern end of the Roman defences was no more and the only bulwark against the barbarian invasion was Luguvalium on the west coast.

"Now brothers, we will not make the same mistakes. When we last came here we left a trail of brave warriors in our wake. This time I want to leave Roman bones to rot. Go with your chiefs, they know where they are to raid. We return with slaves and plunder. Kill every Roman and burn every building."

The cheer from his warriors was an affirmation of the popularity of his actions. He and his father had spent a long months in the winter deciding upon this strategy. If they made the mistake of one warband then the Governor would send out forces from Eboracum and they knew that they could not defeat the Roman behemoth in open battle. By using smaller bands they could still defeat the patrols they met and flee before being caught. Their only fear was the cavalry, Marcus' Horse and Lulach knew that it was the weak part of the strategy. They had yet to defeat these thousand horsemen who could move swiftly and bring deadly retribution on raiders. He just hoped that they would not run into them.

Five years had passed since the most northerly fortress in the Roman Empire, Inchtuthil, had been abandoned and since that time northern Britannia had seen a series of reverses and misfortunes. The line of forts between Luguvalium and Coriosopitum now represented the uneasy northern frontier of the Roman world. Five years in which the relentless Caledonii had ravaged and destroyed the Roman presence north of the Tinea. Many forts and their garrisons had been destroyed whilst others had been withdrawn further south where rebellion was fermenting.

Prefect Julius Demetrius now showed the signs of his time in Britannia and, as he looked northwards, he couldn't help but think of what they had held and what they had lost. The charred line of forts was just a reminder that the frontier had receded. A little like his own receding hairline which made him look much older than his thirty eight years and appeared to be receding at the same rate as the frontier. He had lost many friends, family and brother officers since he had first joined Marcus' Horse almost twenty years previously. As he removed his helmet to let the cooler air refresh him, he peered along the bleak moor land rising away to the west. He had crossed this land many times; he had fought and bled in this land many times but he had always thought that one day it would be safe. It would be a place where the people who farmed the savage uplands would be able to do so without worrying about enemies coming on slave raids. The land was more dangerous now than at any time since the Brigante revolt of twenty five years ago. He had not even been in Britannia then but Gaius, the old Decurion Princeps, had told him of those dangerous times when the only law was the cavalry of the Pannonian Ala.

"Sir?" He turned to see the new Decurion Lentius Gaius Servius. He was one of the many new, unfamiliar faces who had replaced some of the older officers who had served with him for so many years. He found it hard not to call him Gaius, for he commanded Gaius' old Second Turma.

"Yes Decurion? What is it?"

The Decurion had come from one of the southern tribes and he had only known Roman rule and Roman peace. In the sixth months he had been in the north he had found it hard to adjust to the frontier way of life. "Why doesn't the Governor or the Legate just bring the legions up from the south and stop these raids once and for all? We aren't doing much good are we sir? We are like the man trying to plug leaks in an old barrel, as soon as one is plugged another erupts."

Julius remembered when he had first arrived and been full of aggression. "The Legions are guarding those parts of the land which we have conquered, ensuring that the Roman businesses in that part of Britannia prosper. Here we have yet to conquer and believe me, Lentius, if we were not here then the Caledonii would raid all the way to Deva and Eboracum and the barrel would not just have leaks, it would burst."

"Sorry sir. I didn't mean any offence."

"None taken. I, too, long for the day when we march north with legions and auxiliaries side by side and retake the land we once won with so much blood but that may not be for some time."

"Is that why we are split into three groups and patrol so far apart?"

"Yes Decurion it makes the most of what we have got. Decurion Princeps Cilo patrols the south and west whilst Decurion Lucullus covers the east and the north. Four turmae can cover more ground than the whole ala. It keeps our presence over a wider area of this vast and empty land." He glanced around to make sure that the turmae, men and horses, were rested and then signalled for them to follow. "Keep a keen eye out for those raiders. I know they may have returned north but something tells me they are still close by and watch out for ambushes; we have to travel close to the trees and they have learned that horses do not cope with the narrow trails in these dense woods."

They dropped down from the windswept ridge top and followed a small trail through the pine trees. Someone had cut some down at some point and in places they almost found space to breathe. This was where Julius missed Gaelwyn, for the Brigante scout would have been able to smell the Caledonii. Julius and his men would have to make do with their eyes and their mounts that would whinny if they were afraid of something or smelled something alien.

Down in the valley the raiders watched the horsemen disappear into the forest. Their leader, a huge grey haired giant called Modius, had once been a member of the ala until he had deserted. His knowledge of the ala and the way they operated had saved his little band of robbers and brigands on more than one occasion. They had slipped over from the west a month earlier and had spent their time quite profitably robbing caravans of merchants moving small, but valuable cargoes like jet and copper. Some had even had gold taken, ironically, from the rivers close to Modius' camp and following Modius' route to Eboracum. He was a cunning leader and he knew when he ought to cut his losses. Since the ala had sent their patrols out for him he had found the pickings harder to come by. Turmae escorted the larger caravans and kept the main routes open. Modius knew the Prefect; he had served with his brother and, later, been one of the warband which killed him. As much as he would have like to do the same to his little brother he could not take on two turmae with the bandits he controlled. Now he was an independent as he styled himself, a robber baron who answered to no-one but took advantage of the unrest and the raids from the warlike tribes further north.

"Right. They are out of sight. Single file back along this track. I want no noise and I want the last man to clear the trail. Now let's move."

There was no loyalty amongst the band but Modius was an effective leader. As long as he brought them success and cowed them with his strength of arms, they would follow him. They were not warriors as Modius had once led, but they served his purpose. When they were sure that they had lost the patrol Modius headed them up the rocky gully which would eventually take them to the high waterfall. The route was hard for his men but he knew that they would fare much better than the horses of the ala.

Seonag was the wise woman of the village. Nestled in a little dell close to the sea moors the prosperous little village made a good living mining the much sought after jet. Prized by both royalty and mystics its value exceeded that of gold. In the last three years they had sold much to traders from the area around the holy mountain of Wyddfa. Seonag had her own theory about this but she kept her counsel for she was the last of the priestesses in this part of the world. In her heart she knew her sisters were once again rising to take back the power they had once possessed. Despite being a widow, her husband having died young in Venutius' first rising, she was not poor for her medicines and wise words were much sought after by the people of the village and nearby valleys.

Despite her age she was the one who sensed when the band of Caledonii raiders was close by. She was afraid neither of them nor of death. She had outlived all those with whom she grew up and she knew she still had a power over men. She went to her secret place and took out her magic amulet made of intricately carved pieces of jet skilfully shaped into ravens and crows. She walked out into the daylight prepared to meet whoever came.

Manus, as his name suggested, was a big warrior; he was one of the biggest warriors in Caledonia. At his birth his prodigious size had given him his name as soon as he emerged screaming into the world. He had loyally served Lulach for many years as a bodyguard and had earned the right to choose his own warband. Once they had crossed the Dunum he had made straight for this village despite its proximity to Cataractonium. He was gambling that the dreaded ala would be elsewhere but he had visited the place to buy jet many years earlier and he knew of high and steep paths which would enable him to escape pursuit should they stumble upon him.

He and his men rose like wraiths from the tree line. The village was totally surrounded and the fifteen or so men unarmed. They were slaughtered where they stood. "Round up the women and the children kill the old. You eight go and gather the jet it will be in that hut over there then burn the houses and huts."

Just then he noticed Seonag who just stood like a rock, her old piercing eyes taking in the murder and mayhem around her. One of his men was walking up to her, his sax already ready drawn.
"Hold!"
"But you said to kill the old and this one is older than the rocks, and as ugly."
Manus backhanded the shocked warrior to the ground. "You are a fool Lugh! Do you not see she is a holy woman! Would you bring the curse of the Mother on to us? I am sorry mother we mean you no harm."
"I know. Take not all of the jet for the sisters will need some."
Nodding he shouted to his men. "Bring the jet to me."
When the slaves were tethered and the jet packed on to the two small horses used in the village Manus handed over a large quantity of jet. "Thank you. The Mother will watch over you."
The warband headed north at a steady lope heading for the river crossing. Manus was already thinking about the three villages he had skirted whilst heading south. He had lost no men so far and he could gather more plunder there.

Decurion Livius Lucullus had grown up since he had languished in a cell awaiting the whim of an Emperor. Having faced death at close hand he was a far more mature leader than his age would suggest. He had spent much time with Tribune Marcus Aurelius Maximunius and picked up not only wisdom but intimate knowledge of how the ala could and should be used in Britannia. As a native of the island and a relative of the last king, Cunobelinus, he was passionate about protecting its people. His turmae trusted his judgement implicitly. His scout had reported the smoke as they were descending from the eastern moors heading back to Cataractonium. He sensed that his men were ready to return to barracks and a little comfort after a week in the saddle but he knew that it was his duty to find out what had caused the pall of black smoke on the horizon. He wondered if the

Prefect and the Decurion Princeps felt the same. He also knew he would have to investigate.

They rode warily into the still burning village. They saw some bodies near the road and an old woman laying others into a hole in the ground. “Let us help you mother.”

“Thank you. I am too old for this.”

“When did they leave?”

“They came just after dawn and they did not stay long. We were a small village and it did not take them long.”

“Caledonii?” She nodded, there was little point denying it although she did not want to help the Romans if she could avoid it. “Which way did they go?” She waved a hand in the vague direction of north. “Thank you. Would you like my men to escort you to the fort?”

“Thank you for your offer but I have a journey to make and it will be my last.” The young Decurion thought that this was a journey to die and he nodded sadly but Seonag had no intention of relinquishing her hold on life until she had delivered her precious cargo to the sisters who had re-invested Mona. Her journey was not one of death but of rebirth. She would rejoin the community on Mona. Her life was far from over.

“May the gods watch over you.”

“She will.”

His men had finished burying the bodies and they awaited his orders. Decurion Cassius chewed idly on a liquorice root he had taken from his bag. “Will they head for Morbium do you think?”

“Possibly but there is a garrison there.”

“There was a garrison there.”

“True but I think we will follow their trail for a while. If Morbium is their destination then the Prefect will intercept them, for that is his patrol area no we will follow them for I feel they will head for the Dunum and the narrow place.”

“The water there can be deep.”

"I know but in high summer it is often low, especially at low tide and there are bluffs on the other side to afford protection. It is but two extra days in the saddle. I think it is worth it."

Cassius sniffed. "Just means the turmae of the Decurion Princeps will have first choice of food and we will be left with scraps. They will get back to the fort before we do."

Livius laughed. "Always thinking of your stomach."

"If I don't then who will?"

As the troopers rode away the old woman waited in the village. When she saw that they were out of sight she gathered her possessions together. She was leaving the settlement and leaving forever. Before she left she needed to make sure she had enough money to support her on her journey west. She went to the headman's hut and moved away the dead ashes from the fire; taking a mattock she scraped away until she struck wood. The villager's money and valuables had been hidden there in case of such a raid. She felt neither guilt nor remorse in taking the wealth of the village for the inhabitants were either dead or enslaved and the money would do them no good. She would be able to pay for herself to be transported on a merchant's wagon leaving Eboracum for Deva and once there it was but a short journey to Mona and her sisters.

Decurion Princeps Cilo was a very contented leader. As a trooper he had incurred the wrath of a martinet Decurion and almost been dismissed from the ala. If it were not for the weapon's trainer, Decurion Macro, then he would have had to do something else other than this job that he loved. He, like the whole ala, loved Decurion Macro for both his skill as a warrior and his genial good humour; he was great fun to be around. Decurion Macro did not resent the fact that one of his protégés had been promoted he preferred to be weapons trainer and to be given all the dangerous jobs. His turma were all as madcap as he was and were both feared and respected by the rest of the ala.

Macro also had a son to think about and that was more than enough responsibility for him.

The Decurion Princeps had brought his quartet of turmae further north than he would normally because he had heard of bandits and raiders operating west of Cataractonium. The burnt out villages and dead Brigante were a clear trail to follow. Decurion Macro had been more than happy to take his turma north west to find the trail and might also bring him along the line of the Prefect's patrol. The only nagging doubt in his mind was that two thirds of the ala were being dragged north west leaving only Livius and his four turmae to protect the rest. Cilo reminded himself that Livius was well over to the east. The central vale was devoid of cavalry. He shook his head, angry with the Imperial penny pinchers who begrudged paying for more troops for Britannia. Perhaps the new Emperor, Nerva, might be different but the Decurion Princeps had heard that the new Emperor was having difficulties in Rome so it was likely they would have to make do with what they had.

The trooper from Macro's turma came galloping up.

"Decurion's compliments sir and we have found the trail of the bandits. They are about five miles across the moors."

"Right column of twos." Perhaps their luck was about to change and they were actually going to catch these elusive bandits. But at the back of Cilo's mind was the thought that they may be a Caledonii warband trying to draw the ala away.

"Modius!" Without bothering to speak the giant glared around.

"Roman cavalry, to the south."

"Did they see you?" The downward glance told the leader all he needed to know. "Shit!" He had one patrol to the east and now there was another one to the south. "How far away?"

"Three or four miles."

"Damn!" That meant they could be with him in less than thirty minutes. "Ditch everything that is too heavy and double time. We have cavalry after us. If we can make the waterfall we stand a chance. If not then we die. Anyone left behind…." The unspoken reality was that they would die.

There was no loyalty in this band. For a big man who was aging, Modius could move swiftly. He had no need to discard anything as the only plunder he carried was the gold he had taken. The ten men who formed his bodyguard had also done the same. Soon the eleven men were pulling away from their weaker comrades. As the path began to climb towards the falls the gap became even greater. Half way up Modius paused behind a straggly thin elder to survey the horizon. He could see the cavalry now; it was a turma and even from that distance he recognised the enormous figure of Decurion Macro. He remembered him from his days in the ala. He was surprised that the big man was still alive; he had always been volunteering and Modius had convinced himself that he would be dead by now. The turma was within four hundred paces of the rearmost men and, further away Modius could see the rest of the ala. Perhaps the tail enders would hold up the pursuit but he determined to make the most of the gap. "Run you whoresons! Run!"

Decurion Princeps Cilo could just see figures climbing the precipitous path adjoining the waterfall. If they managed to cross it then they would gain a lead. "Trooper. Ride north east. Find the Prefect tell him we think we are on the trail of bandits. He will know what to do." As the trooper galloped off Cilo felt confident that they could catch and destroy most of the raiders but it irked him that some might get away.

A small party of the bandits had decided that they were too exhausted to climb the steep rocky path, in addition to which these fifty had been loath to leave their hard earned loot behind. The large lump of a warrior who fancied himself leader should anything happen to Modius took charge of the rabble who remained. "There's only twenty or so we can have these." They turned and faced the approaching cavalry with weapons at the ready. They had an eclectic mixture of weapons from spears and axes to swords and bows.

Macro had already ascertained what they were going to do; it is what he would have done. He would have to dismount at the bottom of the falls and pursue on foot. He glanced over his shoulder and, in the distance; he could see the red plumes of his comrades. That decided him he would destroy these and then pursue the rest up the path. “Thin them out with arrows but be quick we want to catch the others.”

His men grinned; this was why they loved their leader, it was either death or glory with Macro, there was no halfway. Their arrows did indeed thin them out and when they hit them with their horses and swords the survivors threw their weapons away and prostrated themselves on the ground. “You four guard them until the Decurion Princeps arrives. The rest of you follow me on foot. When the others have taken over the guarding of the prisoners you four take the horses around the bluff and meet us at the top of the waterfall.”

The shell shocked survivors huddled in the midst of their slaughtered comrades. Any thought of escape had ended with the first flurry of arrows. Macro glanced up. The bandits were spread out in a long line negotiating the treacherous and slippery path which wound up the steep sides. The pursuers had barely gone twenty paces when they saw how treacherous it was as a bandit fell screaming to a bone crushing death amongst the rocks at the bottom of the falls which waited like some huge predator with its sharp and jagged teeth bared.

Modius had reached the top of the falls. One of his men started to cross. “No not here they will find our trail too easily. It will take them some time to get to us. We go upstream and then cross.”

The first few bandits encountered by Macro proved to be no problem. They did not know he was behind and he was able to cut them down as they struggled to escape. The screams of the dying rose above the stormy thunder of the falls and three of them turned to face the foe who stalked them up this rocky ladder of death. They had spears and the advantage of height. With any other turma it might have gone ill for the leader but Macro's men raced to fight, perilously close to the edge of the falls, to give support to their enigmatic Decurion. Climbing the falls with three men together slowed up their pursuit but ensured that all that they caught died.

The situation was clear to the highly experienced Decurion Princeps Cilo as he rode up to the bundle of bandits sitting miserably at the foot of the falls. Macro's chosen man told him what Macro had asked. "Good plan."He turned to his own chosen man. "We will join Decurion Macro on the other side. You escort these vermin back to Cataractonium." He dismounted and walked up to the sullen looking prisoners. "Where are you from?" There was a silence more from bravado than any conviction that they would not tell. None of them wanted to be the first to betray their comrades. Nodding Cilo pointed to the large ugly warrior, the erstwhile leader, who looked more sullen than the rest. "You where are you from and who is your leader? Are you Caledonii? Is your leader Lulach?" The man shrugged and gave a half grin to his comrades. "That is your choice is it? Silence?" The man, still grinning, nodded. With almost no effort Cilo sliced his spatha backhand and removed the man's head, still grinning. After a few moments the body crashed to the ground and rolled into the river whilst the unseeing eyes stared at the clouds.

Cilo said to two of his men. "Pick him up." They both grabbed the nearest man whose eyes rolled pleading into his head.

"No please, please!" He screamed.

"Same questions; where are you from, and who is your leader?"

The terrified man looked at his comrades, all of whom looked at the ground. "We came from the west, the land of the lakes and our leader is Modius."

Suddenly Decurion Princeps Cilo stopped and stared as did the older members of the turmae. "This Modius. Did he fight with the Romans?" Having given some information the man found it easy to give more and he nodded, pleased to be alive still. "Well, the Prefect will be interested. Rest your horses and then escort these back."

The last thirty warriors had no energy left when they reached the top of the falls and they could see no sign of their leader who appeared to have been swallowed up by the river. Below them they could see the fifteen troopers struggling up the side and a few of them decided to brave the stones which made a crude, if dangerous path across the shallow bed of the falls. The rest decided to see if they could despatch the fifteen and then continue more safely. It was an uneven contest. The bandits had only fought farmers and merchants; they were facing the hardened elite troopers of Marcus' Horse.

Macro, although out of breath was keen to follow the ones who had half waded, half run across the river. The small rearguard died to a man. Before he pursued the rest Macro glanced down the path and saw Cilo leading the rest of the turmae around the bluff. As he had expected, Macro would be leading the pursuit with his fourteen troopers. "Well lads, until they bring our horses up we are going to have to run. Rip up some of the bandits clothes and we will leave a trail for them to follow." Already the ones across the river were making good their flight and opening up a lead. Unencumbered as they were by arms and armour they thought to make good their escape.

Further up the river Modius watched as the auxiliaries crossed the river in pursuit of the last of his men. "Looks like we made a good decision. We'll stay this side of the river a bit longer and then head south towards Brocauum. Another few days and we'll be home and safe.

The end of the foot race was inevitable; Macro and his troopers were far fitter than the bandits they were chasing. Inexorably they caught them up one by one and they were despatched one by one. Macro could afford no mercy for he only had fourteen men. Once he could see there were only four remaining he shouted over his shoulder, “We take these prisoners. Find out where they are from and who their leader is.”

The last four accepted the inevitable when they heard the shout to stop. At first they had thought they would escape but as they had heard their fellows being killed they knew it was only a matter of time. As they squatted on the ground trying to catch their breath all of them wondered what had happened to their leader.

“Good run lads. If you had been auxiliaries you might have outrun us. Now I’ll give you a while to get your breath but then I want two questions answering. Which of you is the leader and where is your home?”

The looks on their faces and the blank looks they gave each other told Macro that none of these was the leader. Resentful of the fact that they had been abandoned to slow down the pursuit, they all happily volunteered the information requested. “We come from the land of the lakes and none of us is the leader, he is Modius who fought with the horse warriors.”

“So the treacherous bastard is still alive. Right if you can talk you can walk. Let’s get back to our horses.”

Decurion Princeps Cilo was waiting with their mounts when they arrived back at the falls. They were both pleased that their information matched but both surprised at the leader. “Last I knew he was still with Aed.”

“Aye and I thought he died in that last battle.”

“No-one found his body did they and the Prefect had a good look.”

“I didn’t see him. He wasn’t with the ones we killed or captured, which means he went along the river. Do we follow?”

“As much as I would love to catch and crucify that treacherous snake I don’t think we can leave the east of the province unprotected. There is no one else left. Livius only has four turmae.”

“I could go on my own.”

Cilo grinned, "Still volunteering eh? Maybe that isn't a bad idea. What we will do is ride up both sides of the river until we find where they crossed and then I will return to Cataractonium and you can pursue. How does that sound?"

"It sounds good to me."

They travelled four miles before they found the place where they had crossed. "He's still as crafty and cunning as ever."

"Aye Macro and heading south."

Just then a trooper rode up. "Prefect sir."

Julius was tired and he dismounted to greet his friends. "Are these all of the bandits then?"

"No sir we sent twenty or so back to Cataractonium. Macro here, with your permission, is going after the rest. Their leader and a small band he has with him."

"How many are there?"

"We don't know sir. We chased them hard and the survivors don't know who escaped with Modius."

"Modius?" Julius face became filled with anger and hate. The younger troopers had never seen the mild mannered Prefect react in such a way before.

"Yes sir, the same. The old treacherous snake is till alive. Two of the prisoners corroborated the story; they called him Modius who rode with the Roman cavalry."

"I knew the bastard wasn't dead! How many men did you say he had with him?"

"Don't know sir. Looking at the prints it could be anything from ten to twenty."

"Heading back into the land of the lakes. Back to the same place he hid before. Right let's follow him then."

Decurion Princeps Cilo was shocked. "You can't do that sir we would leave most of our patrol area unprotected. We have the only ala in this part of the world and we cannot afford to chase a few men."

Even Macro, who knew Julius better than any, was shocked by his reaction. "I do not care! That man betrayed the ala and my father and killed my brother not to mention all the other innocent deaths he caused."

"I know sir. I was there. But the patrol area… the Caledonii is always raiding. Let Macro go. You know he will catch him."

Julius' face softened. "I know he probably will but I want certainties. Morbium can hold up any incursions from the north. Decurion Princeps Cilo, take Decurion Galeo and your two turmae. Escort the prisoners to Morbium and station yourselves there, we will rejoin you when we have captured this renegade."

Macro shrugged at his friend as much as to say, 'that is all you are going to get' and indeed the Decurion Princeps had resigned himself to the fact that he would have to patrol Brigantia with six turmae not twelve. "Very well sir. I just hope the Caledonii don't raid."

Chapter 2

"Do you miss the ala now Gaius? Do you miss the danger of riding to war and commanding men?"

"Macro is forever asking me that and, in truth, no. The time I spend with Ailis and the boys is precious to me. I love watching them grow up. "

"Are you not bored?"

"Well Marcus let me ask you, are you not bored? "

"No I asked you because I find more to do each day; whether that is talking to Annius about the crops or the house or just watching the land change. I wondered if it was just me or all old soldiers."

Gaelwyn snorted. "You two are like a pair of old women. We are here to hunt and not gossip."

"And hunt we shall Gaelwyn. We are suitably apologetic." Marcus winked at Gaius who smiled. Their weekly hunts were one of the highlights of the week for the two ex-soldiers and, despite his moaning, Gaelwyn looked forward to them. They could talk of the old days and the old ways and know that when they returned home Ailis would have cooked some spectacular meal for Ailis also enjoyed the times when the four of them could sit around the table, eat, drink, laugh and enjoy life. Today they were hunting wild boar, which probably explained Gaelwyn's grumpiness for the last time they had failed to bring home a kill and he had blamed their chatter rather than his poor aim.

"Now be quiet. I found their tracks the other day. They have settled in the thick wood five miles from here. "

"I thought we were almost there. We have already tramped at least five miles from the villa."

"Getting soft you are. It'll do you good. I brought you five miles because I want to be downwind of them. I don't want to spook them. Now come on as you soldiers would say,' *double time.*'"

When Gaelwyn held up his hand they both became serious; he had spotted sign. He waved Gaius to the left and Marcus to the right. In their left hands they held three javelins but in their right they held the mighty boar spear with the metal bar just below the head to stop the boar eating its way down the shaft. Gaelwyn had had the blacksmith work for days until he was satisfied with the mighty spears. The wicked looking heads were half as long as a man's arm and honed sharp enough to shave with. The undergrowth through which they were moving was thick with bramble and wild raspberry bushes, which even Gaius knew were attractive to the boar. They also made it very hard to see them and when you did finally spy one the hunter normally had moments to throw his spear.

Gaelwyn's hand went up again and they stopped. In the silence of the wild they could hear snuffling ahead. It could mean only one thing, wild boar. They all crouched and Marcus and Gaius watched as Gaelwyn moved gently forwards checking the ground for anything which would give them away. Although none of them heard a sound, the boar did and it leapt towards Gaelwyn. The old Brigante bravely stood his ground and hurled his spear. It caught the boar in the throat but it was not a killing blow and it threw itself at the old scout. Marcus threw his spear and it hit the boar in the side. He threw with such force that it caused the wild pig to falter giving Gaelwyn time to roll clear. His respite was only momentary for the boar wheeled around, its savage snout and sharp tusks searching for Gaelwyn's throat. Even as the two men were preparing javelins to throw, Gaius had stood his ground and, as the boar passed him intent on getting to Gaelwyn, Gaius stabbed down though its eye and into its brain. It fell in a heaving heap of blood and fur, a hand span from Gaelwyn.

The old man looked up at Gaius. "Good shot Gaius." He put one finger on his right nostril and shot a plume of mucus at the ground. "I taught you well!"

"Lucky for you! You old fraud. He nearly gutted you then."

Shrugging Gaelwyn added, "He didn't. The Allfather has a different end for me."

They quickly cut down a sapling and thrust it through the boar's snout and out of its anus. They managed, with some difficulty, to lift it onto their shoulders. "I hope that Ailis isn't expecting us soon. It will take us longer to get home than it took to get here for this is a mighty beast."

"Stop moaning old man. The food will taste all the better after a healthy walk and besides think of the taste of this fine beast when we come to eat him."

"Lead on then you old Brigante and try to find a shorter route or we will still be eating our food at breakfast time."

Ailis loved it when the three young boys played amongst themselves and she could just watch then whilst she and the cook prepared the evening meal. The two years that Gaius had been home were the happiest of her life. Her whole world was perfection. Her two sons were healthy and no trouble at all while Macro's son, Decius was even more pleasant. He was a lovely little boy who was as much her child as her own two. She loved the hunting days when the three men in her life would return full of tales of heroic hunting and full of praise for her food and they would sit until the early hours drinking mead and wine and, in typical old man's style, making the world a much better place. For her part she was happy to bring their drinks and just listen to them smiling at their banter and their humour. When she wanted the company of women she would go to her kitchen and talk with the slaves who helped her prepare the food. She had been a slave once and went out of her way to make life as pleasant for them as possible. For their part they adored both her and the children. To Ailis, after so many years in captivity, it was like being in heaven already. Life was good.

Outside the warband had surrounded the stockaded settlement. The warband leader remembered leaving a dead brother here the last time they had raided, years earlier, and he was taking no chances this time. There would be guards and sentries, that he knew, but because it was protected there were things inside worth stealing, animals, women, treasure. He had brought fifty men with him and he had watched as the three men had left before dawn. They waited until just past noon when he saw that the men who were guarding the villa had been fed. As two of them relieved themselves and two others walked off into the woods he dropped his arm as the signal. The two men entering the woods were grabbed and stabbed by four warriors. The two sentries relieving themselves were struck by arrows as were the two also in plain sight. The rest of the warband just raced through the open gate, blades drawn and ready to kill any man that they saw.

The first that Ailis knew of the raid was when one of the farm's guards, standing at the door, watching the boys play, fell through the opening, an arrow through his neck. She was so shocked that she did not even begin to react, she couldn't understand what was happening in her peaceful part of the province of Britannia ;there had been peace for so many years that this was impossible, it was a nightmare from which she would soon awake. Suddenly she heard the screams of men dying and the clash of sword on sword. She yelled at the cook, "Get Decius!"

The two of them grabbed the three boys and ran for the doorway. The sight which greeted them was their worst nightmare and worse than anything Ailis might have dreamed; a Caledonii warband had managed to get close to the perimeter and attacked without warning. The guards already lay dying and the farm workers were busy trying to defend themselves with whatever came to hand, farm tools, sticks, even leather belts were used. Ailis and the cook ran in the opposite direction from the fighting. In Ailis' mind she was just hoping that Gaius and Marcus would return, and return soon. It was later that she became glad that her wish had not come true. As they turned the corner, towards the rear gate, Ailis' hopes began to rise; once through the gate there were many places they could hide until the terror was gone.

Suddenly ten bearded and heavily armed warriors stepped in front of them. The children and their protectors were all unceremoniously grabbed and in a few moments their hands were tied and halters tightened around their necks. The cook was sobbing uncontrollably but miraculously the boys were too shocked to react and Ailis was determined to keep as calm as possible to avoid upsetting her children.

The warband quickly set fire to the homestead and then, with captives tied together, and the captured animals herded, began to trot back north up the Roman road towards Morbium. The leaders sat astride Gaius' and Gaelwyn's precious horses carrying their spare weapons. It had been a good haul, a better haul than they had hoped. Lulach would be pleased and they only had a few miles to go to get to Morbium where others held the bridge for them to cross in safety. It was as they were struggling up the road that Ailis realised that the warband was not hurrying but making their way purposefully up the Roman road to the Roman fort. If they were bold enough to come down the road and travel back so leisurely then they had no fear of the Romans, Morbium had been captured.

It was Gaelwyn who knew something was amiss when he saw the glow in the night sky. The journey back had indeed taken longer than they would have hoped and it was very dark with a heavy overcast sky when they finally arrived at the track which led the two miles to the settlement.

"There is a fire and it is at the farm." The three men dropped their boar and ran up the lane. What greeted them was an even bigger shock than it had been for Ailis. They could see, even as they approached, the bodies littered around the perimeter lit by the light from the raging inferno which had engulfed the main building..

"Ailis!" Gaius' piteous cry erupted from his throat as though ripped by some unseen hand. The three of them ran to each body to see who it was and if they were alive. By the time they had searched the whole complex the fire had abated somewhat and Gaelwyn made his assessment. “It is only the men who are dead, no boys and no women.” He looked at Gaius, “Unless we find bodies in the main house.”

Marcus shook his head. “No Gaelwyn, we saw this in the north west. It is a captive raid. The Caledonii have come for slaves.”

Gaelwyn nodded his agreement. “I have found Caledonii weapons. But I cannot understand why they were not stopped at the fort, unless they headed south.”

“Let us go to my farm”, said Marcus. “It may tell us more.” As they jogged their way the five miles to his farm Marcus just worried that his farm manager and all his people would be dead. They had been with him for a long time. The dogs began howling when they approached and Annius and the salves were armed and prepared.

“Oh it is you master. We thought it was those raiders.”

“Did they come here?”

“No, a rider came from Morbium. It has been surrounded and many of the garrison put to the sword. There are a few men in the fort holding on but the road to the north is no longer guarded and the messenger said that Coriosopitum had fallen too.”

Gaelwyn and Marcus both looked intently at Gaius. “We can do nothing tonight. We will leave in the morning and follow.”

“I cannot ask you two to come into such danger. They are my family. I will follow alone.”

Gaelwyn’s face became suffused with anger. “Your family! Is not Ailis my sister son? And are not her children my family? Besides, boy, you could not follow their trail, you need Gaelwyn.”

“And remember Gaius that Ailis was Macha’s cousin it is my family too.”

“How will you get through the dangerous country north of here master?”

“I think Annius that we will pretend to be merchants. I will dig up some of my gold and we will buy…what would we buy from the Caledonii?”

Gaelwyn suddenly looked dark. “Slaves! We will pose as slavers.”

Distasteful as they all found the idea it seemed the most logical. “In that case we had better take some fetters and lengths of rope.”

“Have you two thought how big Caledonia is? How will we find them?”

“This is why you need me Gaius for I noticed on some of the bodies the clan markings of Calgathus.”

“And we know where he lives Gaius, north of Veluniate. All we need is to find them and then…”

“Get them out and that will not be easy.”

“Neither will getting them but let us complete one before we worry about the other. We leave before dawn for they have over a day’s lead. Annius send a messenger to Cataractonium and inform the Camp Prefect of this disaster.”

It was two days since they had found the trail of Modius but he was proving to be an elusive prey. The land over which they travelled had many gullies and sudden drops which often meant the turmae had to detour. As they dropped down towards the land of the lakes the pursuit became quicker. “Sir I think we can split up and have a better chance of catching him.”

“How so Macro?”

“The long valley is coming up. He has two choices, down the valley or over the top to the valley of the two lakes. If I take my turma to the valley of the two lakes then I can catch him coming down from the top…”

“Otherwise I can easily catch him in the valley of the long lake. Good plan. I will send a rider to you if we apprehend him first.”

“And I will do the same if he comes my way.”

Modius was surprised by the persistence of his pursuers. He had assumed that they would have just given up when they had caught the rest of his band. His hardy band was now struggling, having eaten little and barely rested in the long race. Now that he was nearing his base in the hills above the valley of two lakes he had a dilemma. If he climbed the steep dark mountain he could drop down into the next valley and lose the horsemen who would not be able to pursue him along the narrow edge of the ridge but, looking at his men, he knew that they could not face the long climb and so he continued down the long lake.

"Sir! They are barely a mile ahead."

The Prefect felt a cruel pleasure that he would get to end the life of the man who had killed his brother and betrayed so many fine troopers. "Decurion take your turma and ride up the hillside. If I flush him out he may try to climb up. You six ride along the edge of the water. Prevent him from escaping that way. The rest of you in column of fours." Knowing that they were so close and that he had secured any possible escape Julius could now use speed. Modius could not escape.

As he heard the thundering of the hooves Modius knew that he had nowhere left to run. "Let's face them." His men looked at each other and contemplated surrender; Modius could see it in their eyes. "They do not take prisoners. Our only hope is to kill them." Resigned to their fate the small band spread out and prepared to meet the approaching horsemen.

As Julius came over the ridge he recognised Modius. "Leave the grey haired one. Kill the rest!"

It was not even a contest. The troopers took no chances and their javelins took out the unarmoured men in moments leaving Modius, sword in hand looking helpless."Come on you bastards which of you is willing to fight me?"

Julius sensed some of his younger troopers relishing the challenge of hand to hand combat but the Prefect wanted a sweeter revenge than that. If Modius died in hand to hand then, in his eyes, he would go to the Allfather. Julius wanted him to die slowly and to be punished for his crimes. He turned to the archer next to him. "An arrow in each arm!"

The helpless Modius looked at the feathered missiles protruding from his arms and the swords on the floor. "You coward Demetrius. You are just like your brother! He squealed like a stuck pig when he died."

The cold eyed Prefect ignored the taunts for that was what they were, taunts to anger him but he had a cold anger inside him. "Trooper ride to Decurion Macro and bring him here. You two secure the prisoner make sure he cannot escape. You six cut down two trees and build me a cross."

Modius looked with pure hate at the Prefect for he knew what his fate would be. He would be tied to a cross and left to die a slow death, picked at by the carrion which, like him, preyed on the weak in this wild land.

The cross had been built and was ready to be buried in the ground by the time that Macro arrived. He just stared at the bully who had nearly caused his death. He nodded his approval at the Prefect's punishment. He had worried that his friend would have killed the bandit out of hand. "Tie him to the cross." Modius struggled as they tied him tightly to the rough wooden cross but to no avail, his bleeding arms were no use and his legs were easily controlled. "Break his legs and his ankles." The trooper who had the hammer normally despatched injured horses and he swung the hammer as hard as he always did. The crack of the break was masked by the scream of the bandit and after the third strike he, mercifully, passed out.

By the time he came to, Modius was on the cross looking down on the camp of the Roman cavalry. He could see Julius watching him; he had obviously been waiting for him to wake. He made the mistake of trying to move and, as he did so he felt the broken ends of his bones grate together and he screamed in agony, making some of the horses whinny in fear. "You see Modius the punishment is the pain. Each time you move it will be agony. Your blood will seep very slowly from your body. There is no quick way for you to hurry your end. When we leave tomorrow you will still be alive. You may be alive the following day but I think that the wolves will have descended from the woods and be jumping up to take pieces from you. If you notice the bottom of the cross is just low enough for a wolf to jump up and bite at your foot. If you are lucky he may take a foot and hasten you death but I hope he doesn't and you die slowly, piece by piece."

In a low voice which Julius could barely hear the defeated Modius said, "You cruel, heartless bastard."

"True but compared to a treacherous traitor like you I am as pure as a new born babe. Enjoy your death Modius."

The Caledonii had surprised Ailis for she had been their prisoner before and had been cruelly treated. It was only when she thought back to her time as a prisoner that she remembered that it had been the women folk who had abused her and here there were only warriors. They did neither her nor the other slaves any kindness but they were not unnecessarily cruel. As they had passed the burnt fort and the destruction of the settlement of Morbium she had begun to lose hope. She could see a few soldiers on the walls but there were too few to be of aid. Even had the fort been fully garrisoned they would have found it difficult to affect a rescue for the warband had grown overnight with others coming from the east and the west. This had been a major raid. She had prayed to the Allfather that the ala would be there, waiting, and they would be rescued. Instead they were joined by another tethered troop of slaves. She also noticed the livestock which had been gathered, pigs and cattle and mules. Perhaps therein lay hope for the cavalry could easily overtake this slow moving group. She had contemplated leaving markers for Gaius but the swathe they cut through the land would leave all in no doubt in which direction they had gone. What she could not see was the small band hidden in the woods above the bridge ready to ambush any soldiers foolish enough to pursue the mighty

Caledonii. The horses they had taken from Ailis' and other's farms would facilitate their escape.

"Don't worry mother I will protect you until father comes."

She smiled at young Decius who had puffed himself up to look bigger. The taller and elder of the three boys he had taken on the role of young warrior to protect them. "And your father will come Decius, believe me. We must all stay alive until he can find us and rescue us."

Livius and his men soon picked up the trail of the raiders. "Looks like they are heading north as you said sir."

"I know Gnaeus. I just hope that the river is too high for them to cross." Livius had come to know the land between Morbium and the sea very well. Once the band crossed the river the land was flat for many miles and the cavalry should have a better chance of catching them up. The problem lay at the river for there was no chance that Livius could cross if the enemy held the other bank.

As they approached the river they could see that the raiders had rid themselves of some of the heavier items of plunder. When they reached the water's edge they could see why. The raiders had used six logs tied together to ferry themselves across the narrow river. Those logs were drawn up on the other bank. The Caledonii would have needed to make sure the load was as light as possible to make the crossing. "Cassius you have the best eyes. Can you see any unpleasant surprises awaiting us on the other side?"

Cassius rode to the river's edge and peered along its wood lined bluffs. "No Decurion, it looks clear."

"Troopers we are going to cross the river by letting our horses swim. Just hang on to their manes and they will get you across."

The water was shallow enough that the horses only had to swim for the middle twenty paces. As they emerged from the placid waters Gnaeus spotted the trail. "Heading north east sir."

"That means they are heading for our road."

"That's good isn't it sir?"

"Not really. They should be avoiding the road because of our patrols. If there are no patrols then this is a larger raid than just the fifty or so we are following." He turned to the turmae. "When we find them I would like at least one prisoner. Do not put yourselves in harm's way but if you can just disable one for me we may find out where these raiders are from."

The men laughed and one wag shouted, "Which leg should we disable sir?"

They followed the obvious trail right up to the point where it entered a small stream. The stream was no more than fifteen paces wide and only knee deep but the raiders had either walked downstream or upstream to avoid detection. Livius split his force in two to enable him to cover both banks. He took his men down stream. The banks were covered in willow, brambles and elder making an impenetrable screen. His lead scout shouted back, "At least we can see that they didn't leave the stream here."

Just then an arrow flew from the undergrowth and hit him in the neck. Within moments they were being attacked on both sides. Manus had spotted his pursuers and tried to buy some time with his ambush. It succeeded for the troopers could see nothing at which to shoot and Livius had no alternative but to retreat. Once they emerged into a clear area he sent a trooper back for the other turmae. In the ambush he had lost five troopers. He would have to recover their bodies later. He now had even more reason to catch his prey.

When Decurion Cassius arrived with the rest of the turmae Livius outlined his plan. "You take your turma right of the stream. Ride on the ridge where the trees as thinner. Poor Metellus was right; they had to have come out of the stream where it is open. When we find an open section we investigate until we find out which way they went."

An hour later they found the trail where the stream cut sharply east towards the Dunum. The wooded hillside rose above them gently undulating. "Well sir the road is two miles up there. That is where they are heading but night is falling."

“I know Cassius and I don’t want to risk another night attack. We will make a camp here and follow in the morning. They have captives and they are afoot. We should catch them when our mounts are fresh.”

The next morning they found the clear trail driving like a straight line north. One of the flank scouts rode up. “Sir, another band has joined them.”

“Looks like you were right sir; this is bigger than just one raid.”

“We could have upwards of a hundred barbarians ahead so be careful.”

Manus had taken charge when the raiders from the eastern settlements joined him. They had many cattle, sheep and pigs. Manus would not be held up by those and he pushed on relentlessly. Soon the whole column was nearly a mile from start to finish but they made good time on the hard surface of the road.

Livius caught up with them just after one of the steeper slopes which the animals had found difficult to negotiate. His men formed up in a two line crescent formation. Manus saw the enemy and decided that he could not outrun cavalry with prisoners. “Tie them up from tree to tree. They will have to cut them free if they are to catch us. Now run you whoresons! Run!”

Livius and his men made short work of the men guarding the rear of the train but the numbers of captives and animals they found meant that further pursuit was out of the question. They did, however, have some luck. Five of the raiders surrendered and were able to talk.

The five were questioned separately so that Livius could compare answers. Inevitably some of them lied but they found enough common ground to piece together the whole picture. “So this Manus and his band raided the jet mines whilst the rest were raining north of the Dunum to the east. Lulach, Calgathus’ son raided Morbium and the south.”

“Don’t forget they destroyed Coriosopitum as well.”

"The sooner we get back the better. The Prefect must have had his hands full with a full warband on the loose. Let's get these people safely home."

Chapter 3

Decurion Princeps Cilo arrived back at Cataractonium half a day after Annius' messenger. Even as he was leaving the fort Livius' messenger arrived from the east. The Camp Prefect shook his head. "This has come out of nowhere."

"It is worse than that Camp Prefect, for half the ala is on the other side of Brigantia chasing bandits; we have three under strength turmae available."

"Did not Decurion Macro have family in that farm?"

"Aye. What exactly did the messenger say?"

"It was a message from Marcus Aurelius Maximunius. The farm of Gaius Metellus Aurelius had been burned to the ground and the women and children taken captive. The Tribune, Gaius and Gaelwyn the scout were pursuing the raiders. Who are they?"

"You are new here Prefect so you would not know that Marcus is the Marcus of Marcus' Horse. He was the Tribune and Gaius was Decurion Princeps before me."

"Oh I have heard of them."

"And the third one is the Brigante scout Gaelwyn; believe me he has the nose of a hound and is tenacious as they come. I would not like him to be on my scent. They must have the trail of the raiders. When did this happen? "

The day before yesterday."

"And Decurion Lucullus reported his raid yesterday too. I will take my turmae up to Morbium tomorrow. It is rather like shutting the stable door after the horse has bolted but it is all we can do until the Prefect returns. We must let Eboracum know too for we will need new garrisons to replace those killed. Keep the camp on high alert. We may not have rid ourselves of all these raiders yet. I will write a report for him tonight in case anything untoward happens to me."

"Like what?"

"Like getting killed by a warband which will probably outnumber us by at least five to one. Believe me your wooden walls may not look much but they will give you more protection than my turmae. Our horses are our only protection."

The two halves of the ala still in the east met close to Stanwyck. The Decurion Princeps and Livius shared information. Livius and his men looked exhausted having pursued raiders around the hills south of the Dunum. "I know your men are tired Livius but I would be happier with six turmae if we are to encounter the Caledonii."

"It is Lulach."

"Lulach again? How do you know?"

"We spoke with a dying prisoner. He was proud of the fact that Lulach was able to come and go as he chose. He boasted that they had destroyed Coriosopitum and now there would be nothing to stop them returning at will."

"Coriosopitum is the gateway from Caledonia. With its destruction there is nothing to stop them flooding into the soft underbelly of the province; it means they are rising again."

They rode north in silence. "Does Macro know of his son and his abduction?"

"No I only found out yesterday. The Prefect and Macro were still hunting Modius. I think if he had known of the invasion he would not have gone off on a wild chase."

"It seems unlike the Prefect to be so…"

"So forgetful of his duty?"

"Well I wasn't going to say that but you are right. It is to do with his brother. I hope he ends it now and not continue to pursue this spectre from the past."

"Who is this Modius?"

"He was a vicious, sadistic trooper who was optio under the Prefect's brother. He turned traitor and betrayed the ala but more than that he led the Prefect's brother into an ambush and killed him."

The further north that they went the more that signs of the raid became evident. There were burning farms and bodies littering the countryside. Carrion birds circled in the distance showing where travellers had met their end. Discarded belongings showed where the people had tried to flee and the fact that their belongings lay like autumn leaves showed that they had failed and were now Caledonii captives. They headed for the tribune's farm which was on the route to Morbium. The whole ala knew of the farm as most of them had their gold buried in various parts of the villa. "Marcus was lucky that they didn't decide to come here."

"I think, Livius that he would have preferred they had sacked this farm and left Ailis alone."

"You are right. I was not thinking, the Tribune always cared more for people than possessions. Can we do anything to help the three of them?"

"I think not. The Prefect may decide to follow but, in my view, that would achieve nothing. The three of them will be less visible but they are taking a risk. If they are caught, as ex-Roman soldiers, their deaths will be particularly unpleasant. The three of them are now in the hands of the Allfather. If he wills it, their quest will succeed. If not then we shall see them at the end of our time."

Having spent some months in a condemned cell with Marcus, Livius felt a closer bond with the Tribune than anyone else he had met. He knew that the ex-tribune was a stoically brave man but he did not deserve the Fate he had been handed. He had already lost one family, murdered by Brigante rebels; to have to suffer the same fate with a second family was more than one man should have to bear.

Annius retold the troopers what Marcus had said. "So they are going to pose as slave traders."

"It might work. It would give them a good excuse to seek out slaves."

“The problem, Livius, is that Marcus and Gaius are well known by the Caledonii. They fought against them many times. I hope that their disguises are good.”

“Sirs the master asked, before he left, if you wished to take any of the spare horses.”

Sergeant Cato trotted his horse up to Decurion Princeps Cilo. “Not a bad idea sir. The Tribune has a good eye for horses and some of these we are riding are out on their legs; we have over used them.” The criticism in the Sergeant’s voice was not hidden. Everyone in the ala knew that Cato preferred horses to men.

“But are they trained? The last thing we want is to lose a trooper because of a half trained mount.”

Cato laughed, “Trust me sir if the Tribune offered them then they are ready to ride. He knows more about horses than any man I know.”

Livius laughed, “Apart from you of course.” Cato shrugged a half smile on his lips.

“Very well then. Sergeant you choose which mounts but don’t waste time; the longer we wait, the further away they get.”

The depleted garrison at Morbium had taken in some stragglers from forts further north who had made their way to the half burned outpost. Some had managed to make it all the way from Coriosopitum. The centurion who walked proudly in with the last exhausted fifty men of his century looked ruefully north. ”This is now the frontier Decurion Princeps. You are the first organised unit we have seen. Between here and Coriosopitum it is nothing but raiders and opportunists taking what they can while the garrisons are slaughtered.”

The troopers helped to rebuild the fort. As Cilo and Lucullus checked the horse lines the Decurion Princeps confided in Livius. “This has decided me Livius. Until I receive further orders we will wait here and help garrison and rebuild the fort. This is the main route south and we are all that stands between Calgathus and the fertile south. I just wish that the Prefect were here, for a thousand men would be a better deterrent than the handful we have now."

"It will not be a happy meeting when the Prefect and Macro hear news of the raid."

"No. I am glad that we are here for Macro loved his son as much as the Prefect loved his brother and that will not be happy for either of them."

By the time the Prefect returned to Cataractonium with his prisoners the men and horses were exhausted. Julius peered around wondering where the rest of the ala was. The Camp Prefect had not been looking forward to this meeting. An old bluff soldier he had never had a family of his own but he liked the genial giant, Macro, and he wondered how he would take the loss. He was grateful that the Decurion led off the horses and turmae to the stable leaving the Camp Prefect with Julius alone. Something on the camp Prefect's face warned him that there was a problem of some description.

"Spit it out Lucius what has happened and where is the rest of the ala."

"The Caledonii raided south of the Dunum. Coriosopitum has been razed and Morbium badly damaged."

"That is bad news. I take it the Decurion Princeps rode north to do what he could?" The Caledonii were always raiding; it was just worrying that a few had got as far as Morbium.

"It is worse than that Prefect. It was a major warband and they were able to raid at will." The unspoken criticism was not lost on Julius who looked up sharply at the comment. "They raided Stanwyck. The farm of Gaius Aurelius was burned, the men slaughtered and everyone else taken into captivity." He repeated for emphasis, "everyone!"

"Decurion Macro's son too?" Lucius nodded. "Does Gaius know about this?"

"Yes he and the Tribune and that Brigante scout Gaelwyn have chased north after them. I don't hold out much hope for any of them." The old soldier had fought the Caledonii and knew the country; he thought it unlikely that they would ever see any of them again.

Julius shook his head. "If there are three men in the province who could get the job done it is those three. And the Decurion Princeps?"

"He went north to Morbium, he left you a report." He handed over the wax tablet which Julius quickly read.

"Does Eboracum know of the situation?"

"We sent riders with the news but there has been no word."

"In that case I will write a report detailing my analysis of the situation and my intentions. I am afraid Lucius that I will be leaving you short-handed again until Eboracum sends reinforcements. I intend to take the ala, tomorrow, north of the Dunum. It is probably hopeless but I may be able to return some of the captives. I take it Gaius' wasn't the only settlement hit?"

"Every farm, town, fort and hamlet between here and Coriosopitum appears to have been raided. We have had local Brigante chiefs complaining about the lack of security. They are not a happy people."

"I can understand that. When we have been to Corio we will have a better idea of the problem and then I will return." He turned to go.

"I don't envy your next task Julius."

"You don't know just how hard it is going to be. I kept the ala out longer than necessary because I was chasing my brother's killer. I can never forgive myself. For the first time in my career I have put something before military consideration. When we have Ailis and the boys back I will have to consider my position."

"Don't do anything hasty Julius. We all make mistakes."

"True but my mistakes may have caused more pain to the people I love than I can live with."

Decurion Macro had his usual boyish smile as he walked back from the stables. The young, adoring troopers were enjoying the banter with the warrior they all wished to emulate. Seeing the

Prefect they all dispersed leaving Macro alone with his friend. "They are a good bunch of lads aren't they sir? We seem to be getting better volunteers these days."

"I think our reputation has something to do with that."

"Where are Cilo and Livius? I expected them to be here when we returned."

"There have been Caledonii incursions into Brigante land. Coriosopitum and Morbium have been attacked."

"So they are chasing the bands eh? Well aren't we going to follow them and give them a hand? Ten turmae will be better than six."

"There's more and no easy way to tell you." Macro's face screwed up as he tried to work out how it could be worse. "They have sacked Gaius farm and taken the women and children as captives."

"Decius?"

"Yes it looks like all three boys were taken. Gaius, Marcus and Gaelwyn are following them." Macro turned to run back to the stables but Julius restrained him. "Where do you think you are going?"

"To find my son."

Taking a deep breath Julius said, "Decurion you are not like Gaius and Marcus you serve Rome and I cannot allow you to go off on your own. You have a duty to serve Rome and the ala."

Macro's eyes hardened. "I might have taken that sir!" he emphasised the sir, "If you hadn't taken us all over Brigantia searching for your brother's killer. If we had been where we should have been, doing our duty, then we might have stopped the Caledonii before they could have taken the captives. I don't care what you say, I am off!"

"Macro! You are right, I was derelict in my duty which is why I will not allow you to make the same mistake. Troopers!" He called over to eight troopers who were heading for the gate. "Arrest Decurion Macro. Put him in chains and confine him to his barracks."

All around the camp troopers heard the command and could not believe their ears. The eight troopers looked at each other wondering if this was some kind of joke. "Do not disobey me! Do it now!"

Macro suddenly flexed his shoulders as though he was going to resist and then the discipline of a lifetime took over and he resigned himself to his fate. "Julius, I will neither forget nor forgive."

As they took him away the Prefect said to himself, "And neither will I Macro, for I blame myself more than you do."

Morwenna had grown into a beautiful woman in the years she had been on Mona. Aodh her lover and guard found himself more entranced and enchanted every day. When he asked her about her beauty she modestly credited the isle and the power of the Mother. Certainly she had bloomed and blossomed and since her three girls had been born she had a wonderful aura about her which was apparent to everyone. Aodh was convinced that she actually glowed although Morwenna mocked him. "You are a man and every man can be bewitched by any woman. It is that little piece of manhood dangling between your legs that enables us to work our magic."

The community had also grown in the years since they had crossed the narrow Menai Straits. Blissfully ignored by Roman patrols, which thought the Druidic religion gone and were far too busy protecting the gold shipments from the new mines close to Wyddfa, the sisters all flocked to the island where their combined knowledge and power made each witch even more powerful. Morwenna knew that soon they would be able to leave the island and begin the revolt against Rome. They had meditated and communed many times; Morwenna had dreamed dreams but still she waited for a sign.

The only man in the community, Aodh, was confused. "What sign?"

"I know not."

"Then how will you know?"
Enigmatically Morwenna said, "I will know when the sign comes."
Aodh was also confused about the three girls he had fathered. They had been born in three consecutive years and he had expected that as they regularly made love, for Morwenna said that it was part of her religion, they had no more children. Morwenna had looked at him as one might look at a cooking utensil or farm implement. "Three is a mystical number we have no need of other girls."
"How do you stop… I mean how can you know we will have no more children?"
"Because it is in my power and not yours. You have served your purpose. Your seed was female and for that I give you thanks."
Other men may have been hurt that they were used as a sire, a breeding bull, but Aodh was so smitten by Morwenna that he accepted these few crumbs of affection. The three girls also showed themselves to be almost identical to their mother and Aodh was barely tolerated by them. In the community he was seen as the provider of food and nothing more. As long as he shared his bed with Morwenna, Aodh cared not.

On the other side of Wyddfa Decius Lucullus was looking very pleased with himself. He had hit upon the idea of dressing his guards in Roman uniforms. This simple deception enabled him to ensure that the workers behaved themselves and stopped any other Romans from interfering. He had worked for his uncle, the deceased Governor of Britannia, Sallustius Lucullus, long enough to understand that if you gave someone the right title and appeared to have documentation then the bureaucratic Romans would leave you alone. The miners thought that the gold they extracted was going to Rome. They did not care for they were paid better than they had been in the mines to the south. What they did not know was that the gold was taken to Decius' partner, Aula Lucullus who was busy buying land both in Rome and in

Britannia. Decius was enough of a realist to know that they would eventually be caught out which was why he had purchased a boat which he kept at Deva; he was ready to get away to Rome as soon as danger threatened.

His senior guard came over. He was jokingly referred to by Decius and the other mock Romans as Centurion. "Yes Centurion?"

"Are you sure you don't want me to take some lads out and frighten the locals a bit. It's what regular Romans would do."

"I know but I want us to be seen as harmless. Let them play at witchcraft on their little island, we will be gone within the year." The Centurion trudged away shaking his head. Decius knew that the real reason he had wanted to take out a patrol was to be violent with someone. The last thing that Decius wanted was the locals causing trouble. He had, of course, lied to the Centurion; he and Aula would have left the hell hole which was Britannia by the spring thaw and then they would enjoy the heat and opulence of Rome.

Chapter 4

The three hunters caught up with the tail end of the retreating Caledonii. Gaelwyn had found their camp and reported back to the others. "There are no captives and they are well armed although few in numbers."

"You mean if we had a turma we could dispose of them?"

"Yes Gaius but we do not want to dispose of anyone do we?"

The three of them were camped downwind and upstream from the raiders. It had been an easy ride to catch them for Marcus was keen to conserve their mounts until they needed to ride them hard. "So we have a dilemma; do we follow these or move on and catch up with the others."

Gaelwyn spat the gristle from his meat into the trees. "It is obvious isn't it? We keep going until we find some captives."

"Good but what about this band? Are we going to be looking over our shoulders?"

"Gaius is right and what do we do when we find captives?"

Gaelwyn shook his head and gave a quiet chuckle. "The trouble is you think like Romans and not barbarians. This bunch of barbarians is making so much noise that we will easily hear them and we are mounted, moving much faster than they are. When we find some captives then we cut out a guard and find out if they were the ones who raided your farms."

"What if he won't talk?"

Gaius you are thinking like a Roman. I will make him talk." The evil leer on the old scout's face left them in no doubt that whoever they captured would gladly tell them anything. "I know you both speak a little of the language but let me speak as though I am the slave master. That way we may live through the negotiations."

"When we do find Ailis and the boys what then?" Gaelwyn looked at Marcus quizzically. "Well you seem to be making all the decisions."

"It looks like I have to for you two are too busy thinking with your hearts and not your heads. When we find the band with the captives then we approach them further along the trail, heading south, and ask if we can buy some captives. If they agree then we win for we will have what we want if they do not then we follow them and rescue them."

"Isn't that a huge risk?"

"Life is a huge risk Gaius." There was no answer to that and the three of them went to sleep knowing that they could be on a fruitless and ultimately heartbreaking quest. All of them could die because they were all beyond the land controlled by Rome. Up in the far north there were no rules. They went to sleep early for they would have to leave in the middle of the night if they were to put some distance between the band commanded by Manus and find their loved ones.

Many miles up the Roman road, for the raid on the farm had been one of the first, Ailis and the boys appeared to be the only ones amongst the captives who were taking the journey well. Ailis had told the boys that it was a game and their fathers would judge, at the end of it who had been the winner. The boys loved games and took pride in being stoic. The Caledonii guards, for their part, were impressed by the bravery of the young boys and took to calling them 'the little warriors'.

Ailis had been worried for the first few days that some of the warriors might have decided to use her but it appeared they were under strict instructions from Lulach to bring the captives whole and unharmed back to his homeland. Ailis was not comforted by this order for it merely meant Lulach wanted the goods he intended to sell to be in the best condition. She had not let on that she could speak their language; having been a captive before she was fluent and understood all that she heard. She knew that they would have a long journey if they were to return to the land north of Veluniate and, in a way, that helped her for it meant her husband had more opportunities to rescue her. She never doubted for one moment that he and Gaelwyn would be tracking them. She smiled to herself; there had been no need to leave extra clues for their trail was so wide that even she could have followed it. Even so whenever they came to an open area she made sure that she left a small piece of cloth torn from her shift. Of all the fcmale captives, hers was of the highest quality and was a distinctive blue. Gaelwyn would know.

"It is her dress. I recognise it."

"Of course it is. Do you think I showed it to you to confirm it? I just wanted you to know she is still alive."

Tetchily Gaius snapped, "I know she is alive and I don't need you to prove it to me. I am her husband and I know she is alive!"

Gaelwyn shrugged and Marcus could see the tension between them. It was an uneasy balance. They needed Gaelwyn to track and to follow but it galled Gaius more than Marcus that he was impotent and relying on someone else to find his wife and children. "Can we work out how far ahead they are?"

"We have just crossed the Vedra which means the old fort at Vindomora should be just ahead. I would say that they probably passed the old fort not long after dawn."

Marcus looked up at the sky. "They will probably camp near to what is left of Coriosopitum then."

"I would say so."

"Let us get there first then. We can make better time than they can and the land closer to the coast is not hard for horses. The sooner we can gain an advantage the better."

The three of them swiftly mounted and rode down the small valley until they came to the mighty Tinea. They followed its banks all the way to Coriosopitum and saw, with heavy hearts, the burnt out ruin which had once been the bastion of the east coast. The bodies of the dead Romans had been stripped and left for the animals to ravage. It chilled them to the core to know that they could not honour their comrades with burial. They would have to leave them where they lay. "We can push on north then?"

"Yes Gaius but first I want to bury a little of our money here." They both looked at him as though he had gone mad. "We have brought much gold and copper I know. We do not know how much we will need but we also do not know if they will let us buy them. They may decide to take the money and the captives."

"So how does burying the money help?"

"If we lose horses, or we lose money then we can return here to dig up the hoard and we know they will not build here." Gaius still looked doubtful. "If anything happens to any of us the others can still have the money to buy back Ailis and the boys."

They found an area which had been disturbed by wild animals and they dug a deep hole and then buried the small amphora containing the silver and copper. By the time they had buried it and scuffed up the surface it was well hidden.

"Now we have wasted enough time. Let us move north."

"Very well Gaelwyn I am contented now." The snort told Marcus what he thought about that.

They camped some miles from the deserted fort. For the first time in several days they were not hiding and Gaelwyn shot them a small doe which they roasted over a fire. "With luck, "Gaelwyn said, "they will scout us and be interested enough to approach us."

"They could also decide we look like easy pickings and slit our throats."

"Which is why tonight, young Gaius, we each take a watch and sleep with our horses tethered to our feet."

Marcus smiled and Gaius asked, "What is so funny? Here we are stuck at the back end of the Roman Empire surrounded by enemies and with no friends within a week's march."

"I was just thinking back to all the times we rode up and down this road with the turma or the ala and never gave a moment's thought to how pretty the land is around here. Gaelwyn has caught us a delicious meal and here we are, three old friends lying beneath the stars. I don't know about you Gaius but that makes me feel good."

Gaelwyn nodded but Gaius would not let it go. "But Ailis and my children are in danger."

"And that is why we are here and tomorrow we may all die. Your family would still be captives and we would be dead so let us enjoy this night for it may be our last but it does not have to be filled with dire and dreadful thoughts eh?"

"He is right Gaius. You are blaming yourself for the raid. Do not deny it. You have been itching for a fight with someone since we left the farm. You are not to blame. The barbarians have been raiding Brigantia since… well so far back we cannot count the years. If you want to avoid the raids then move your family, when we rescue them, to the far south for there it is safe. Would you do that?"

Gaius looked for all the world like a truculent little boy with pouted lips, "No of course not."

"Well?"

"Well what?"

"Accept that we do what we can, we do our best but we take each moment as though it were our last for remember Gaius, none of us are young anymore. When Decius Flavius died I swore then that I would enjoy life and by the Allfather I have. I do not want to be here because my family is in danger but if I am to be here then I will make the best of it and hope that someone is watching over us."

"And as you are so full of evil thoughts you can have the first watch. Wake the Tribune next and then me. Goodnight."

He was asleep in moments. "You have been a little irritable with Gaelwyn you know."

"I know it's just that he didn't seem to care."

"Oh he cares but he doesn't upset himself or others, he keeps it inside. We will find them and we will save them."

"What about dying tomorrow then?"

"Oh we could die tomorrow but that makes me determined even more that we don't and then that will make tomorrow night even sweeter. Goodnight and stop worrying. Trust in Gaelwyn and the Allfather."

Lulach's men left Coriosopitum and did not follow the road north as Gaelwyn had anticipated. Instead they followed the road built by the Romans towards Luguvalium. Lulach and his other warbands had been looting the lands of the Carvetii and the Novontae. His chiefs were wary of attacks from the south and the east. Marcus' Horse had a fearsome reputation and Lulach had impressed upon his leaders that they had to avoid the ala at all costs.

As soon as Ailis realised that they had left the northernmost road she, once again, placed a piece of her dress in an obvious place. As they trudged along the road, tucked behind the ridge rising to the north she said to the boys, "Today we must play a new game."

"I like games," said a very serious looking Marcus. Decius, Macro's son, always liked to copy Marcus and he too tried a serious face but it didn't quite work; it came out as a lopsided grin making Ailis smile.

"Today's game is to make our people smile."

Marcus' brother Decius looked at the cook and the other slaves and saw how sad they looked. "Why do they look sad mother?"

"Because they are captives as we are and they are going to be slaves in Caledonia." Ailis had decided right at the start of this ordeal that she would try to be truthful with the boys wherever possible.

Decius pondered on this and then asked, "But I thought they were slaves already? Aren't they our slaves?"

"Yes they are but we treat them well do we not Ula?"

Ula, the cook, gave a half-hearted gap toothed smile. She had been listening to the children talk and found her own troubles receding. "Yes young master Decius your mother and father are kind, even grumpy old Gaelwyn is kind in his own bad tempered way but we are going to a strange land and I fear that we will be treated badly."

Ailis flashed her a sharp look, "But we are together are we not?"

"Yes mistress."

"Well in that we have hope and they have not mistreated us yet. So boys let us see if we can make the people smile today."

Gaius was almost disappointed when the night passed without incident. He was even more perplexed when no-one came up the road from the fort. "You two break camp and I will ride back and see where they are."

Gaelwyn galloped off and, after they had packed their equipment away they took the opportunity of taking out the swords they had secreted in the saddle cloths. Gaius had brought the Sword of Cartimandua for, as he said to Marcus when questioned, "If I cannot use the sword to save the last of the Brigante royal family then what is the point of the sword? Besides I believe it will protect us. It always protected you when you used it did it not?"

Now as they checked the edges of their blades it was brought home to them just how perilous their journey was. They were indeed on a knife's edge themselves and one slip could end in disaster.

Gaelwyn rode in a short while later. "They have headed west, I found their trail and this," he held up the piece of dress.

"She is still alive then?" The relief in Gaius' voice brought a smile to Marcus' face.

"She is still alive."

"Let us follow. When we are closer I will try to see where they are exactly in the column. They had been joined by many more raiders and captives. They must have sent a mighty force south."

Marcus looked down the road to the distant and unseen fort of Morbium. "I wonder where the ala is?"

"And I wonder how the Prefect has tethered Macro for surely he would want to be here."
"He would. Gaius he would."

Back at Cataractonium Macro was cursing his own honour and training as a soldier. He could have broken free of the troopers, they would not have held him but he obeyed orders. He had spent his life obeying orders. He had no wife, the bitch had betrayed him and killed his friend, but he had a son and he would protect his son, with his life if needs be. He made a momentous decision; he would desert and find his son. Once he had come to that conclusion he felt much better. It would be a small task to escape. They had merely tied his hands and the room he was in was not locked. The trooper on guard outside would never hear him when he did escape

He chose his moment well. It was just before the guards were due to be changed. It would give him a short time to escape but it meant that the guard would be tired. He broke out of his tethers for they had not used the chains ordered by the Prefect and although the rope was a good rope it was no match for the strength of mighty Macro. He retied them loosely. Pretending to be asleep the guard closed the door and stood outside the cell bored and cold. Macro opened the door silently, as he had planned. He grabbed the trooper with one hand around his mouth and dragged him into the room. Once inside he spun him around and hit him with his other mighty fist right on the point of his chin. He went down like a sack of apples. He took his helmet, sword, pugeo and shield and walked calmly from the room towards the stables. All the sentries were busy watching the perimeter; raiding barbarians had focussed their attention on the outside. He chose his own horse and, grabbing a water skin, he headed for the Porta Decumana. He mounted the horse and, with the cloak, wrapped tightly around his shoulders rode slowly up to the sentry on the gate. The trooper was tired and saw what he expected to see, a messenger with despatches. As he looked up for the pass he saw, with shock, that it was Macro. Before he could shout a warning Macro had kicked him in the head rendering him unconscious. He dismounted and opened the gate. The new guards would be coming soon so he just pushed the gate shut and walked his mount away from the fort. As soon as he heard the shout from the tower he mounted his horse and galloped quickly north.

He skirted the fort and headed straight for Morbium. He was risking meeting the ala but, riding at night meant that they would likely be in camp anyway. Now that he was racing along the main road north he began to work out what he ought to do. He had no idea where his family was and he just hoped that by heading north he would meet up with Marcus and the others. He felt certain that Gaelwyn would be on their trail but that trail was almost five days old and very cold.

Prefect Demetrius viewed the devastation that was Morbium. The auxiliaries from the raids north and the survivors had all made their way there and Julius worked out that he had a cohort to man it. "Come on men. Let us get these walls up." It was imperative that the fort became defensible. Decurion Princeps Cilo had suggested a mobile barrier across the bridge. If the raiders returned then they would be slowed at least. For himself Julius was desperate to move north. To say he felt guilty about delaying his return because of some misguided view of honour was ridiculous. He had determined that, once he had secured the captives he would resign. As a patrician it was his right to do so and he would retire to Rome. He had let down his ala; he had let down Rome but worst of all he had let down his friends. The enemy might be three days up the road but he would pursue them and, when he returned Macro's son to him he would resign with honour knowing he had done his best.

Seonag arrived at Mona even as the hunters were creeping their way north. She had, with her purloined gold, secured passage with an unctuously bejewelled merchant taking jet to Deva. She found it ironical that she held, in her casket, more jet than the merchant had ever seen in his life. His pomposity had amused her as he told her of how he had cheated the villagers of their money as he gave them a much lower price for their jet. She almost laughed aloud when he confided in her that he hoped to sell much jet to the sisters, the worshippers of the Mother. She knew that, once she arrived in Mona, the sisters would want for neither gold nor jet.

Morwenna greeted her like the long lost sister she was. The signs, the symbols, the secret handshakes were unnecessary as the old woman and the young woman greeted each other. They both knew instinctively who the other was. "Mother I bring you great treasure and great news."

"Sister I was looking for a sign and I see it in your eyes."

"The north is rebelling. The Caledonii have come south and have devastated the border."

"Calgathus?"

"Mother I believe so."

"The Romans have moved all their troops south, to safer, richer lands. The Brigante are ready to rebel. They have suffered too many privations and raids. When their children are taken then they will act and the Caledonii have taken all the children."

Morwenna grabbed the old woman to her breasts and hugged her. "You do not know how long I have waited and this is the sign."

Seonag's eyes filled with tears. "I am a sign?"

"Sister you are the stone which begins the avalanche which sweeps the Romans from our land."

Macro did not head for Morbium for he knew he might run into the ala or at the very least the barrier that he thought they would have erected. Instead he headed east to where the Dunum was narrow and slow. He would swim his mount across and then head up the partly built road which went north. He needed to get around the raiders and their pursuers it he was to meet up with Gaelwyn and Gaius. Having languished in a cell for a few days he was not tired and his only concern was for his mount. To spare the beast he walked up the hills leading his horse; it was an old trick and he thanked Sergeant Cato for his horse wisdom.

He was able to reflect, as he trudged up the hills, on his rash action. He had, almost certainly, ended his career in the ala and, quite possible he had signed his own death warrant. It was a rash act but in the cold light of day he knew that he would do it again. There came a time in a man's life when some things became more important. He had had the glory he had sought when he joined the ala but, since the birth of his son and his betrayal by Morwenna he had had a different perspective. His son was his immortality and he needed protecting. Ailis was a wonderful foster mother and she would see that he was brought up as he should be to be a fine young man but Ailis too was in danger. He cursed the powers that be for leaving Britannia in such a perilous state. He had known that Roman politics was dangerous when the Tribune and Livius had been arrested on a trumped up charge and almost suffered an Imperial death. He resolved that, once he had rescued his son he would have no more to do with the world of Roman politics but would dedicate his life to bringing up his son. Mounting his horse he smiled wryly to himself, how he would escape punishment to be able to do so was beyond him. He looked up at the heavens and spoke to his dead friend Decius Flavius, "You always said I was better with my hands than my brain and you were right Decius but I have cast the dice and for good or ill this is my course."

The miles flew by and the big man lived from his energy. His child was in danger and nothing would stand in his way. The road and the terrain were so familiar to someone who had fought in this land for so many years. Riding was second nature to Macro and he was able to ride and think at the same time. He thought not of his pain but of his son lost and alone; if the Allfather would let him change places with his son then he would do so in an instant.

When his horse began to foam, as he approached Vinovia, he rested. He found a small steam where his exhausted mount could drink and then he took her up to a secluded dell where he slept the sleep of the dead; a sleep haunted by a tiny child crying for his father to rescue him.

The Prefect and the ala had picked up the trail of the raiders and found the group led by Manus. Livius recognised the huge man from the crossing of the Dunum. "This is the band that raided the jet mines. They have no captives and they were not the ones who took Ailis."

"I know."

Livius looked questioningly at his leader who appeared to have aged in the past few days. "Then we can go around these and find Ailis."

"No Livius. I forgot my duty once before, I will not do so again. These men raided Roman land and they will pay the price." He held his hand up to prevent further argument. "Besides we may get valuable information about the direction that Ailis' captors took. We are now heading west and if they are meeting up with a larger band then we may have to stop our pursuit and return to the new border at Morbium."

Livius' shoulders sank in resignation. He knew that the Prefect was right and the chances that the one thousand men of the ala could effect a rescue was dubious but his heart felt like lead at the thought of the lovely Ailis and the three boys being slaves in a Caledonian camp for the rest of their lives. He prayed to the Allfather that Marcus was having better fortune.

Chapter 5

Gaelwyn slipped back into their hidden camp. They were north of the abandoned fort of Blatobulgium in the land of the Novontae. Although it was some years since they had been in the area, when they followed Julius Agricola to glory, the land was still familiar. "They have scouts out. I think we take one and question him."

"Is that wise?"

Gaelwyn shrugged, "We know not which direction they are taking and the further we are from home the harder it will be to get back."

Marcus nodded his agreement. "Let us leave the horses here then and proceed on foot."

The three men were well used to moving silently through the woods and the scouts were busy looking behind them for pursuit. Gaelwyn identified their target, a young boy of fifteen or so summers. To him it was exciting to be with the older warriors and the raid had made him believe that he too was a warrior and he made the cardinal error of moving out of the sight line of the next scout. When he stopped to relieve himself they pounced for he had left his spear propped against the tree and, rather than keeping watch, he looked down. Marcus swung the thick branch at his head and Gaelwyn and Gaius caught the unconscious boy.

When he came to he was tied against a tree and there was a sword a hand span from his groin. "Right boy we need some information." When he heard his own language he was confused for these were not Caledonii. From their hair they were Romans, or at least two were but from their clothes they looked to be bandits. "Whose clan are you?" He shook his head bravely and Gaelwyn shook his own grey and grizzled mane sadly. "We will get the information boy but if I have to use pain I will. Who is your leader?" Gaelwyn slapped him across the face.

Spitting out blood the boy said, "It is Lulach and he will eat your hearts out Romans."

"That's better now we know your clan. And where are you heading?"

With tears in his eyes at his own betrayal he shook his head again. "First you will have to kill me Roman."

When Gaelwyn smiled his cruel smile the boy shuddered, "Oh you will die but it is a question of how. Another question then. Is there a mother and three young boys amongst your captives?"

His eyes lit up with the remembrance of the pretty and cheerful captive, "Oh Ail…"

In horror he realised he had confirmed what they wished to know and he shut his mouth as tight as a beached clam. The knife sliced through the boy's ear as though it were butter. Gaius' hand over the boy's mouth stopped the cry. Still he would not speak and it took three fingers before he relented and told Gaelwyn all that he needed to know. As Gaius put the sword in the boy's damaged hand Gaelwyn slit his throat saying, as the blade slipped in, "You were a brave boy, go to the Allfather with honour."

After they had roughly hidden the body some way from the trail they considered their options. "We need to rescue them before they get to the land of the Selgovae for there we have no allies."

"True but it will be difficult to get by the column in this narrow valley. We shall have to trail them until we can find a way ahead."

The Prefect was determined that the patrol would boast some success. He knew they would have to return soon to Morbium, their horses were exhausted and they had run out of supplies. He was equally certain that he did not want to lose men unnecessarily. The Decurion Princeps took half the ala to ambush the rebels when they ran from the attack of the remainder of the ala. "Decurion, if we can I would like prisoners if only to find out who they are and where they are going. This is the first of many raids and we need to be prepared."

The ambush was prepared in the unique style of Marcus' Horse. Half the turmae were dismounted and spread out in a half circle whilst the mounted portion was a few paces behind. As soon as the barbarians began to flee in their direction they hurled their javelins and fired their bows. It was a slaughter for most of the Caledonii were watching behind them for any pursuit and trying to avoid the obstacles in the woods. When they suddenly tripped over the bodies of those first to flee they saw the line of armoured horsemen behind the wall of steel. Many chose to prostrate themselves on the ground and take whatever mercy was on offer. Manus was one of those. He had decided that he could always escape whilst on the road but there was no chance to escape the horse warriors who heavily outnumbered them.

"Tie them up and let us get back to Morbium. We have done all that we can here."

The troopers looked at their Decurions. They all knew of the abduction and, despite the short rations and exhausted horses, were all prepared to keep going until they found Ailis and the boys. Decurion Pontius, the most outspoken of the officers voiced his concern. "What about the bairns and Ailis? Aren't we going after them?"

"No, we are not. This is a huge warband. We have picked off the minnows but do you think that, if we managed to surprise them, they would not kill the captives?" Each trooper dropped his head for they knew he spoke the truth and yet they could not leave those children as captives. "And what of the rest of the province? What of the land which has not been raided? Who is there to protect it? You saw the garrison we passed as we rode north. We are the only defence for the province and we are a thin defence at best. As much as I want to rescue Ailis, and by all the gods I do! I cannot jeopardise everything we have won so dearly." His shoulders sagged and his voice broke a little. "If the Parcae allow then Gaius and his comrades will do what a thousand men cannot. When you pray to the Allfather ask him to watch over our comrades."

Macro had slept in a small dell not far from Coriosopitum. He had not seen any sign of either raiders or Romans. As he left the dell and came to the fort he looked at the tracks; they had all gone west. He decided he would have to risk the road. He discarded his helmet and rolled his cloak up. He had to look like a deserter, which of course he was, or a mercenary. For the first time in his life he regretted being such a larger than life character that people remembered. Every battle in which he had fought had been a backdrop for his heroics and he knew that friend and foe alike remembered him. The beard he was growing could not disguise the shoulders and his size but they might make an enemy think he had deserted.

He found the field of battle where the ala had destroyed Manus' band. As he gingerly inspected the bodies he could tell that it was the ala which had destroyed them. He recognised the arrows and the design of the javelins. He could see no evidence of small feet and he deduced that this band had had no captives with them. From the tracks he could see that the ala had moved south; that decided him. Now there were only four warriors who could rescue his family and he was one of them. The sooner he found the other three the better. The trail of the main warband cut a huge swathe through the landscape. Gaelwyn would have to be blind not to deduce the direction. He needed to find a way to observe the barbarians and find Ailis without the enemy finding him. He rode a parallel course to the band. When it was nightfall he would move closer to the camp and spy upon them. He was confident that he could dispose of any scout or guard whom he met.

He rode along the ridge way skirting in and out of the trees. It was not an easy route but it afforded him a clear view of the narrow valley that he knew both his friends and his prey would be taking. When he saw the spiral of smoke in the distance he almost shouted with joy. Such a column of smoke meant a large camp; his friends would never advertise themselves so clearly. With luck it would be the barbarians. He gently nudged his weary mount down the hillside his route clearly marked by the smoke. Within the hour he would know if his son was there and within a couple of hours he might have saved his son.

Gaelwyn the hunter had finally seen Ailis. Gaius had to be restrained for his immediate reaction was to run to her. "No Gaius, let us watch. We know where she is kept and the children. We can spend a day or two watching how they guard her and then we can work out how to rescue them all."

Over the next two days, as the ponderous column of raiders and captives crept ever northward they saw how difficult a rescue might be. The captives were tethered together and four guards surrounded them during the night. "Just too many of them. We could take three guards but with four one would see us and then the alarm would be sounded."

"We will have to try and negotiate then Marcus."

"It will have to be me who goes, Gaius, for the boy recognised you two as Romans, even in these clothes and with your beards and many of these warriors would have fought you in the Caledonii wars."

"Very well we will try your way."

The next day Gaelwyn rode into the camp from the north, trailing their spare horse. He had left his comrades south of the camp and he arrived just as the Caledonii were preparing their food. The guards were alert but did not appear to be worried. The leader of the warband was one of Lulach's cousins, Ael. He was a powerful warrior who ruled the band with a fist of iron. The scar which ran down his cheek was the result of a wound at Mons Graupius and, as a result, he hated all things Roman. His guards brought the mounted stranger to him.

"Welcome to my camp stranger. You are not Caledonii." It was a statement not a question and Gaelwyn knew that his answer would determine if he lived or died. He sensed some of the younger warriors, bored with escorting plunder and captives, itching for a fight.

"I am of the Brigante oh chief."

"What brings you to this land so far away from your homeland? Do you seek your family?"

Gaelwyn could see that this chief was perceptive and no fool; he shook his head. "I seek slaves for my master." He waved his hand expansively in the direction of the captives who were some distance away. "I see that you have a rich haul. Would you consider selling some to me? I can pay a good price and save you having to take them further north."

Shaking his head Ael spat out a fatty piece of meat. "No my lord, Lulach, has determined that we sell none until he has inspected them."

"This is a difficult road you take. I could take some off your hands and make your journey easier. I have much money."

"Did I not make myself clear Brigante? I said that my lord has said that we sell none until he has seen the worth of them. I do not betray my lord."

Gaelwyn knew he had offended the honour of the man and decided that he would get nowhere. "I am sorry chief and I will continue my journey. If I am unsuccessful in my endeavours where will the sale of these captives be held?"

Slightly mollified Ael pointed vaguely north. "If you come, at the time of the burning of the bones, north of the Clota then my lord will sell those whom he does not wish to keep."

"Thank you."

"Will you not share our camp?"

"Thank you for your hospitality but it is not yet dark and I can journey further south."

As he rode by the captives he surreptitiously glanced towards them, hoping to catch Ailis' eye. He had almost given up hope when he saw her walking from the stream carrying a jug of water, guarded by a bored young warrior. Neither Ailis nor Gaelwyn showed recognition but their eyes locked for an instant and, suddenly, Ailis had hope, if Gaelwyn were there then her husband could not be far away.

Gaelwyn was well aware of the six warriors trailing him. When he had mentioned money he had noticed their shared smiles. He must have looked like an easy target, an old man, alone and far away from his homeland. It would have seemed like easy pickings. Rather than heading straight for Marcus and Gaius he led his would be robbers further down the trail. He made sure that he made plenty of noise for he wished to alert Marcus and Gaius. He knew them well enough to know that they would watch his back. With luck their arrows could take two of the six and they could defeat four barbarians, especially four who thought they were robbing an old man. He slowly eased his sword from its scabbard as he felt them closing in on him.

The six young warriors had not told Ael what they intended, indeed they hoped he would not find out for they would keep the old man's gold for themselves. Their clan was from the far north and they were not of Lulach and Ael's people; they felt no dishonour in trying to watch out for their own. Lulach might reward them when he sold the slaves but this way they could return to their village richer. They spread out in a half circle; they had come far enough from the camp to avoid detection. They drew their swords and prepared to attack the helpless old man from behind. As their horses were urged forward two of them were plucked from their backs by the arrows of Marcus and Gaius. Suddenly the hunted had become the hunter and they saw, with horror, their victim turn and charge towards them with a long sword in his hand. Two of them tried to turn but found themselves facing two other warriors equally armed. As Gaelwyn attacked the leader, the last member of the group decided that discretion was the better part of valour and headed off to the side. The three men fighting Gaelwyn and the others were no match for the experienced fighters and soon died. "After him!" Gaelwyn yelled as the final survivor hurtled through the woods.

Gaius had the best horse and he set off on what he knew would be a hopeless pursuit; the warrior had too much of a start. His target glanced over his shoulder to gauge the distance and Gaius saw, annoyance and frustration, the grin on his face as he saw that Gaius would never catch him. It was a shock when he looked up only to see a huge warrior slicing with a wickedly long spatha towards his head. The look of shock was still on his face as his lifeless skull rolled gently through the trees.

"Macro!"

"As usual I am here just in time!"

After they had stripped and hidden the bodies the four comrades took the captured horses up into the trees well away from the trail and the scene of the ambush. Macro stood grinning like a naughty boy caught stealing apples. Marcus looked at him and then embraced him. "It is good to see you but I know there will be a story behind this." He waved a hand at the unkempt look.

"Wait until we have food before we begin this tale."

"Good idea Gaelwyn for it is two days since I ate."

Later as they sat, hidden in a small dell many miles from the barbarian camp, Macro told them his story. "We found Modius and killed him in the land of the lakes but it meant that, when we arrived at Cataractonium the raiders had already left and you were many miles away in pursuit. I asked to follow you but the Prefect threw me in a cell. He took the ala out to follow the raiders and I escaped."

Marcus shook his head. "That was foolish, old friend for you have given yourself the death sentence."

"I know but when we have found my son then I will leave this land and we will build a new life. I have thought to going across the water to find that Irish king, Tuanthal. He liked me and I could train his troops."

"But you have thrown everything away and the king may be dead, that was some time ago."

Gaius shook his head, "No Marcus; you are wrong. I would have done exactly as our young hot headed friend did although I might have hidden my intentions more effectively so that I did not get thrown into a cell."

Macro laughed. “Decius always said I acted first and thought later.”
“I am not sure that Decius ever credited you with actually thinking.”
“Besides which we have yet to recapture these captives Tribune. Let us catch the horse before we talk of riding him.”
“Wise words Gaelwyn.”
“Do we go tonight or tomorrow night to rescue them?”
Gaelwyn and the others exchanged looks. “Neither Macro. We could have gone tomorrow night, for with four of us we could have affected a rescue but the six warriors we killed will be missed and they will be wary for they will remember the Brigante warrior who tried to buy captives. There will be more guards tomorrow.”
Gaius’ shoulders slumped in resignation. “So they are lost?”
“Not so. I have yet to tell of my visit to the camp. First I saw Ailis and she saw me; she has hope now for I saw it in her eyes. Secondly they will not be sold until the burning of the bones.”
Macro looked at Gaelwyn as though he spoke a foreign language. “Burning of the bones?”
“When the crops and harvests are gathered in they kill any animals which they cannot keep over the winter and the preserve the meat. The bones which are left are burned with leaves and dead wood to spread on the land and bring forth better crops. Lulach will use the captives before he sells them and he will know their worth. This Lulach is a clever man; he is not the usual mindless barbarian.”
“So we have time then?”
“Yes and now we have more horses. With four of us we have a better number to overcome any guards and we can wait for them to become less vigilant and then rescue them.”
Gaelwyn held up a warning finger, “They will now be watching for us along the trail. We will need to move far ahead of them.”
Marcus had been quiet for some time. “I have been thinking on Macro’s words. He said the Irish king. Remember when we met

him, we travelled up the west side of this island and we came to the Clota. We know that is where they are going."

"But why the west?"

"This valley is narrow all the way to the Clota and we could be spied more easily besides the Classis Britannica still patrols on this side of the land. If we were to signal one of the ships it might mean we could escape a little easier."

Gaius looked doubtful. Macro nodded, "I like it and the land is easier on that coast and as I recall the Novontae was friendly towards us."

"They were then who knows now."

Gaelwyn stood up. "It is decided. We head for the sea." Gaius looked as though he was going to argue but a quick look from Marcus reminded him of their earlier conversation.

"Well at least we have made a decision."

Far to the south Morwenna gathered her sisters together. Aodh stood behind her uninvited but wanting to know why she had called the conclave. "Sisters, Seonag has brought us a sign." The old woman brimmed with joy at her fame. "It is now time for us to go back into the world of men and bring the word of rebellion to their ears. The precious stone our sister brought is also a sign for now we have our symbol to carry with us, the symbol of the black bird of death. We go to the north and make the Brigante, the Carvetii and the Novontae see that the rule of the Romans is over. We now have gold to buy horses and make the journey quickly." She walked over to Seonag and touched her hand. "Sister I would ask that you raise my girls and the acolytes until I return."

With tears of joy in her eyes the old woman kissed the hand of the young witch. "It is my honour to do so."

"I am not only your leader but, through my father Aed I am a Brigante princess. We will use that to inspire the people of the north."

With a cacophony of screams, screeches and squeals the sisters embraced and kissed each other. Aodh stood to the side feeling as though he was in a different world. He was the outsider in this world of women but as long as he could be close to Morwenna, the woman he worshipped, then he would happily live in that world and pick up the odd crumb of affection.

Decurion Princeps Cilo had seen many more sides to Prefect Julius Demetrius over the past weeks. When they returned with the prisoners he saw a Prefect angrier than he had ever seen him. The blazing row he had with the Camp Prefect could be heard all over Cataractonium and when he eventually came out, red faced, no-one dared to approach him. He slammed into his office and the Decurion Princeps took a deep breath. Someone had to go and talk to the Prefect. Macro, Gaius and Marcus were all closer to the Prefect but it was their absence, and Macro's escape which had angered him He decided he would wait for a short while before he broached the lion's den.

Inside his office Julius held his head in his hands. All of this was his fault. Had he not followed Modius, against every precept he had held then, perhaps, Ailis might not have been captured and, certainly, Macro would not have gone off as a deserter. He could not believe he had handled it so badly. He had ranted and railed at a good man, the Camp Prefect, when it was not his fault that Macro had escaped. In his heart Julius had known that the big man would escape, in fact, it was hard to see how he would not escape. He took his sword from its scabbard. Perhaps the best thing, the noble thing, the honourable thing would be to take the sword and end his own life. Just then there was a knock at his door. "Yes."

The door opened and Decurion Princeps Cilo stood there looking apprehensive. "Sir? If I could have a word?"

Julius was about to shout at him when he remembered that none of this was anyone else's fault but his own. The only person he should be taking it out on was himself. "Yes, come in Salvius."

Once he was in the room he was not certain where to start but once he saw the pain in his commander's eyes he knew what he had to do. "Sir, begging your pardon but you are not being yourself."

Julius looked up, surprised both at the comments and the apparent impertinence. "Go on Decurion Princeps."

"You cannot change the past. Whatever happened it doesn't matter now. What matters is how we deal with this. I think that you blame yourself because Macro went off after his wife. You have to post him as a deserter and that makes you unhappy because you think you drove him to it." Salvius stepped back because he thought he had overstepped the mark. In his mind he had expected the Prefect to interrupt him and stop him but he hadn't and Cilo had just spoken what was in his head.

Surprisingly the Prefect smiled slightly, "Go on Salvius. Perhaps you are gaining second sight for those were my thoughts."

Sighing, the Decurion Princeps continued, "Well sir if we don't post him as a deserter he isn't one is he?"

"I don't follow."

"He could be on a scouting expedition, or compassionate leave or any other mission ordered by his Prefect."

"Yes but the guards, the Camp Prefect…"

"Sir the guards are the young troopers trained by Macro; they love the man. They would not say a word and believe me the Camp Prefect would not want to see Macro punished for something every soldier in the fort would have done."

"That's fine as far as it goes and Macro might not be punished where does it leave us?"

"It's like I said sir. You think too much, beg pardon and you shouldn't. Let's get back to doing what we do best, being the best ala in Britannia. Before we knew Macro had gone we were going to base the ala at Morbium and make the province quieter. We should do that."

"That leaves south of the Dunum without a military presence."

"The Brigante are quiet enough sir. If we can stop the raids and the captives being taken they will all be happier."

“Very well give the orders and Salvius?”
“Sir?”
“Thank you?”
“You’re welcome and if you don’t mind me saying so it is what Decius Flavius would have done.”

Chapter 6

The hard part of the journey to the coast was the first part. They left in the late part of the night but even so Ael had sent searchers out to find either his lost warriors or those who had killed his men. Macro and Gaelwyn had spent some hours before they left laying deadfalls and traps to slow up their pursuit. They had to cross a thick forest and rising, rocky uplands. "If they catch us here we are dead men for they can go quicker on foot than we can with this string of horses."

They heard, from the valley below the sounds of pain as warriors set off the traps while in the distance they could see the column of captives and raiders sinuously snaking northwards. Macro's heart sank as he realised they were going further from his son, not closer.

"Sometimes Macro you have to take a step back to take two steps forwards. Marcus' plan is the best we have; it is the only one we have."

"But I feel so angry Gaius. That young child amongst the barbarians."

"Gaelwyn observed them from a distance and they did not look to be suffering. My Ailis is a good woman and our people are good people they will not let harm come to our children."

"I am sorry Gaius I should have realised that this is worse for you than it is for me. You have two children and your wife."

"Numbers do not increase the loss Macro. Your one child will hurt you as much as the three that I have lost. The Allfather has protected them so far and brought you to aid us. I am more hopeful now that this quest will end happily."

"I hope so."

"Did you mean what you said about Ireland?"

Shrugging he said philosophically, "King Tuanthal, if he was a king, seemed to like me and he did ask us to go over with him to train up his warriors. If he is still alive then I think that the training and the tactics of the ala could make his kingdom secure. After all General Agricola believed he could conquer it with just auxiliaries."

"Yes but it is ten years since we met him, anything could have happened."

"My son and I will take our chances. Even if I have to take on a champion I think I can beat any man alive in single combat." He said the words without any boasting, it was a matter of fact and Gaius had to agree that Macro could beat any warrior that Gaius had ever met or seen, Roman or barbarian.

Once they reached the bleak and windswept top of the hilly forest Gaelwyn allowed them to slow the pace. Marcus was always amazed at the mental map which Gaelwyn carried with him. It had been ten years since they had been in the land of the Novontae and yet it seemed as familiar to the old scout as his own farm. Marcus was not worried about Gaelwyn and his plan, he would get them to the place where Ailis and the children were being held but he could not see how they could rescue the captives and escape with their lives. It would take an extraordinary set of circumstances for them to manage, what seemed a Herculean feat. If the fleet was off the coast that might just give them the edge they were seeking. As he looked up at the sky he also worried about the weather. They had another month to get to the Clota but in that time the weather could and would worsen.

Three days later, when they finally dropped down to the coast and they could see the grey choppy sea, their hopes began to rise. They could see the sails of ships out at sea; none of them looked Roman but a ship of any type might be useful, even an Irish raider. "We still have all our gold and silver, we could buy a boat or pay a captain to take us."

Gaelwyn, the landsman, looked sceptical but he held his counsel about the wisdom of trusting to ships. "We still need to find their camp. I will push on with these two, Tribune, if you are determined to try to get a boat."

As much as he hated to be parted from his comrades, Marcus could see the wisdom in the old man's words. "Very well. I will meet you where the Clota meets the sea in ten days. That should give you time to locate their camp."

"May the Allfather be with you."

Morwenna and Aodh used some of the gold brought by Seonag to buy horses. They took with them two of Morwenna's witches as an entourage. "I intend to let the Brigante people know that their queen has returned. As such I need to have a presence."

"How will they know that you are indeed Aed's daughter?"

"We go first to the cave in which I was brought up. Hidden beneath a large stone is the torc which belonged to Venutius and then to Aed. Once my warriors see that they will know who I am." She glared darkly at some hidden point in the west. "Would that I had the Sword of Cartimandua that the horse warrior carries for with that I could unite not only the Brigante but every tribe in Britannia. When we have raised the people we will visit the Roman and retake what is rightfully mine." Although a bright sunny, day, Aodh shivered at the ice and the unspoken threat in her words.

"Do you know where it is then?"

"Aye it is on the farm with Ailis and Gaius. I lived there for a while but Gaius was still serving the ala. I think he is older now, mayhap, he may have left the ala and be but a farmer. That would make it easier."

"The Roman cavalry may be a problem my love for did they not defeat your father?"

"They did and for that they will be the first to die and when they are gone there will be none to stop me."

Prefect Julius Demetrius had committed the ala to controlling the land north of the Dunum. The tribes north of the river were not as pacified as they had been and the raids from the north had made them apprehensive perhaps even a little resentful of the

Roman presence. For the first time since he had come to Britannia, the Prefect wondered if the people of the island actually wanted Roman rule.

Livius felt confused. His mentor, Marcus was off in the north trying to find his family and his hero, Macro was a deserter. All that he had known and trusted in; all that he had believed in and valued had been turned upside down. He had been betrayed by his uncle. Governor Sallustius Lucullus and by his cousin but he had come to the ala and found a rock in an uncertain world. Suddenly that rock was shown to be insubstantial and ephemeral. All he could do, as Decurion Princeps Cilo had told him, was to do his duty and focus on the turma under his command. His role was to patrol the eastern side of the province. The Votadini had already revolted and Livius had helped to put down the revolt. This latest incursion from the north had caused all the uncertainties about Roman rule to the surface. Livius found distrust and hooded eyes when he took his turmae on patrol. No longer did he feel safe as he travelled through the valleys and rich farmland of the coastal strip. His camps were those that one would build in a hostile environment. The burning of Coriosopitum had cast a long and black shadow. There was nothing in the east to stop an invasion, just a small damaged fort and a bridge at Morbium.

They stopped at a small settlement in the Ituna valley. The eyes of the headman were cold and scathing. Livius smiled, as he always smiled, to ferment concord but there was none. "What of my children, taken by these Caledonii? When will they be retuned to me? When will you stop the rape of my land? When the eagle came we were promised peace and calm. Where is the peace? Perhaps we need to rebuild our forts and arm our young men."

"We will stop these barbarians chief but it will take time." Even as he uttered the words he realised the futility and inanity of them. The truth was the ala, on its own, could do nothing without reinforcements and Livius felt as impotent as a castrated bullock. He hoped that the new governor, Tiberius Avidius Quietus, would do what his uncle, his predecessor had not done, concentrate on ruling Britannia and stopping the barbarian incursions. "We will do as we promised. My men and I will ride the roads and try to bring peace."

The grudging nod told Livius that he had bought some time but that was all. "Gratius take your men north to what remains of Coriosopitum. It may be that not all the raiders have returned north." He shrugged his shoulders. "It may be that some more are coming south. Either way you will be our warning."

"But the Prefect wanted four turmae together."

"I know but we need to do something to gain an advantage."

As the single turma headed north Livius thanked the Allfather that he had this part of the frontier to patrol. It was perfectly suited to cavalry with not too many forests and slopes which his mounts could master. The Prefect had given himself the harder task riding the spine of the country where, even in summer, the winds howled and made it feel far colder than it actually was.

The Prefect was finding it hard going. His men were not just exhausted, they were demoralised and exhausted. He had always known what a shadow Macro had cast, now he knew just how important the Decurion was and had been. No man voiced his disapproval of his actions but Julius could tell from the slight delay in following orders, from the veiled looks he received and the chilly response he got from any kind of humour; they blamed him for Macro's desertion. Gazing northwards the Prefect hoped beyond all hope that Macro was still alive and able to help Marcus and Gaius. "Sir, scout returning."

The two scouts had been sent by Julius to investigate a small plume of smoke in the north west. He had hoped secretly, that it was a friend and he could ride in and find Macro and Gaius sharing a meal. In his heart he knew that this would not be.

"Sir it is a small band of warriors."

"What tribe?"

"We were too far away to see sir."

Not for the first time the Prefect regretted that he did not have Gaelwyn as a scout. Had Gaelwyn been the scout he would have identified not only the tribe but the settlement in which they lived. "Very well. We will ride in as though they are hostile. Cassius take two turmae and fan out east. We will approach from the west."

The gorse and undergrowth came up to the horse's haunches and the troopers found it difficult to navigate an even line. "Keep together!" The warriors stood as the turmae surrounded the camp. Julius could immediately see that they were Selgovae and the hairs on the back of his neck prickled. The Selgovae were an untrustworthy bunch and even when they were pacified could still stab you in the back.

The chief, for the Prefect could see the torc around his neck, stepped forward, his palms open in a sign of peace. "Welcome Romans rest and eat with us."

Even as his men began to relax the Prefect's sword was coming from its scabbard, he had seen movement in the gorse and noticed that all the weapons of the tribesmen were handily placed. "It is a trap!" The trap was sprung and the hundreds of warriors hiding in the gorse rose up behind the troopers. The warriors had the advantage and, as the ala tried to turn to fight their foes swords and axes were hamstringing the helpless horses. Julius's sword was out and he took the chief's head off in one blow. Turning he urged his horse towards four men surrounding his signifier. His blade sliced down the unarmoured back of one warrior cutting him open to his backbone. His horse trampled a second. The third broke and the signifier killed the fourth. "Sound the retreat!" This was not a battle which could be won for they were outnumbered and surprised. Julius needed to regroup his men and then attack the Selgovae on grounds of his choosing, not theirs.

He and the aquilifer hacked their way through the warriors, other troopers falling in behind until suddenly there were no more warriors before him. He halted and said to the signifier, "Sound recall!" Although few would hear the call for the remnants of the turmae were with Julius, it would tell those further away that there were survivors. He glanced around and saw, to his dismay that there were less than sixty men in their saddles. He had lost half his command in a few moments. The Selgovae were busy desecrating the dead and suddenly Julius was angry; the pent up frustration of the past weeks erupted. "Marcus' Horse let's show them what we can do! Charge!"

The tiny line of troopers was a mere sixty men wide but this time they had the advantage of space in which to build up speed. In addition the Selgovae had made the cardinal error of assuming they had won the battle when they had merely won the first encounter. The troopers were as angry and vengeful as Julius; each blow they struck was a blow for their dead and dying friends, and more importantly, for their lost hero Macro. The Selgovae fell to their blades as a wall of sand before the incoming tide. Each trooper was filled with a rush of blood which brooked no defence and soon the only Selgovae remaining on the field were the dead. "Find our wounded and tend to them. Cassius find the dead and let us burn them."

Later, as the Prefect led the remnants of his turmae south to Morbium he felt that they had, at least acquitted themselves well. They had found ten of their comrades wounded and counted over a hundred dead barbarians. But as Julius felt every blow and cut he knew that this meant the Selgovae had joined the revolt it was going to become more difficult before it became easier. Leading his weary warriors south Julius could only pray that his comrades in the north were faring better than his beleaguered ala.

Gaelwyn came hurtling down the trail. "Hide! Caledonii!" Ever used to instinctive reactions his two comrades raced into the trees with their mounts, pulling swords from scabbards in anticipation of action. The three of them were as stationary as statues when the barbarians raced down the trail. Gaius noticed that they were all afoot which meant that they could probably outrun them if they had to but at the same time he didn't want their presence advertised. They were so close to the Clota that they could smell the sea but they had also encountered many bands of warriors patrolling the estuary to protect their prince, Lulach. When they had passed by Macro was the first to speak. "We will be spotted soon."

"I know."

"We need to find their base and then seek a place of seclusion before we meet with the tribune."

Gaelwyn shook his head. "You two still look like Romans. Take the horses to the meeting place and camp. I will find where they are keeping Ailis."

Gaius could see Macro reddening and about to argue. He had come to realise, after Marcus' advice, that Gaelwyn was looking out for all of them and they had to obey the scout. They were no longer in the world of the ala with orders and regimentation, they were in the barbarian world and the old scout was king. What they would do without him Gaius could not begin to imagine. "He is right Macro. Let us go."

Gaelwyn left the two younger men. Perhaps this would be his last ride, perhaps he would die in this quest but it would be an honourable death. He would be serving, as he had always served, the Brigante royal family and Ailis and Gaius were as much his children as any. He was resigned to his fate. The Allfather had been kind to him; the past few years had been the happiest of his life. He had loved every minute he had spent with the extended family. The three boys had been a joy to the old man, listening to his every word watching him, even copying him. If he could return them to their happy life south of the Dunum then any price was worth paying, even his life.

Far to the west Marcus approached the small settlement carefully. He remembered that the Novontae had welcomed the ala in the past but things changed and people moved on. The raids by the Caledonii and Irish may have turned them from allies to foes. He felt the weight of responsibility on his shoulders more than at any other time; even when he had been Tribune he had not held so many lives in his hand. He was under no illusions, if they could not acquire a boat then they would not escape; three children and a woman would not escape the horde that was Lulach's warband. They were deep in enemy territory and so far from home that the journey did not bear thinking about. Winter was bad enough in the rest of the province, up here it was lethal. So far he had seen no sign of the Classis Britannica. He had almost given up hope of finding any boat Roman or Novontae. This small settlement with the tiny boats drawn up like crabs upon the beach was his only chance.

He dismounted and dug a shallow hole. In the hole he buried two thirds of his gold and his spare sword. He had thought he would bury all his weapons but then he realised that they would respect him more if he had a sword. If he had had more time he would have waited until the morning but he had only one day to make the rendezvous with the others. He had to secure a boat and, in the darkening twilight this was his best chance.

There were ten families who eked a living from the sea. They would never have money but they were well fed and they traded enough to ensure that they could buy those items they could not make. The stranger who rode into their village looked strange. He was not a Novontae and the old man spat into the fire and said, "Roman!" It had been many years since the Romans had passed through on their way to Caledonia and few of the villagers had seen them let alone met them. The men took out their spears although they needed them not for just one man but, as the old man said, "Romans rarely travel alone."

"Welcome Roman what brings you to our little village?"

"I have not been here for some years, friends but when I came through here with my ala of cavalry I was welcomed and I thought to spend the night here."

His eyes scanned the men looking for fingers easing towards weapons. The old man stepped forward. "I remember a sword Roman; a sword of legend carried by a Roman warrior."

Marcus nodded, a smile playing on his lips at the remembrance, "Yes the Sword of Cartimandua, it is no longer mine for I passed it on to the heir of Cartimandua as was right and proper."

The old man nodded. "It is as I remembered. You are welcome Roman and you shall spend the night here."

Marcus dismounted and, taking a small bag of silver from his belt said, "I am not here as a thief, I will pay for my food and my roof."

The old man smiled, "You are the man I remember and I will enjoy sharing tales of times past."

After they had eaten well on a dish of shellfish and flatfish Marcus turned to the old man. "I have money and I would like to buy a boat."

There was an exchange of looks between the men sipping the water of life. "Boats are expensive."Marcus threw down an extravagant amount of gold which the men ignored. "And sailing them is even harder. " Marcus threw down a second bag.

"Friends, for I feel I may call you friends. I have no wish to own a boat, I merely wish to give you money to sail a boat and pick up some friends of mine and take them south. After that I have no need of the boat and I would give it as a gift to those who helped me."

"We will need to speak." The men spoke in the language of the Novontae. Marcus picked up some words but not enough to discern the direction the conversation was taking. It mattered not, they would either help him or not. After much arguing and gesticulation the old man said, "We will help you. Where do you need the ship and when?"

There was relief and consternation in Marcus' mind. "As it will be my ship, for however short a time, I will need it where the Clota meets the sea. When? Take me there tomorrow and then I will tell you when." The men discussed, debated and argued a little more. "My horse I will leave here for I shall not need it now that I own a boat." Later when sailing north Marcus reflected that the horse, Marcus' own horse raised by him from a foal was the deciding factor in the deal for it was a good horse which was probably worth as much as the boat itself.

"It is agreed and now we drink!"

As they sailed into the estuary Marcus was very impressed with the skills of the three men who sailed the boat. The old man had insisted on coming with them, Marcus felt it was a point of honour. Marcus scanned the shore but he could not see his companions. "If you take me in shore I will await my companions. Meet me again here, in seven days." He paused, unsure of how to continue.

"We will be here Roman. We have given our word."

"I know for you are a wise man and you will be rewarded."

"You have paid enough for an honourable man, to pay us more would make me think we were not doing an honourable thing." The clear blue eyes bored into Marcus' and he returned the gaze.

"It is honourable and the Allfather would give it his blessing."

The old man nodded. "Then we shall be here."

As he waded ashore Marcus wondered if his friends would be there or if he would have a lonely night waiting for their return. Climbing the wooded bank he glanced around hoping to catch a glimpse of a familiar face. Suddenly from out of nowhere came a huge fist and a chuckling voice which said, "Thought you would never get here."

"Macro!"

Gaius stepped out from behind the tree, an arrow notched in his bow. "We have found their camp. Gaelwyn is watching." He gestured towards the boat. "Do we have transport?"

"They will return for us. They will come back here in seven days. Now we just need a plan."

Gaelwyn looked at each of them in turn, "A plan which secures the captives and gets us back here safely."

Chapter 7

"We will go to Brocauum." When Morwenna spoke there was no discussion. Aodh felt a little uneasy as there had been a Roman garrison at the old Carvetii stronghold but he did not risk the wrath of the witch. She smiled at him, the smile a mother gives to a small troubled child. "The Romans will not be there Aodh and now that we have the torc we will soon gain the support of the people."

The two acolytes also smiled at Aodh; he rarely saw Morwenna speak with them but they seemed to know all that she planned whilst he, the man, was excluded. He shrugged his shoulders. If this was the way his life would be then so be it. He had chosen to worship and serve the sorceress and the pains and trials were more than outweighed by the pleasures.

He had been a little wary when they had first left the safety of the cave hidden deep in the land of the lakes and travelled so close to Morbium; he remembered the horse warriors who patrolled there and they were but a day's ride away from their destination in the land of the Carvetii. Morwenna was adamant; she wanted to visit the farm where she had lived with Ailis. She had told Aodh that he could approach the farm for he was unknown but, in the event, it was unnecessary. The blackened remains of the main building told the cruel story quite clearly as did the neatly laid graves. When Aodh had found the broken charred arrows he was able to confirm that it had been his clan. He had been reluctant to follow Morwenna's orders and dig up the graves but such was her power that he had no choice. The grisly task was unpleasant enough but when the decomposing bodies were uncovered the smell almost knocked him from his feet. When she had been satisfied that they were all males, and none of them was Gaius she had allowed them to move on, towards Brocauum.

The settlement was stockaded but a small party of protected women did not warrant a rigorous inspection. The men at the gate merely checked what weapons Aodh carried. When Morwenna came next to them they almost shrank from her gaze. There was no hostility in her eyes, merely a power and a knowledge which made men quake. "Who is the leader here?"

The authoritative voice brooked no dissention and the men volunteered the information readily. "It is Colla, "and they pointed up the main avenue to the largest building; a rectangular building partly made with stone.

The small party rode on. Aodh noticed that there were more rectangular buildings here that in other Brigante villages. The Roman influence was clear to see. He worried that a love of Roman buildings might also reflect a friendly disposition towards the Romans. As they dismounted he saw that the two acolytes had not followed them but ridden to another hut some distance away. Aodh had learned never to question; he would discover where they had been later, if Morwenna chose to tell him.

An imposing warrior came to the door, taller than Aodh and with a decorated helmet. As he looked closer Aodh saw that he had been imposing but his waist was bulging and his jowls showed that he liked a drink. "I am Colla, headman of this town who are you?"

Morwenna did not speak but walked closer to him and said, very quietly, "Do you discuss all business on the steps of your home? When you have made us welcome then we will talk."

His guards slipped their hands towards their swords for their chief was not spoken to in this manner, especially by a woman. Aodh did not move, he merely smiled. Morwenna did not need his protection, yet. Her eyes flashed a glare at the men who shrank back. "I am forgetting myself please enter." Colla's voice was humbler and he half bowed as Morwenna entered.

When they were seated Morwenna scanned the men before her. There was obviously some sort of meeting taking place and Aodh noticed that some of the men looked unhappy that it had been interrupted especially as the interruption was from a woman. When Morwenna felt that the silence had gone on long enough she stood looking, to all who saw her, as a regal figure. "I am Morwenna, daughter of the last heir to the Brigante crown, Aed and his wife, the sorceress Fainch." There was an audible intake of breath. The lie about wife could not be disproved. She waited and then held her hand out. Aodh knew his role in this drama and he took out the golden torc and placed it reverently into her waiting hand. "This is the royal torc of the Brigante and I wear it now as a symbol of the power and lineage which is rightfully mine."

As soon as she placed it around her neck Aodh dropped to his knees. The warriors and Colla looked at each other in a confused manner. Some started to half bend and then seeing their peers still standing, straightened their backs. Morwenna nodded as though she had expected some dissension of this sort.

Colla gave a half cough and said, almost apologetically, "We see the torc but it takes more than a piece of gold to prove you are the rightful heir. We know of the sorceress Fainch. What sign have you that she was your mother?"

Morwenna took the jet raven from beneath her white shift and displayed it below the shining torc. To Aodh it seemed that the white shift seemed to glow and it affected some of the warriors who did drop to their knees.

One angry looking warrior stepped forward. "I am Ownie and I fought with Aed. It will take more than a piece of black stone and a golden ring to make me drop to my knees."

Morwenna stepped towards the haughty warrior, her eyes never leaving his. Even though she was smaller than the powerfully built warrior she seemed to grow in stature the closer she came to him and he seemed to shrink. When she was very close to him she hissed, "I am Morwenna. My father was Aed and my mother was Fainch. Do not doubt my power Ownie the Brigante for if I become as angry as you then all will see my true power."

He held her gaze for but a moment and then dropped to his knees. As soon as he did the rest fell to their knees. Suddenly the room was filled with the women of the town who also dropped to their knees their chanting becoming more audible with each chant, "Mother, Mother, Mother!" Finally they all raised their arms and gave a shout of "Mother!"

The men looked around in shock and Aodh finally saw the two acolytes behind the women. Morwenna had left nothing to chance, her women had worked their own wondrous magic and ensured that Morwenna would have the support of the wives of the elders.

She sat down and Colla found his voice again, "What is it you would have us do Queen Morwenna?"

"The time has come for us to throw off the shackles of this Roman yoke. The Caledonii raid you with impunity and there is no protection. Soon they will be followed by the Selgovae and the Votadini. The Irish will come from across the seas and steal your children. We are the Brigante and the Carvetii. We ruled this land from far to the north all the way to the mighty rivers in the south, even to the borders of holy Mona. Why can we not be powerful again?"

"What of the Sword of Cartimandua?" A quiet warrior who had kept to the back spoke up. "If we had the sword, as in the days before the Romans came, then all would fall before us. We have been a beaten people since the sword was taken by the Romans."

"I know," her voice was hard and cold, "but the sword has been lost. I will find the sword and I will wield it but we must rise up quickly for the Romans are weak now and are busy defending the north from the privations of the Caledonii. While they are weak with few soldiers let us rise up and take back that which was stolen from us."

The quiet warrior nodded. "You are right Queen Morwenna for I have seen the empty forts. I, Parthalan, will follow you but hear this mighty Queen, without the sword we cannot win."

Others looked at the quiet warrior whose voice carried such power. "He is right. We must find the sword."

"Yes Colla and we will. But the sword is no longer close by."

"How do you know?"

Her eyes flashed dangerously and Colla shrank a little. "I am the Romans worst nightmare for not only am I Queen but I am the sorceress who can see beyond the hills, who can see into men's hearts and bring the power of the Mother against the invader. The sword has travelled north but it will return south and when it does it will be mine and we will use it to finally rid us of these Roman overlords."

Satisfied Colla said, "What would you have us do?"

"Begin to train our warriors. Send out riders for the other chiefs to come here. By the new moon we will be ready and we will put Cataractonium and Eboracum to the sword."

Every voice was raised in a cheer for they all felt the power of her words and believed in the darkness of her magic. Even Aodh was impressed. Lulach and Calgathus were powerful speakers but this young woman had more power in a look than they had in their armies.

Lulach and his father embraced. It was many months since he had been north of the Bodotria and Lulach could see that his father had aged. The grey now covered his head like winter snow and he looked a little thinner as though he was being eaten from within. "You have done well my son." Even his voice showed the signs of age. "Warriors have told me of the captives and treasure you have amassed and the Romans you have slaughtered."

"We did not kill as many Romans as I would have wished but this was but a trial. We have learned how to defeat them without losing many warriors. We have learned their weaknesses and where they are vulnerable."

"Where are the captives for I see you have come with just your guards?"

This was the reason Lulach had come back. He had a difficult speech to make and he hoped that his father would understand. The deterioration in his father gave him hope. "I intend, father, to build a new stronghold north of the Clota. The Selgovae see me as their leader and, with the warriors I have amassed I can build a bigger kingdom in the west than we have in the east." Lulach watched his father to see if he detected any anger but there appeared to be none.

His father stroked his grey beard. "Do you do this to create Lulach's kingdom or do you still serve Calgathus and the Caledonii?"

Lulach dropped to his knees. "King Calgathus I serve only you and the people of Caledonia. By making the west as strong as the east we make all our people safer. When we have defeated the Romans I will go across the waters to the Irish and punish them for their raids on our lands and we will add to the land of the Caledonii, the land of King Calgathus."

"That is good my son for I have grieved for the lost ones taken by those pirates. You have my blessing but we will need those warriors you took for your raids." Lulach looked up sharply. "We are weaker now because of the losses. If the Votadini or those raiders from across the eastern seas come we will not be able to defend our people."

Lulach knew then that his father might be greyer but he had not lost any of his acumen. By reclaiming his warriors he was making Lulach rely on his new allies and keeping his own army stronger. "Very well father when I return to my new lands I will send your warriors back to defend this land."

Prefect Julius Demetrius had withdrawn his depleted ala to Morbium. "You see Salvius we have not replaced mounts and we have had no recruits. I believe we need to reorganise the ala. We do not have enough troopers for twelve turmae."

Decurion Princeps Cilo shook his head, "Nor do we have enough Decurions. I think we can muster eight turmae."

"I agree. You can command four and I will take the other four. When they are remounted and re-equipped we will patrol again. You can take the east and I will take the west."

"It leaves Morbium and the road south vulnerable Prefect."

"I know but until the new Governor travels north and reorganises the garrisons we are helpless."

"I cannot understand it. We sent the news of the raids weeks ago."

"Sadly, Salvius, unless it affects them directly and their lands are threatened then they will move slowly. I just pray that the barbarians have raided enough this year and have satisfied their greed and lust."

Livius watched the Prefect as he went with the Quartermaster and Sergeant Cilo examining every mount and every piece of equipment. The side of his job which Livius, who aspired to lead the ala, would not relish was the mind numbingly complex area of logistics. He would have loved to lead the ala in battle but not this. Walking back to his quarters he reflected that the ala was but a shadow of its former self. The departure of Macro had left a hole which no one could fill. It was as though the big man was the heart of the ala. Taking off his armour he wondered if he would have dealt with Macro the same way as the Prefect had. That the Prefect regretted all of his actions since pursuing Modius was obvious but once the chain of events had started there was little that any of them could do. The Parcae were fickle creatures indeed.

Aodh was impressed at the large number of Brigante and Carvetii chiefs who arrived over the next few days. It showed that they were dissatisfied with Roman rule. The Caledonii raids had worked in their favour. All of them wanted to speak with this new Queen and Aodh was privy to every conversation. He stood behind Morwenna as each man came for an audience. Perhaps why they wondered why this Caledonii warrior was guarding the Brigante queen but none dared ask the question. Each man was ensnared the moment they met her. She seemed to know something about each man as they entered. It took him some time to work out how she did the seemingly magical trick of telling each warrior about himself the first they met. Each chief took it as confirmation that she was, indeed a sorceress. Aodh spotted the trick when an acolyte brought in a beaker of a liquid for Morwenna prior to each audience. She would whisper something in her ear and then the other acolyte would bring in the chief.

Rather than the knowledge diminishing his approval and adoration of Morwenna, it actually added to it. She soon had every chief of the Brigante and Carvetii not only behind her but willing her to greatness. They all wished for the heady days of Queen Cartimandua, now a tale told around fires by old men; a time when Brigantia was independent and not reliant on the crumbs from the Roman table. That she was a woman and a sorceress were taken to be good things for Queen Cartimandua herself had appeared to have magical traits. The Sword of Cartimandua was the only point over which they were uneasy. The story of the sword being lost did not sit well with them for if lost it could be found and used against them.

Late in the evening when Aodh, Morwenna and the two acolytes were resting Morwenna summed it up. "We have to find the sword. I curse myself for when I lived with Ailis I had it almost in my grasp. Would that I had realised its significance. The Mother weaves complex and complicated baskets for our dreams and she makes us seek that which is most precious. Now we know what is precious we can seek it."

"I could go north to my home and find it for you."

Smiling maternally at the eager young warrior Morwenna explained, as though to a child, "I am afraid that Lulach would not be happy about your desertion. You left him to follow me. No we will go to war without it and, when we win, I will ask Lulach to find the sword for me."

The next day all the chiefs stood in a semi-circle around Morwenna; she was dressed simply in a white shift but the golden torc and the black raven seemed to accentuate her green eyes and red hair. Each chief knelt with his sword pointing upwards so that they all touched. She walked up to the blades, to the very point where they touched and she put her breast so close that one would have sworn the points entered her. "Today the land of Brigante goes to war. I will lead you and we will drive these invaders from our shore. It will not just be the men who fight for, as with Boudicca and the Iceni, all will fight for it is our war and our land and we must all fight to free it." The ululation from the women was louder than the cheers and roars from the men and Aodh fully understood the power which the sorceress had unleashed. "Go for your fighters and your warriors. Rediscover your weapons and your warrior hearts. The day after tomorrow we destroy Cataractonium and then on to Eboracum!"

The Camp Prefect at Cataractonium was just grateful that the cohort of Tungrians on their way north to Morbium had spent the night at the fort. The Governor had finally reacted to the news of the Caledonii raids. It was too late to stop the raids but it boosted the number of soldiers in the north. At least he had not been worried about attack for with Marcus' Horse constantly on patrol he was understaffed quite heavily. As he watched the autumn mist creeping along the ground he did not envy them their march north. Although he had not heard of any more raids the quiet was a little worrying. The Caledonii were unpredictable and the Selgovae and the Votadini appeared to be every bit as belligerent. The First Spear of the Tungrians waved his hand in salute, "Thank you Camp Prefect. When we are settled in to our new fort you must enjoy our hospitality/"

"I will do. Beware of ambushes, especially just out side Morbium."

"Thanks for the warning. Come on step out lively there."Smacking one of his recruits on the back the smiling centurion headed out at the back of the column. Behind him the mules were still leaving the fort when suddenly the mist erupted in a sea of blades and savage blue painted barbarians. The young recruits stood no chance. As far as they were concerned they were safe for they were still in a fort. The disaster which ensued could have been minimised if they could have shut the gates of the fort but the recruits panicked and ran back, all semblance of order gone. The barbarians poured in after them. The Tungrian First Spear managed to form a thin line with the first century, all of whom were experienced.

The Camp Prefect turned to his aquilifer. "Grab a horse and get a message to Eboracum, tell them the Brigante have revolted and Cataractonium is no more." The man looked at him in shock. "Go on get on with you or Eboracum will fall too." Grabbing his sword and his shield the old centurion ran down the steps to the mayhem in the Praetorium. It had been many years since he had wielded a sword in anger he hope he still had it.

He stepped into the gap next to the Tungrian centurion. "The ambush came a little early!"

"Sorry about that. Well let's see if we can thin these out a little." The two centurions became the rock around which the sea of rebels broke. Had there been more soldiers of their calibre and fortitude they may have stemmed the tide but all around them the Tungrians were being assailed and assaulted from all sides. The auxiliaries had never faced an enemy before and their training had been in the open. The confined space of the fort suited the barbarians. The young soldiers did not use their weapons as well as their officers and the casualties mounted as they were hacked, chopped and slashed by four warriors to every soldier. The Brigante and Carvetii were venting all their anger and frustrations upon the hapless Roman defenders. Their walls no longer protected them, they enclosed and imprisoned them. Gradually the Roman line fell back to the Porta Decumana, the last exit from the camp and the last hope of the Romans. Some of the weaker and fearful members of the cohort had opened it and fled south. As they came closer to the open gate the Tungrian First Spear said to the Camp Prefect. "If we hold them at the gate, it might give some of these lads the chance to escape."

The Camp Prefect had lived a long life and a good life. He had survived all those who had joined with him over thirty years ago. A sacrifice now might enable some of these young untried soldiers to become the veterans who would save Britannia. It would be a worthy death, an honourable death, a death with a sword in his hand. "You're right and I am not running anywhere." He gestured with his eyes to his leg which had been sliced from the ankle to the knee and pieces of bone protruded. "Right then. They're your boys you tell them."

"Tungrians here is my last order. Get out of the fort and go to Eboracum tell them what has happened." The two centurions were still falling back and fighting for their lives yet the auxiliaries did not move. "Run! Now!" Like a dam which suddenly bursts the survivors fled around the two centurions who moved backwards to fill the gate. Brigante warriors hurled themselves at the two but each was beaten back. The barbarians had not fought seriously for years and there was neither order nor method in their fighting. The Tungrian centurion used his shield and sword in perfect harmony. He punched with the shield and stabbed with the gladius. The Camp Prefect covered his sword side and he too found his opponents less than skilful. Had they an experienced century then the two men might have held the enemy off indefinitely. Their end would come, inevitably, through tiredness but the gate was still filled by the two heroes and, in front of them the ground was filling up with the dead and dying warriors who continued to hurl themselves at the two rocks.

Finally Ownie had had enough and he hurled a mighty war axe. It caught the Camp Prefect on the side of his helmet and as he staggered back, a young warrior thrust his spear into the unprotected throat of the veteran. The First Spear had no chance then for they were on him like a pack of wolves and, like a pack of wolves, they tore and hacked at his dying body as a punishment for holding them up for so long. Finally Ownie raised the decapitated head of the Tungrian Centurion who had held them and saved some of the garrison.

The eighty men who escaped thanked the Allfather for the courage of their two leaders and each swore that they would revenge themselves on the treacherous Brigante. Elsewhere in the troubled province of Britannia other Roman garrisons found the people they were there to protect rising against them and the only force which could have done anything was patrolling north of the Dunum; unaware of the disaster in the south.

Chapter 8

At Eboracum the Legate, Appius Mocius Camillus could not believe the news but the battered, wounded Tungrians who trudged through the main gate proved to be a powerful argument. The garrison commander shook his head, "We haven't got enough troops here to launch a counterattack. You will need to bring troops from further south." Vibius Duilius Scaeva was a cautious man. He had spent many years dragging himself up the ranks to his present position of power. The last thing he wanted was for a disaster on his record. The Brigante were a dangerous tribe and if he marched his cohort off and lost then it would be remembered for all time.

The Camp Prefect looked off towards Cataractonium as though he could actually see the hordes of barbarians flooding south. "You could always recall the ala operating north of the Dunum. There seems little point protecting that part of Britannia if we are in danger."

The Legate was new to the province and he did not need a minor problem like a fort or two being overrun becoming a major disaster with a legionary fortress like Eboracum falling. His two advisors had been in Britannia for some time. Until the Governor came north and gave him orders he would take the advice of the two local experts. "Very well. Send to Lindum for the rest of the Ninth and recall the cavalry; once they are here we can put down this little rebellion." He hoped that he would be able to put down the rebellion. He had served in the east and there wars were fought in a very different manner; control of water and passes was much more important than here where any barbarian band could travel in any direction. Here enemies could attack at any time with impunity. Nowhere was safe.

Morwenna was angry and frustrated. The Brigante chiefs had made much of their conquest of one fort. They celebrated long into the night burning every hated symbol of Roman rule. She had urged them to follow the Romans she knew had fled but this was war they said and men needed to rest after such a magnificent victory. She knew that they would not have had the victory but for Aodh; he had proved his worth with the plan to hide in the fog and attack when the gates opened. The chiefs had been most impressed that Morwenna had conjured the fog and summoned the power of the Mother. Morwenna and Aodh had merely exchanged knowing looks; the fog was predictable in the vale at this time of year.

The two of them sat, with the acolytes, apart from the whooping and celebratory Brigante and Carvetii. Aodh tried to placate the seething sorceress. “One day’s delay will not hurt us. Even if the Romans get to Eboracum before nightfall they cannot leave until the morrow and we could catch them on the road.”

“They will not leave Eboracum. I am more concerned that the refugees alert other forces and bring them to their aid. If the chiefs had pursued the Romans and stopped them from reaching Eboracum then we would have had total surprise. That is why I am angry. We have to fire the other tribes and make them join our rebellion. One little fort will not do so but Eboracum? That is a mighty prize. If that fell think of the effect on the rest of the province. The Silures and Ordovice could rise against Deva and the legions would be stretched. No Aodh, you did well with your plan but we had surprise. Eboracum has been warned and we will need a better strategy now.”

Aodh pointed to the west. “But the victory is bringing us more warriors.” A line of torches showed where other tribes, from further afield were coming to join, what looked like becoming a rout of the Romans.

“We will need more, especially when they bring the legions north.”

The messenger entered Morbium just as the ala was about to go out on the new patrols. "Prefect! Cataractonium has fallen, the Brigante have revolted."

Dismounting Julius called, "Officers to my office. You come with me." The messenger joined the ten men into the office, "well give us the worst."

"Yesterday morning the relief column for Morbium was surprised by a huge force of Brigante as they were leaving Cataractonium. The barbarians broke into the fort and killed the garrison. There were less than fifty survivors. The Legate wants you to go to Eboracum where he will make a stand."

"How many men does he have there?"

"A cohort of the Ninth and a cohort of Gauls."

Livius burst out, "Less than a thousand men against the Brigante."

"Let us not panic yet, we do not know how many Brigante there are."

"As I came north I saw great burning to the west."

"But none to the east?" The messenger shook his head. "Then there is a cohort of auxiliaries at Derventio and another at Vinovia. Camp Prefect, Aulus, I will send a rider north and bring the garrison of Vinovia here. I can then take this garrison south and join with the garrison of Derventio. That will give us a force of almost two thousand men."

"But Prefect that will leave Morbium undefended!"

"There will be those soldiers who have injuries and it will only be until the garrison joins you. Think on it Aulus if Eboracum falls then there will be nothing to stop the Brigante from raiding south and north. It will not matter about Morbium if Eboracum falls. We will await the garrison from Vinovia before we set off"

"You are right. May the Allfather help us."

Finally the Brigante horde began to move ponderously south; their numbers swollen by hundreds who had come from the west. Colla was preening himself in his new armour liberated from the dead Camp Prefect. "We will cut through the walls of Eboracum like a knife through butter."

Morwenna looked scornfully at the warrior who, until seven days ago had just been the headman of a small town and now he was Venutius reborn. "I hope that the Romans do not realise that the warriors who come against them are so shallow and easily satisfied with minor victories."

"They are keen and they are brave," Aodh had been in the thickest of the battle and knew how well and bravely the Brigante warriors had fought. "They are new to war for it has been a generation since they have had to do so. They will improve and remember my love the garrisons have not fought for a generation. The only Romans who have experience of fighting are north of Morbium. We are like a stone rolling down the hill. We are slow now but, as the people flock to fight for you then we will become unstoppable."

"You are right but I want my revenge now not when I am old and grey."

"You will have it now and the people have begun to worship you. They believe in your magic."

Aodh was right for warriors would ask, shyly for Morwenna to touch their blades or their amulets just to have some of her magic rub off on them. She rode at the head of the column with Aodh at her side but to call it a column was generous for it was more like an enormous crowd spilling off the road along its sides with a straggling tail which stretched almost a mile behind the leading warband of warriors. Aodh had insisted that Colla put scouts out but the chief was full of his recent success and convinced that the Romans were fleeing and would not stand against such a mighty host. Aodh pulled the man to one side and spoke quietly and threateningly in his ear. "You are the Queen's servant, I am her military adviser, you will put scouts out and you will listen to me. Do I make myself clear?"

Colla looked at the clear blue eyes and saw the threat. It had been many years since he had fought in a battle and the success at

Cataractonium had made him forget that man to man, anyone could lose. In the battle he had managed to avoid striking a blow whilst still being in the forefront. This Aodh was a dangerous man and he decided that he would heed his words, for the time being. "Of course. I will send out scouts but we do not have many horses."

"Which is why we use them for scouting and then we can have warning of an ambush or an enemy." Colla wandered back to the mounted men muttering to himself. Aodh thought of how Lulach would have reacted and he knew that Colla would be missing his head.

The Prefect rode with his turma to Derventio. Technically he outranked the centurion at the small fort but he knew that, sometimes, petty leaders would baulk at following orders from a stranger. They made good time and arrived at midday. As he approached the gate Julius thought that the Vinovian garrison should have reached Morbium, enabling Salvius to start the column moving down the road. They had to move at the speed of the infantry but in his heart Julius knew that the barbarian raiders could only move at foot pace themselves. Travelling down the main road should give them the edge that they needed. If the barbarians laid siege to Eboracum then so much the better for that would take time to encircle. Julius was confident that the fortress could withstand the early attacks, especially if they had warning but the river could be used against them. He remembered Decius Brutus the former First Spear of the Ninth, telling him of the floods caused by the river. Although there were no rains in the skies a wily opponent could easily dam the narrow river. He wondered, not for the first time since hearing the news of the revolt, who the leader was. He had known the Brigante well and neither Gaelwyn nor Marcus had mentioned any leader rising as a new Venutius. Speculation was a luxury he could not afford. Decius Flavius always said that he thought too much.

The sentries summoned the First Spear once they had admitted the turma. Julius breathed a sigh of relief when he recognised the Batavian centurion; he had fought alongside the ala at Veluniate. “Centurion, the Brigante have revolted. You must leave half a century to guard your fort and then join us to relieve Eboracum.”

It spoke much for the links between the Batavians and the ala that the Centurion did not question the orders but quickly set about organising his men. Julius peered up into the sky. With luck, and a forced march, the two columns should be able to join up before Cataractonium, or what was left of it.

It was heading towards late afternoon when the Decurion Princeps and the Prefect met at Cataractonium, or what was left of Cataractonium. The rebels had taken all that there was to take and burned everything that could be burned. As for the dead garrison, they were spread over a wide area, dismembered and despoiled, food for the carrion feeders which flew and slunk away as the horsemen approached. “Tell the infantry to rest Livius. Salvius let us go and bury the dead.” The Decurion Princeps looked at Julius strangely as Livius trotted back to the Batavians. “They are infantrymen, the same race as the dead garrison. Would it do any good for them to bury their comrades? We need them angry tomorrow not fearful. Our troopers have seen it all before.”

“You are right Julius but just once I would like someone else to be given the dirty jobs.”

By the time they had finished the troopers were in no mood for food but ready for a fight. They rode back to the auxiliaries. The Batavian Centurion came over to Julius. “Thank you Prefect. My men would have done as yours did but I am not sure how they would have reacted.”

“I think we will march a little longer. I know we have to build a camp but, even as we sit here, they will be attacking Eboracum. I want us there as quickly as possible tomorrow. Besides I would like to be away from the stink of death.”

“I think we can manage another ten miles.”

“Good for that is ten miles less before we fight tomorrow.”

In Eboracum the Legate viewed the hordes arrayed around the walls of the fortress. The first assault had been easily repulsed with bolt throwers but then he saw that the enemy had someone using their head and they pulled back having suffered minimal losses. They were planning something but he could not work out what. He and Vibius Scaeva had assessed the force against them and decided that, with the single legionary cohort in the fortress, a foray was out of the question. They were completely surrounded; fortunately the two rivers met close to the fortress making an assault only possible from the side with the civilian settlement. Scaeva had not wanted the civilians allowed in and argued against the Legate. "They are Brigante. How do you know they are not part of the rebels?"

"I do not but they showed genuine fear and they have more to lose than we do for most of them earn their money through the fortress. Have the auxiliaries keep an eye on them if you wish."

"I will do believe me!"

"What are they up to?"

"They haven't attacked since the morning and I for one am happy."

"Sir! Smoke!"

One of the legionaries pointed south just beyond the settlement. "Now then what does this mean?"

The legate was answered when a flurry of fire arrows plunged into the thatch and wood of the civilian huts and shops. They were as dry as kindling and soon they were a blazing inferno. The Legate nodded appreciating the military mind. "Someone over there has a military mind and they are using it.

Scaeva, who had spent most of his military career in garrisons, looked at him, puzzled. "It just means they can't attack that way and the rivers stop any other attack."

"The wind Vibius, the wind. It is from the south. The flames and the smoke will blow in this direction which means they can close with the walls. And they may even induce the fortress to catch fire. It is a clever move. We cannot see them and our most deadly weapons will have to fire blind."

The Brigante leaders were looking with increasing awe at Morwenna who seemed to be able to summon the wind at will and control the elements. Any doubt about her power as a witch had now gone. "Now my warriors get as close to the buildings as you can for they cannot see you and fire your arrows over the wall." As they raced forward to do her bidding she turned to Aodh. "Take your men to the river at the side of the fort. They will not be able to see you. Cut down the trees and make a dam."

Almost afraid to question her immaculate judgement he asked, "Will that not make it difficult for us to assault on that side?"

"Yes but the water will be lower on this side, we will have a larger area for our attack and the water will flood parts of the fortress. By the time the river has risen it will be dark and they will not be expecting us to be able to assault at night."

Inside Eboracum the initial salvo of missiles had caught many legionaries and auxiliaries unprepared. The Legate himself had only been saved by a quick thinking legionary who had put his shield above the two of them. "Get men to take water from the river we cannot let that fire catch hold. Order the bolt throwers to fire."

"But they cannot see anything."

"Neither can they but they are hitting us."

As dusk approached the fires were dying down but a mixture of water from the defenders and old soaked wood meant that palls of smoke kept drifting into the defender's faces. Aodh reported back to Morwenna, pleased with his dam which had already caused the water level on the Brigante side to drop revealing a gentle bank which could be easily climbed. The smoke had obscured the dam and the defenders could still only shoot blind.

On the north west and north east sides the defenders could see the fires of the Brigante spread out to encircle them. An exhausted Legate shared a beaker of wine with the garrison commander.

"Well Vibius if we do not get help in the next couple of days we could be in trouble."

"We have expended half of our bolts and we have taken many casualties. The extra mouths will mean that we will have to ration food soon."

"I do not think that we will starve. The food will only need to last three days for by then we will either have been relieved or we will be dead."

The stark assessment caused Vibius to down his beaker in one. "Then we had better pray to Mithras that either the legion marches from the south or that famous cavalry ala rides from the north."

"The legions can only set out tomorrow. They will take another day, at least to reach us and even then they will have to face their whole army for they are on the south side of the fortress."

"The men on the towers tell me that they can see bands of warriors arriving hourly and our friends from the north will have to pass their camps and the rivers to aid us."

"Let us hope then that the Prefect knows his business and can unravel this Gordian knot."

The night brought no respite for the defenders as the Brigante moved closer to the walls under the darkening night. The ditches and the traps slowed them slightly but the legionaries and auxiliaries found themselves under constant attack. It was only in the early hours of the morning, when the supply of arrows had diminished and even the most ardent attacker had retired to rest that the Legate was able to assess the damage. "We have less than six hundred defenders left sir. The artillery has enough ammunition for an hour, nothing more. The waters are rising to the west and threatening to undermine the walls."

"Have the engineers strengthen the buttresses. We need to build some barriers inside the walls for when they break through."

The Prefect of auxiliaries looked aghast at the suggestion. "If they break through we will be slaughtered, they outnumber us ten to one."

"As Boudicca did in the early days but the legions held and so will we. When they break through the walls they will have to fight through narrow walkways. We can make them narrower and negate their numbers. We just need to slow them down, Prefect, until relief arrives and it will arrive."

Vibius murmured, to no one in particular, "I just hope that some of us are still alive when that happens, if it happens."

By the time dawn broke Julius and his pitifully small relief column was already marching south. In the sky lightening from the east they could see the pall of smoke. Livius turned to Decurion Cilo. "Are we too late? Do you think that is Eboracum?"

"I would be surprised for they had warning and the Ninth are a good outfit but it does not bode well Livius."

"If the whole of the Brigante have revolted we stand no chance."

"I don't think it will be all of them. Many are Romanised. If it hadn't been for those Caledonii raids I don't believe this would have happened. I just can't understand where their leaders have come from. No this is a large rebellion but it is not all of the people. I wish Gaelwyn and Marcus were here they knew the Brigante better than anyone and they would have been able to give us a better idea of who is fermenting this discord."

Livius noticed the past tense. "Don't you mean know the Brigante?"

Salvius' eyes suddenly looked much older as he turned to his young comrade. "If they are still alive, which I very much doubt, then they will be in an even worse situation than us. At least we are close to friends and we could head south to Lindum if disaster occurred. There are just three of them against every tribe north of here. Everything has to go perfectly for them to succeed, one piece of bad fortune and they will die. If they are still alive then the Allfather is watching over them."

The scouts returned just as the sun finally cleared the hills to the east. “There are many Brigante with carts and women they are camped between the river and the fortress. South of the fortress the town is burning and the river has risen.”

Julius conferred with the two centurions and Salvius. “It is as I feared they have surrounded it. I was hoping that they would naively attack the main gate.”

“They must have a wise head leading them.”

”Yes Salvius but who? “ He shook his head as though to rid the unwelcome thought from its new home. “It is irrelevant. Centurions I have one hundred men who are good archers; I will place them on this side of the river to harass and annoy the barbarians. They will be expecting support and my one hundred may persuade them that that is where the danger lies. Meanwhile the rest of us will skirt the river and, if it is dammed, it will be lower down, south of the camp, so we could attack them there in numbers. They may draw off warriors to fight my archers, in which case they could mount and retreat. Salvius?”

“As good a plan as any. And when they do pursue me?”

“ Ride north west and then circle around to join us and if they do not pursue you then repeat until they do.”

The Batavian centurion coughed, “But what if they outnumber us? What then?”

“With a little help from the Allfather I am hoping that your cohorts can break in and reinforce the garrison. My horses are best placed outside the walls where we can harass the enemy. I am assuming that there will be reinforcements heading up from Lindum. Someone will need to link with them. It is agreed then? Let us try to save Eboracum and put down this revolt.” He turned to the Decurion Princeps. “It will take at least an hour to get into position. Begin your attack in an hour. Do not risk the men but make them pursue you. Annoy them.”

With a sad smile Salvius said, “That is where we need Macro. He could annoy any barbarian, just by standing there.”

Chapter 9

Close to Wyddfa Decius Lucullus had received word of the Brigante revolt. He had known that there would come a time when he would have to leave in a hurry; he had just assumed it would have come because the Romans had discovered their deception. There was nothing between Brigantia and Deva. Once Eboracum fell they would pour south and Deva would be the next target. He had his men load all the wagons and mules with their ill-gotten gains and while they were securing the beasts he and his lieutenant went to the mine entrance. The beams which held up the entrance had been built while Decius had watched; he knew where the weak points were. He and his companion took their axes and demolished the supports. At first nothing happened and then suddenly the whole of the entrance collapsed in on itself burying the twenty miners and dooming them to a suffocating and slow death.

The murder was justified in Decius' mind as it meant they could leave at leisure with no pursuit. Just as he justified deserting Aula as a necessity and when the time was right he would abandon his men but he needed them until they arrived in Italy. First he had to get to Deva, secure a ship and then avoid the Classis Britannica but he was well satisfied, he had achieved his first aim, he had his fortune. He smiled to himself as they set off down the twisting road from the mountain, perhaps the confusion with the rebellion might actually help to obscure his movements. Aula might believe him dead and the trail would go cold, he could re-invent himself in Rome itself.

Seeing the huge numbers of barbarians gave the auxiliaries the incentive to move swiftly. If this were not nipped in the bud then they would have even greater numbers to face. Julius halted them just where the river was shallower because of the fallen trees and brush. He could see the Brigante trying to scale the newly revealed banks. “This is where we attack. I will charge with my horse and then you can bring your cohorts to join in the attack. Once you join us we will wheel and attack those at the rear. When we have cleared a breach take your cohort and try to join the Legate in the fortress. Your extra numbers should enable him to hold until the Ninth arrives.”

“Look Prefect!” Livius pointed. There was consternation amongst the Brigante and he could see a warband leave the attack and move northwards. “It must be Salvius!”

“Good then we have time to prepare. Form two lines! I will lead the first, Livius you take the second.”

Inside the fort the Legate had been resigned to his last morning in the fort when suddenly they saw Brigante racing north. “Vibius! It must be the reinforcements. Tell the men, there is hope. We just need to hold out when the attack comes.”

Morwenna was calmer than the Brigante leadership who were clucking like hens when the fox is in the farmyard. When the news had come that the ala was attacking north of the river she was pleased for she wanted her mother’s killers in her grasp. It also meant that she knew where they were. “Aodh let Colla and the others race north to fight off this attack of the cavalry we must still breach the gate. We are very close to taking it. You had better stay here and take charge for I fear that these warriors do not have your wise head.”

Inside Aodh was almost bursting with pride although he knew she was right. “Ownie!” The Brigante chief rode over on his pony. “Take charge of the assault. The banks are easy to climb and we have weakened their walls.”

Giving a lopsided grin because of the new scar he had picked up at Cataractonium he hefted his sword from its scabbard. “Tonight we dine on Roman flesh! With me!” With a roar he leapt from his mount and raced at the head of his warriors to begin what the whole Brigante horde thought was the end of Eboracum.

The timing from the ala was perfect for so intent was the mass of screaming warriors on massacring their victims that they did not notice the line of grim faced horsemen racing towards them across the lowered banks of the now shallow water. Although denied archers, the troopers were just as adept with their javelins and they managed to throw two each before they wheeled. Two lines of over two hundred troopers meant that the attack that was meant to be from a barbarian army already tasting victory, withered and died before it even started. Julius swept them around in a perfect half circle to crash into the mob that was waiting to pour into the gap created by the attackers. The long spathas of the Roman cavalry found no armour to impede their progress and vicious, deadly wounds were created, the attackers had no defence. The warriors at the front of the lines had had shields but those at the back had merely swords and spears; they were cut down like wheat. As the sheer weight of opponents slowed down the mounted horse warriors, the nine hundred auxiliaries, foot and horse, smashed, like a huge battering ram, into the remnants of the first attack and then the mob burst open by the cavalry like a ripe plum.

Morwenna was, for the first time, surprised. She had not expected the attack to come from that quarter. Aodh, as a seasoned warrior who had already fought against Marcus' Horse, reacted the quickest. "Form a line of spears and stand shoulder to shoulder!" He roughly pushed into line, with the flat of his sword, those who looked as though they were fleeing.

Morwenna realised that she had to play her part and she screamed out an invocation. "Mother come to our aid and show our enemies your vengeance! Devour these unbelievers and give your people victory!"

To a primitive mob that had seen wind and fog created by the sorceress and seen her read men's minds this was enough to stiffen the sinews and strengthen the line. Suddenly the barbarian horde became solid again and the horses of the ala found themselves facing a solid line of steel. The huge mass of men which thrust from the back forced those at the front into the horses and the troopers found it difficult, on the upslope, to control their horses. Blades, knives, clubs all struck the horses which reared and snorted in panic and in pain. As horses fell so did riders, to be torn apart by an angry multitude intent on revenge. The momentum all gone the line foundered and collapsed in on itself. Livius' second line became embroiled in the first and Livius had to lay about him with both his sword and his shield. Using only his knees and his heels he extricated himself from the front line and tried to reorganise his men. "Second line hold!"

Julius heard the command and knew, for he had fought in enough battles to know that a horse will not charge unbroken men, that they were doomed if they stayed where they were and he shouted, above the din and wreck of war, "Wheel and withdraw!" All of the troopers grabbed the reins with their left hand and tugged back to make their screaming, rearing and bucking horses withdraw. With their right hands they used the long reach of the spatha to hold at bay the unruly warband armed with much shorter weapons. As the horses withdrew from the angry blades they became much calmer and more controllable. "First line withdraw behind the second!"

"Second line, if you have javelins use them!" Livius strident voice carried and the last javelins flew over the head of the retreating front line to create a small gap.

There were thousands of barbarians poised on the slight slope and, seeing the ala pull back hurtled down after them. Julius was aware that the two cohorts were still some way from the gate and he had to withdraw slowly. "Second line retreat behind the first. Javelins!" There were far fewer javelins this time and it was like throwing snowballs into a firestorm, they did nothing and soon the two lines were intermingled again and troopers were fighting enemies on both sides of their mounts.

The two centurions had been watching the charge as they despatched the last of the attackers and saw the line of horses judder to a halt. The Prefect's orders had been quite clear and the buccina sounded the retreat. Inside the fortress they heard the retreat and the centurions on the walls sent down the order to open the gates. Such had been the speed of the Roman attack that there were no Brigante near to the gate and the two cohorts made it inside almost intact. Marcus' Horse was not so lucky. Julius roared, "Retreat!" As they tried to disengage the barbarian archers took their toll and arrows rained down striking both shields and horses. Those on the edges were plucked from their saddles by spears as they tried to wheel away from the danger and a fearsome mass of infuriated Brigante desperate to wreak revenge on these horse warriors who had killed so many and frustrated their attack. When they finally reformed and were clear of both missiles and enemies Julius saw that they had left almost a hundred of their comrades on the field but they had achieved their aim. "Back to the Decurion Princeps!" The frothing bleeding horses lurched and limped away from the blood soaked battlefield carrying troopers, every one of whom carried at least one wound.

Far to the north Gaelwyn was outlining his plans. "Since they have built their camp and returned closer to their homeland they are more relaxed. The captives are no longer fettered but they are closely watched. At night they have one guard on the gate which is but loosely latched. Lulach arrived yesterday with some Selgovae and many of the Caledonii left. We will never have a better chance for it will soon be the time of the bone burning."

"The boat will be off the coast tomorrow night. We must strike this evening or in the morning."

"Morning."

They all looked at Macro for there had been no discussion. "Why?"

"If there is pursuit then I do not want to be waiting with our backs to the sea for too long. If we take them in the morning and then head south, we can cut back west once they are following the trail. We have horses and should be able to out run them."

"Good and perhaps we can lay some traps today when we scout the route."

Gaelwyn snorted, "If you have all finished deciding what you will do when we have them could we come back to the problem of how we rescue them." Suitably admonished they listened. "Macro you will take out the sentry with an arrow. Marcus you will wait with the horses. Gaius we will enter the round hut in which they are kept and get the children and Ailis. Macro you will cover our retreat. There is but one gate and if there is a pursuit you should be able to hold long enough for us to escape and then you can follow."

"Where is Lulach?"

"He and his men have a large camp up river. Probably five miles away."

"Which gives us an hour at the most. That is not long."

"It is all we have."

"Very well."

Marcus looked sharply at Macro. He had expected more of an argument. And the giant was right, an hour was not long enough to lay a false trail and evade pursuit. But as Gaelwyn had said those are the bones cast by the Parcae and man has no control over them.

Gaelwyn and Macro created a few nasty surprises on the trail south from the captive camp. "We want to make sure that they cannot follow quickly. The more time they spend looking for traps the more time we have to escape with a woman and three bairns." Gaius was the most nervous of the four men. He was close to regaining his family.

Macro, in contrast, was the most relaxed. "You worry too much Gaius. Gaelwyn's plan is a good one. The guards will be less alert, after all they are close to their homeland and there was no pursuit. We'll be in and out before they know."

"We have three small children remember."

"Which is why there will be two of you and Ailis, each one can carry a child. Ailis is a good horsewoman. You should know that better than anyone."

"And what if Marcus or the boat is not there?"

"And what if my sister was my brother!! Listen to yourself. We have planned this as well as we can. Short of going back in time and preventing their abduction there is not a great deal we can do." Gaelwyn watched the two Romans arguing. There was nothing else anyone could do so why not just accept it. "Look Gaius," Macro's voice became quite gentle and soothing, "we all have things in our past we want to change. Like if I hadn't taken up with Morwenna then Decius would still be alive. You have to live with things like that. It is life. All you can do is your best and try to make amends. The Allfather knows I have tried to make amends for my mistake and I promise you this, Gaius, you will get your family back. You have my word, for your family has looked after my son and I would do anything in my power to protect them and give my life to do so."

"Well if you two girls have finished your argument, kiss and make up and then we can get back to the camp. We have to be in position well before dawn."

The Prefect led his weary men to meet up with Salvius. Livius brought up the rear, one of only two Decurions to survive the battle. Cassius, the other survivor had a long cut running from his knee to his ankle and Livius knew that he had cuts to his arms but there was so much blood he could not tell which was his and which the enemies. The ala had suffered greatly but Livius had seen, as he led the second line that they had broken the back of the enemy. They would not attack for at least another day as their braver warriors, those who had led the assault, now lay dead and dying in the ditches surrounding Eboracum. If the Ninth arrived, as Julius had predicted, then the Brigante would have to lift the siege. The Decurion Princeps and his archers looked to have fared better than Julius and Livius could see no empty saddles. The eight turmae of the ala were no more. They would be lucky to field six and the mounts were looking the worse for wear.

"Well Prefect it looks as though we halted the attack."

"Yes Salvius but at a great cost."

Decurion Princeps Cilo pointed beyond the remnants of Julius' charge. "Look yonder, some of the Brigante have had enough. They are leaving." They could see knots of people fleeing west from the carnage.

"True but they still outnumber the garrison. Livius when you and what remains of your turma have rested take them towards Lindum to meet with the Ninth. I would be happier knowing that they were on their way."

"Let me send one of my turma, they are fresher and Livius is wounded."

"No Salvius yours are the turmae who will have to fight tomorrow for I believe the Brigante on this side of the fortress may either attack the fortress or us and either way I need your one hundred warriors to combat whatever comes at us."

"Very well. We will camp yonder, well away from any surprise attack."

The trail and traps they created took them a long way south before they turned west. It was a fine balance they were trying to achieve. In a perfect world their pursuers would not realise that they had turned off and they would have all the time in the world to get to the boat. They all knew, however, that the Caledonii would send their best trackers and they would find their trail which would be heading north west. Their hope was that they would slow them down enough to get to the coast well before the pursuers but just in time for the ship. None of the three cared to think what would happen to them if the boat did not arrive but the Tribune had assured them that the boat would be there and Marcus had never let them down before.

When the first hint of a lightening of the sky appeared in the east the three men tied their horses securely to the tree. The last thing they needed was to make good their escape from the camp only to find their horses gone. Gaelwyn and Gaius just had their swords and daggers. Macro had his bow. They halted at the edge of the wood and looked over to the gate guarded by a single sentry. There was no bar on the gate it could be opened from the inside or the outside, the sentry was the barrier. The three of them made sure that there were no other guards and then Gaelwyn nodded to Macro. He pulled back the bow and aimed for the guard's neck. At only forty paces distance Macro was confident he could make the killing blow. Gaius and Gaelwyn were poised for the arrow's flight. As soon as it struck they ran but the man fell silently in a heap with no more noise than a loud sigh. The early dawn was still as silent as could be. Even the early morning birds had yet to make their dawn chorus. Macro easily dragged the body off while Gaius and Gaelwyn opened the gate slowly and peered in. They had to pass between two other huts before they reached Ailis' and Gaelwyn had warned Gaius that there were guards in the others. Gaelwyn had not seen any dogs but that was the one problem they had no solution to. They could hear the men snoring as they moved alongside the first and second huts but no-one stirred. They glanced back to see Macro with his bow notched, the smiling face nodding.

Gaelwyn opened the door and the two men slipped inside. They were so silent that none of the sleepers moved. Gaius went to Ailis and putting his hand over her mouth awoke her. The shock turned to joy as she saw her husband. He put his finger to his mouth and she nodded. He point to her and then Marcus, to himself and Decius and to Gaelwyn and Macro's son, Decius. When he knew she understood the three of them put their hands over their child's mouth and lifted them. Still no-one else had stirred. The two men knew that the hard part would be when they crept, hopefully unseen, into the settlement where every warrior was an enemy and every sound a weapon.

As they moved quickly through the huts they kept their eye on Macro for he would be the first sign that there was danger. They almost breathed a collective sigh of relief when they passed Macro but Gaelwyn kept them moving into the woods. Once they reached the horses they quickly mounted. The three boys were so shocked and delighted with the appearance of the friendly faces that they uttered not a sound. Macro was about to join them when the sentry's relief came out of his hut; Gaelwyn had watched on previous nights and this was earlier than before. Was their good fortune deserting them? Macro waved Gaelwyn off and the three adults rode away leaving Macro's horse tied up. They had had this as a back up plan for Macro would be able to move quicker on his own than the others with children. He calmly watched as the new sentry walked to the ramparts and relieved himself. When he had finished he looked curiously towards the open gate. Macro could almost see the thoughts and questions racing through the man's mind; where was the sentry and why was the gate open? The arrow flew straight and true towards the man's throat but as he was turning to shout for his comrade the arrow caught him in the shoulder and did not kill him instantly. He fell with a soft cry.

"Shit!" Macro murmured. They would be on to them as soon as they came to. He raced for his horse and swiftly mounted. Rather than following the others he waited, another arrow notched. The first hut erupted with armed yet sleepy men wondering what had awoken them. The first warrior saw the body of the second guard with the arrow still in his neck and suddenly the alarm was raised. He gave an enormous shout which made even Gaelwyn and the others turn as they fled the scene. The powerful Roman watched to see who gave orders and as an old grey haired warrior shouted something Macro's arrow hit him in the side of the head. The rest dropped to the floor but not before Macro had sent another one to the Allfather. Rather than racing away Macro walked his horse backwards through the woods. The warriors inside did not know how many men were outside and they came out cautiously, peering into the forest which was becoming lighter to see if they could see who had attacked them. When they found the second body in the edge of the forest more men emerged and they began to fan out in the woods. Realising that another arrow would show them the direction he had taken Macro took off down the trail carefully avoiding the deadfalls and traps.

The other three had made good time for Gaelwyn was very familiar with the route and Macro only caught up with them when they had turned west. “Keep going!” Macro put one huge hand out and swept Decius on to his horse. “Did you think I wouldn’t come for you son?”

“I kept telling them; I knew you would come for me.”

The Decurion gripped him tightly to his chest, tears of joy in his eyes; he had never felt such love in his life. He now knew that what he had felt for Morwenna, the boy’s mother was lust and this was love. He knew that he would do anything to save the boy who, he realised, was the single most important thing in his life. All that he had held important, comradeship, honour, fighting, Rome, all was meaningless against the life and future of his son.

Morwenna held counsel with Aodh and her chiefs. “We should attack tonight!”

“Yes Parthalan that makes sense now that they have reinforced the fortress.”

“Ownie do not use that tone with me or we will settle our differences with blades.”

“Any time you wish I am ready.”

“Enough!” Morwenna’s voice silenced them in an instant. This bickering would get them nowhere. “Aodh’s scouts have reported the Roman legion less than a day away. When they arrive we will be caught between two forces that can destroy our warriors.”

“My men are not afraid.”

“I know Parthalan but we do not need to waste warrior’s lives uselessly. My old chief, Lulach taught me that. Make the enemy bleed, not your own warriors.”

“Aodh is correct and we did make them bleed today. Look at how many of their horse warriors lie dead. That was the force we feared. Our warriors are swift enough to evade the legions which are slow and ponderous."

"You are suggesting what then, oh Queen." Colla's voice was less confident than it had been. He had been shocked at the casualties they had suffered. He had thought that the numbers of warriors they had would ensure an easy victory. The tenacious Romans had fought far harder than he remembered from his youth.

"We leave Eboracum." There was a stunned silence.

"After all the warriors we lost we just turn tail and run back to our homes to await the vengeance of the Romans!"

"No Parthalan. We do not run away; we do what we set out to do we remove the Romans from our land. Eboracum is but one town. They have taken troops to fortify this symbol of Roman power from many towns which now lie defenceless. They have people living in them who just need convincing to join with us. When the Roman legion arrives at Eboracum they will spend time rebuilding. In that time we can raise an army twice as big as the one we now have and we can lure the enemy to a battlefield of our choosing and there we can destroy him. You are right Parthalan, the enemy will think we have gone home but they do not know who they fight."

Mollified and intrigued, he asked, "Then what do we do?"

"We divide the army into four. We go north, east, south and west to raise more recruits."

"What if they do not wish to join us?" The dissenting voice of Colla warned Morwenna that he was unreliable.

"Then they die." Her ice cold voice chilled the old chief. "Parthalan you take the south. The legion will be in Lindum and they will not expect us to travel in that direction. If you avoid the Roman road you will avoid any reinforcements they are sending. Take your warriors as far as Lindum if needs be. We must make them fear us. We must make them wonder where we will strike next. Colla take yours west, that is land familiar to you and you can control the land to the sea. Ownie destroy all that lies to the east, especially their signal stations which they will need to use. We will head north to Morbium for Aodh and I know the area well."

"How will we keep each other informed?"

"Aodh has ten trusted messengers and he has trained them well. They are mounted on the finest horses we have captured. Use them to send messages to me and I will pass my orders by them to you."

The three Brigante chiefs noticed the word, orders. Although they were disappointed with the campaign so far they still respected her as a sorceress and the women who now followed her was nearly as great an army as the men. They would all follow her, for the moment.

When they were alone and the camp was being packed up Morwenna surprised Aodh by telling him that she believed her chiefs were less committed. "Then it is over?"

Smiling that secret smile she had she said, "No. It has just begun. You did not think that one battle would win the war did you? Your leader Lulach showed that. The Roman beast is powerful, like a mighty boar. One spear will not kill him. He needs bleeding and slowing down for a wounded Rome is dangerous and, like the hunter we must attack and withdraw, attack and withdraw; each time bleeding him a little more. I do not doubt, my dear Aodh, that your countrymen will take advantage of this revolt and will also come south. They too will bleed the beast."

"That is why you chose north!"

"It is why I chose north so that, if he does come south then I can meet with him and we can join forces. If the chiefs are less than reliable, it will not hurt us in the long run. Parthalan and Ownie are good leaders but they are young and ambitious. They may do much harm and they may kill many Romans but, inevitably, they will fall."

"And Colla?"

"He will hide in his home but we have sown enough seeds amongst his clan to ensure that someone in his home will want to lead. They will be our reserve."

Aodh looked in admiration at his queen, his woman. "You have planned and thought all of this out yourself."

"I had a good teacher. Luigsech spent long nights in darkest winter when the blanket of snow and cold trapped us in our cave, telling me of how the wars had been fought and the mistakes people had made. She made me realise that women are often underestimated. The women of Brigantia will follow me and, as you know my love, men will do anything for the women in their life." The two acolytes giggled as Aodh reddened and left.

Gaelwyn urged them on once they were on the north west leg of the journey. They had not laid traps for they wanted to sow confusion. If the enemy could not find their trail quickly then they might escape. The carefully crafted route took them across every stream and river that they could. Each stream they crossed they went either up or down stream to throw off their pursuers.

Ailis gripped Decius tightly to her chest. She had never given up hope of rescue but, the further north they had travelled, the less hopeful she had become. She knew that, were it not for the children she would have taken her own life for she had been a captive of the cruel Caledonii once before and death was preferable. She glanced over her shoulder to her husband also clinging on tightly to their young son Marcus. He looked older and greyer and yet it had only been a few weeks that they had been apart. She had had it hard but she could see that he had suffered almost as much.

Gaius was more afraid, as they raced as safely as they could through the heavy woods, than he had been so far. They were tantalisingly close to escape. The boat had been a stroke of genius and confirmed, in Gaius' mind, the brilliance of the Tribune. Once at sea they were free and they could escape no matter how perilous the sea was it was nothing compared with the barbarians now pursuing them. His fear was that they would catch them or even anticipate their route and be awaiting them on the beach. To have his sons and wife back was joyous but to have them and then have them snatched away would be cruel beyond measure. He prayed that the Allfather was watching over them.

Chapter 10

"Sir!"

It seemed to Prefect Julius Demetrius that he had only just fallen asleep when he felt the hand of the trooper shaking him.

"Yes what is it?

"Decurion Princeps compliments sir but it is dawn and the Brigante have gone."

He jumped up, almost colliding with the startled sentry. "What? How? When?"

"There was a fog in the night sir and with the rising waters and the bit of smoke left from the fires the guards didn't see anything and then when the sun came up, well they was gone."

"Tell the Decurion Princeps to stand the men to."

By the time he had put his armour on and left the tent the ala was standing ready to ride. "Well Salvius this is, as Decius might have said, a bit of a bugger."

Cilo smiled at the remembrance, "He would too and he would have been right as well. They must have left soon after dark. I have sent a patrol around to the southern gate and they report they are gone from there. The Legate asked if you would go into the fortress for a meeting."

"Right. Well send out the turmae…"

"We only have three Decurions left, sir."

"Of course. Divide the remaining ala into three turmae. Livius is south so send them north, east and west. All they need to do is to find where they are, no engaging. Clear Salvius?"

"Clear. I don't think either the men or the mounts are in any condition to engage."

It felt strange to watch what remained of the ala ride away without him but he knew that a meeting with the Legate was vital if they were to take advantage of this strange withdrawal of their foes.

Riding through the main gate Julius could see the devastation cause by the attack. The fire and the floods had damage so much of the parts of the fortress that the Prefect could see it would need to be rebuilt. Many of the troops in the fort would be engineers before they were soldiers. He nodded to the Batavian Centurion who was leading his men to destroy the half built dam. "I think we came just in time Prefect."

"You are right a longer delay might have seen it destroyed."

The Centurion pointed south to the battlefield. "Your lads did well yesterday. Did you lose many?"

"Too many Centurion and too many who were irreplaceable."

The Legate came down the smoke blackened stairs of the headquarters building his arms outstretched. "Thank you Prefect. Your timely arrival yesterday saved the day."

Vibius Scaeva patted Julius on the shoulder. "I have never seen a more magnificent charge. Two hundred against thousands! Magnificent!"

"Thank you sir but it cost us half my men and today we could have done with those men to find where the rebels have gone."

The Legate looked at Julius. "They have gone home of course. It is over."

Shaking his head firmly Julius said, "They haven't. You do not know the Brigante. They have a wise head this time not a hot head like Venutius. This leader is more like Aed and Maeve who were far more thoughtful. The attack at Cataractonium showed that. No, they left because they knew the Ninth was on its way. If my little cavalry attack could hinder their attack they knew that the Ninth would make mincemeat of them. I believe they have gone elsewhere to make other mischief."

"I think you are giving that woman too much credit."

A sudden chill ran down Julius' spine and a sense of dread filled him. "A woman? Which woman?"

"We caught a prisoner and, after torture he told us that the Brigante chiefs were led by a sorceress the daughter of that Aed chap you mentioned and a witch called…"

"Fainch! Then it is Morwenna."
The legate and the garrison commander were both astounded. "How did you know?"
"She infiltrated the ala a few years ago and murdered the Camp Prefect at Coriosopitum, Decius Flavius. She is an evil and powerful woman. If she leads this army than I can guarantee that it is not over and will not be over until she is on a cross or burned."
The Legate was taken aback by the venom of the young man's words and he no longer doubted them. "But where will they go?"
"I do not know but my turmae are seeking them. She will do all in her considerable power to end Roman rule. At least we now know whom we seek. Would that the Tribune was here."
"The Tribune?"
"Tribune Marcus Maximunius. He was the one who caught and killed her mother and also helped to defeat Calgathus."
Vibius said, "I have heard of him. I was a centurion under Decius Brutus and met him once. He is a good man. Where is he?"
"He has gone north to rescue his family from the Caledonii."
"Then he is dead."
"No commander. He is still alive, I can feel it. And now I must rejoin my men for they will need to know the news. It will anger them even more than the loss yesterday."
As Julius was leaving he heard his name being called. When he turned he saw Livius leading his exhausted men into the fortress. "Sir, the Ninth are an hour behind us."
"Good, tell the Legate and then we will ride."
"But sir my men…"
"The Brigante are led by Morwenna!"
His face hardening Livius said, "We will be right there then sir."

There was barely a half cohort at Morbium but the Centurion was an old frontier hand. He had been at the fort, whilst still in the ranks, when the Caledonii had tried to take it and he had fought with his back to the wall expecting to die. Centurion Decimus Murena felt that every day he had been alive since then had been a bonus. That said he had no intention of having his testicles taken as a souvenir by any rebel whether Caledonii or Brigante. He had barred the bridge. It was a crude barrier and could be removed by determined men but they would have to do so whilst under a barrage of arrows from the fort. In addition he had placed oil soaked rags within the barricade for he remembered the inferno which had burned and killed so many the last time the barbarians had tried to take the fort and the bridge. The banks of the river had been cleared of undergrowth and he had dragged the bottom to make it flow as swiftly as possible. The ditches were doubled and deeper than they had been. His garrison was pulling double shifts, four hours on and four hours off. He had impressed upon them the need for vigilance. "If you don't recognise the man who comes up that road, or the way he sounds! Kill the bastard! They are my orders!" Whenever the rest of the garrison and Marcus' Horse returned, they would find that this crossing had been denied their enemies.

Aodh and his scouts arrived at sunset and saw, with dismay, that the fort had not been abandoned. Morwenna was more phlegmatic. "We can go down stream and cross the Dunum. This is the last garrison. We need not fight until we have more men and have the Romans where we want, not hiding behind their walls where they can kill more of us." Leaving a dozen men to watch the fort they headed downstream to where the river twisted turned and gently slowed. They were easily able to cross with just wet legs and feet as the price. "There is a small settlement to the north of here; we will spend the night there. They may join us, if not…" She turned to the two acolytes, Anchorat and Maban and spoke to them. They both kissed her on the lips, smiled at Aodh and left.

“Where do they go?” As soon as the words were uttered he regretted saying them.

Morwenna held up an admonishing finger. “Do not question me. Know that I do what I do and you know what I tell you. Their work does not concern you but we will see them again within a few days.”

The settlement of Seton was close to the sea hidden from the land by a mighty wood. The people there enjoyed both the fruits of the sea and the fruits of the woods. They were prosperous and contented ignored by both Roman and Caledonii alike. They were also led by a powerful woman, the matriarch of the leading family. When her husband had drowned she had taken over the control of the settlement making both the rules and the laws. Cruatha was a strong minded woman and, with the strongest five men in the village as her sons was impregnable.

“Where is the settlement? I cannot see it?”

“Which is why it is important. It is beyond the forest close to the shore. Have your men follow me.”

“But there may be danger...”

She smiled a thin humourless smile. “I think I will be more danger to those people than they are to me.” She moved swiftly and easily through the trees and emerged on to the beach. The gate of the settlement was open and she walked past the two men lounging there, too surprised to react. She could hear the sounds of shock as people came out of their round huts. The men of the village came out with swords and clubs in their hands. Morwenna kept her hands at her side and, with only Aodh behind her, for the rest waited without the walls , she walked up to the largest hut that she could see.

Cruatha stepped out an angry look on her face. She was still a relatively young woman having seen but thirty three summers and she was still strikingly beautiful with the body of a young girl. Her height made her appear older than she was. She fixed her eyes on Morwenna who did not flinch but stared back with the same intensity. It was as though there were no others for miles around so intent on each where they. Aodh was the only one who did not find it disconcerting for he knew what Morwenna was doing; she was entrancing the head woman and bending her to her will. Cruatha found it both intoxicating and alarming at the same time. Within her she had so many conflicting emotions that she didn't know what to do. Morwenna stepped towards her and Cruatha gave a half bow and taking the younger sorceress by the hand led her within the hut. Aodh stepped to the door, now closed and stood facing the crowd which gathered. The buzz and the conversation came from the crowd for Aodh stood silently on guard.

When the two of them came out, some time later Cruatha was looking at Morwenna with awe, bordering on adoration. He cheeks were flushed and she looked to have become even taller. "We welcome our Queen, Queen Morwenna of the Brigante," and then she bowed. Aodh led the bowing and soon the whole settlement had bowed. "All her people are welcome," with an imperious wave she summoned in the waiting warriors. "My people we will feed them and give them shelter for now we are one people and tomorrow we go to war with the Romans."

Many of the people looked at each other in surprise. Going to war? With the Romans? Aodh smiled to himself. They had captured the settlement without a blow and Morwenna had won the village, how he knew not but he was not surprised. Morwenna had used her magic again and however many warriors they accrued it would increase their numbers but, more importantly give them a safe and secure base.

When the Prefect arrived at Morbium it was with a sense of relief that no one had destroyed it and more no one had even tried. Instead of riding across the barrier Julius and the ala swam the narrow river. "Good to see you sir? We were worried. How did things go at Eboracum?"

“We will camp in your fort and I will tell you over food for, in all honesty centurion it is many days since I ate and slept comfortably. The walls of Morbium will be more than welcome.”

“It was only then that the centurion noticed the wounds on the men and the condition of both men and horses.”I am sorry sir. I was so worried that I forgot my manners. Tribune Furius would have had my guts for garters.”

Julius laughed. “Of that I am certain for he would have had a wild board roasting just on the off chance that some visitors might come.”

“Aye he would, the old bugger loved his food.”

“And his wine,” added Julius. who knew the old tribune well.

“I hope he is feasting with the Allfather even now.”

“To be truthful Centurion I suspect that even the Allfather cannot cope with his appetite.”

As they later sat in the mess Julius proposed a toast, ”To absent friends!”

“Well sir, you’ve been fed and watered. The horses looked after. What has happened?”

“The Brigante have a new Queen, Morwenna. She’s the daughter of the witch Fainch.”

“The one we crucified years ago.”

“Aye. She has raised the Brigante and they tried to capture Eboracum. Well we stopped that but we lost a lot of the ala. When the Ninth came they raised the siege and we are looking for them. We followed their trail north and then lost it around the river nearby. Did you see a large horde?”

“No sir. There were some warriors in the woods across the river, not enough to cause a nuisance but enough for us to keep an eye on.”

“We’ll have a look for them tomorrow. I don’t think it is over. I expect the legate will reinforce you when he can but the barricade was a good idea.”

"The trouble is this fort was built to protect the bridge from raiders in the north not those from the south. We could do with a fortlet on the other side."

"When you get your reinforcements build one. It can't hurt. And now Centurion we will sleep our first peaceful sleep n a while."

The next day Livius and his scout found where they had been observed by the scouts. "It looks like the trail goes east sir towards the coast. There is a good crossing point about twenty miles east."

"There is another one about ten miles east. We will try them both."

They rode along the gentle banks of the Dunum as it meandered between fertile lands on both sides. Suddenly a rider appeared. "Sir, Decurion Princeps sent me sir. He has received reports of a warband in the east towards Stagh-herts."

"Do you think our lot have joined them?"

"It doesn't matter. We head east to where we know a warband is. If the band we were following has crossed north then they are not raiding here and if they have joined Cilo's band then we need to stop them. "He looked ruefully at Livius. "At the moment we do not have enough men anyway. The Decurion Princeps can't contain the larger warband on his own. I am not sure we can either but at least we will have eighty men which gives us a little more to work with."

The settlement at Streonshal had grown well under the stewardship of Atticus the one time Roman helmsmen, shipwrecked just up the shore. He was a thoughtful and compassionate leader who had learned that not all men are what they seemed. He had been badly duped once by the traitorous and murderous Gaius Cresens, ex-quartermaster of the Second Pannonian Horse. Now that Atticus was into his middle age, he had become even wiser. The warriors employed by Cresens in the past were now members of the community and their sons provided the defence for the shore side settlement. Trade with the

Raomans was brisk and had brought great wealth to the community that, a generation ago, had been a few huts and a population slowly starving to death.

Atticus had been receiving reports that Derventio had been all but abandoned and there were signs of burning in the distance. The last time that had occurred Streonshal had nearly been destroyed and Atticus was taking no chances. "Bring the livestock in the stockade and tell Ael to double the sentries. Keep the gate closed and barred."

Ael, who was the defence's leader, appeared concerned when he finally found Atticus who was supervising the storage of the freshly cured fish. "What is wrong leader?"

"As far as I know Ael nothing but Derventio's garrison has left and there are signs of burning. I thought that we could keep watch for a while until we see another Roman patrol."

"The Romans are still in their signal tower. They would know if anything were amiss."

"Perhaps but their job is to pass messages up and down the coast," the grey haired, powerfully built man pointed west, "that is where we saw the burning. It will do no harm to keep the animals in the stockade for a few days."

"But it is inconvenient to have to open and close the gate," grumbled Ael.

Laughing the genial headman pointed at Ael, "You know Ael you sound for all the world like a small child told that they cannot play outside because of the weather. If there is a danger out there and my senses tell me there is then our duty is to keep this community safe. Have I ever been wrong about things like this?"

Shaking his head Ael wandered off mumbling to himself, "It is me they will all complain to when they want to leave."

Ownie's warriors had already destroyed two settlements which refused to join their revolt. They found another two which had been destroyed in the Caledonii raids earlier in the year. He had decided to follow the next instruction from Morwenna. He would destroy the signal towers; the Romans would be blind. He had started in the north and so far it had gone well. His scouts returned with consternation written on their faces. "What is it that you look so worried?"

"There is a settlement in the next bay and they have closed their gates."

"And what of the signal station?"

"It is further south."

Ownie stroked his chin thoughtfully. If this was a stockaded settlement then it was a large one and if they had barricaded it then they expected trouble. The Brigante in this part of the world were an unknown people; they lived from the sea and kept to themselves. On the other hand if they had numbers of men and were rich then his band could be expanded. "We will ride and visit with these people."

"We will have to go some way inland for there is a wide river with steep banks. There is a crossing but it is some miles upstream."

Dismissing the problem with a wave of his hand Ownie led the band of warriors inland. His band had not grown but he had had no losses. His men numbered more than a thousand and everyone acknowledged that they were the best. He grudgingly agreed with those who said that Aodh's elite were the best man for man but they were only fifty. If you were to win a war you needed warriors like Ownie's. He was proud of the fact that at least half of them sported Roman armour and weapons which they had acquired at Cataractonium. They were fiercely loyal to him and he had, of late, begun to wonder about Colla's leadership. In the campaign so far he had not shown himself to be the powerful warrior they all hoped. When he met up again he would challenge Colla for the leadership. With Morwenna as queen and himself as general they would sweep the Romans back to the southern half of the country and the yoke of the past thirty years would be removed.

After they crossed the river and turned the bend of the wide river bed he could see the impressive stockade on the top of the cliffs. The path which led to it was twisting. He noted that the lower end of the path had seaweed upon it; the tide would cut it off at high tide. "Caddell take twenty men and ride south. Approach the settlement from that side. I want to know if there is another path or entrance." Ownie hated the thought of being trapped by the sea. This was an intriguing place. Living on the high moors he had only seen the sea in the distance before and he could see that it could be an ally or a foe. He would not underestimate this place and its leader.

When they reached the top of the path they found themselves in a cleared area, 'a killing place' Ownie thought to himself. His men arrayed behind him bristling with arms and armour. Ownie would intimidate those who were inside. He began to think how he might use this as a base himself in the future. He counted the men on the ramparts. He noticed with some disquiet that they all appeared to be well armed and there were more of them than he had expected. He kicked his horse on and rode with open palms towards the gate. As he drew nearer he saw a grey haired but powerful looking man on the ramparts above the gate. Alarmingly the two men next to him had bows drawn and aimed at him.

"Who are you and what do you wish of us?" The voice from above was calm and without fear.

"I am Ownie, chief of the Brigante and servant of Queen Morwenna."

"Queen Morwenna? I have not heard of her."

"She is the rightful queen of the Brigante and we are here to ask that you join us in our fight against the Roman usurpers."

"I see. Well I have to tell you Ownie, Chief of the Brigante, that we do not believe the Romans to be usurpers. They are our friends and we will not be joining you in your fight."

Ownie was disconcerted by the calm reply. "Will you not ask your people? Ask your council?"

"My people feel as I do. I need not ask them, I know."

Ownie was confused. He had expected, at the very least fear but there was none. “We can take you and your settlement easily for we are many.”

“True you are many but you would lose more than we and Ownie a word of advice. Beware of the tides for as you can see,” he waved his hand to his right, “the water is fast approaching.”

Ownie could see that he and his band would be soon trapped; he turned and rode back to his men.”Sceolan stay here with fifty warriors. We will return when the tide has gone out. Hopefully Caddell has found another route not dominated by the tide.” Turning he shouted to Atticus. “Your last chance to aid us. Refusal will mean that all will be put to the sword.”

Nodding Atticus said, “That will be as the Allfather wishes.”

By the time he had found Caddell the light was fading. “There is a path over the ridge but on the other side there is a gully filled with rocks and a ditch.”

“What of the far side?”

“There is a steep cliff dropping to the sea and the rocks.”

“Could we camp there?”

“Probably.”

“Good then lead us there we will camp there tonight and then decided how we remove this winkle form its shell.”

Julius met up with the Decurion Princeps close to where the Dunum met the sea. Salvius pointed off to the headland where a thin spiral of smoke rose gently. “They have destroyed the signal station and killed the auxiliaries there. It looks like they are heading south.”

“Streonshal.”

“That is what I thought. We can save time by heading due south and approaching from the south west.”

“Yes I remember it well and the signal station is to the south. With luck Salvius this time tomorrow we may have caught up with this elusive little band. Tell me do you know how big it is? Is Morwenna with it?”

Salvius shook his head. "They have left no survivors but from the tracks it is not the whole warband. I think there are less than two thousand."

"I would like to catch that witch."

"It is a good job that Macro is not here isn't it Julius?"

"Aye he would be off trying to defeat the whole Brigante army on his own. Well let us be off. We will soon see if we have caught the queen herself or one of her leaders."

Chapter 11

Gaelwyn halted the band some way along the trail. "The little ones will need some food and we must save the horses. Whilst you feed them I will go back down the trail and try to make it less obvious."

Gaius gave the boys the dried venison to chew on while Macro went round with the water skin. "Where is Marcus?"

Gaius pointed north west. "He is waiting on the beach for a boat to take us south."

Little Marcus looked up in terror. "We are going on the water? To the ends of the world? The monsters will get us."

Macro's son gripped his father's leg tighter and tears welled up in his wide eyes. "I don't want to be eaten by monsters."

Macro laughed. "You need not be afraid of monsters while your father is here. "Why there is no monster out there that I cannot destroy."

"You will frighten them, Macro." Gaius knelt down so that he was face to face with the three small boys. "We will not be sailing past the end of the world; we will see the beach the whole way. There will be no monsters." Little Decius still clung on to his father's leg unsure of the future.

Ailis stroked his golden hair. "The monsters, if there are any, will be so far out to sea that even if you could see to the ends of the world you would not see them. We will be safe and then soon we will be home." She looked at Gaius. "We will be home will we not?"

"We will but I am afraid that we will need to rebuild for all was burned."

"At least we are alive to rebuild; our poor people are lost."

Gaius wondered if there was a criticism in her words. "We could not rescue more my love."

"I know." She put her fingers on his lips. I am so grateful that you came for us and I know that we could not have saved more but I remember what it is like to be a captive. I know."

Gaelwyn came to the horses from a different direction. "Well I have done my best. It is in the Allfather's hands now. Let us go for we need to be at the beach before it is dark."

Lulach arrived at the camp as soon as he heard of the escape. When he dismounted he went to the bodies of the dead men and examined the arrows. "Romans! Which way did they go?"

"We have men trailing them sough. They left a clear trail and they are mounted. But the warriors I sent were also mounted."

"If they were clever enough to get here undetected they must have a plan to escape. Let us go." The twenty men he had brought with him were all mounted and they trotted down the clearly marked trail. They found the first of their injured men half a mile along. He was lying by the side of the trail with a clearly broken leg. Lulach ignored him and turned to one of his warriors, "See Diuran, they are trying to slow us up, to gain a lead." By the time they caught up with the main pursuers they had passed eight injured and one dead warrior.

"We cannot find the trail."

"How long since the traps stopped?"

"About half a mile."

Turning to his men he said, "Diuran go back half a mile and see if they left this trail there. You," He pointed at the tracker before him. "You follow this trail south. The rest of you spread out on both sides of the trail. They have left the track somewhere. There is cunning here."

Gaelwyn had cleverly hidden their trail but eventually Diuran found it. He sent a warrior to fetch Lulach. "Diuran has found a trail heading west."

"West? That may be a false trail. The rest of you continue south for that is their quickest way home. I will examine this other which may be a false trail."

As the twenty warriors tracked through the forest Lulach began to believe that he had found the correct trail until suddenly it stopped. Diuran shield his eyes and looked through the trees at the sky. "It is getting dark. Soon we will not be able to follow the trail. We may have to wait until the morning."

"No Diuran. I am now convinced that this is the trail. "He said loudly so that they could all hear. "Spread out in a circle and walk until you find it."

It was almost an hour later, with the light fading fast when the shout went up. They all raced to the man who was kneeling next to a tree. "Piss and still warm."

"Now we know their trail."

Marcus had lit the fire well before dark so that it would be burning brightly when the old man returned. He was not worried that his companions had not arrived it boded well for if they took this length of time to arrive then their pursuers would be even further behind. He had scouted back and seen that the trail they would take came through a narrow gully in the trees. He waited there, bow in hand, hidden behind a tree. He peered around to see how far down the twisting path and he found he could see a long way but anyone coming up the path would struggle to see a hidden archer. This would be the last roll of the dice should there be a pursuit.

He sat with his back to the tree relying on his ears rather than his eyes. It was so peaceful this close to the shore. The noisy gulls of the morning had departed leaving a gentle shush as the waves lapped up on the beach. In the forest he could hear the birds as they furtively rummaged amongst the dead material to find food. He had imagined, when he finished with his military career that this would be how he would spend his free time, just enjoying sitting and watching. The last time he had been this quiet was just before Ailis and the boys were captured when he and the others were hunting. That was the happy time. Perhaps he was doomed never to have another happy time. When he had been taken as a child from Cantabria he had been too young to remember his parents. The men who had raised him had all left to join other auxiliary forces and he grew up, a young man alone. When he found Macha and he had his son it was but a fleeting moment of companionship too brief for him to get to know either of them and then when they were murdered so soon they became an intangible memory, like his parents. Now, in his third age, he had the chance to make amends to save a family, a family he loved and, as he listened for any footfall or hoof beat, he swore that he would make sure that he saw more of this family and watched over them. They would not become a memory which could not be mourned. He would grow old watching them grow and their children grow. He was tired of death and tired of pain he wanted life.

Hearing something he immediately became alert and chanced a glance around the tree. He could see a horse and then sighed with relief when he saw that Gaius and young Decius were on it. He decided to test his theory about observation; he waited until Gaius and Ailis had passed him before he spoke. "Welcome!"

Gaius almost fell off his horse but before Marcus could laugh he felt a blade at his throat, "Welcome Tribune! You may hide from Romans and women but Gaelwyn the Brigante can smell you!" The old Brigante helped Marcus to his feet. "Come on then you old man. Let us find this boat."

The sun had dropped below the horizon and the red rays of the sunset spilled over the water making it look warm and glowing. "Any sign of your friend?"

"No, but I would not expect him until after dark. There will be less chance of being seen. I killed and cooked a couple of hares this morning."

Ailis came over to kiss the Tribune on the cheek, "That was thoughtful and Marcus, thank you."

"You are my family and I am just glad that we succeeded."

Macro murmured. "We may be out of the trees but we are not out of the woods yet. There will be a pursuit."

Gaelwyn shook his head. “We worry about that when it happens. First I get some hare and then young Macro, you and I will walk down the trail a little and see if we can spot our enemy.”

Macro’s son looked up in panic at his father. “Are you going to leave me again?”

“Son, I am only going down the path with Gaelwyn I will be back. “He looked up at Ailis and Gaius, and if I should be kept a little longer then you know that Ailis and Gaius will be as parents don’t you?” Although talking to Decius he was looking at Gaius who nodded. Ailis gripped her husband’s arm and buried her face in his shoulder. When the two men had left Marcus called over to the tearful boy. “Decius, come here. I have a present for you.”

Sniffling back his tears he wandered over curiously. Marcus and his brother watched equally interested. “What is it?”

“It is something I bought for my son but he, well he doesn’t need it and I wondered if you would like it.” He held out a small pugeo with an intricately carved handle perfectly made for a child’s hand. The short blade was encased in an embroidered tooled leather scabbard. His eyes lit up all thoughts of losing his father gone.

He gently took it from the Tribune’s hand and turned it over to look at the handiwork. Looking up he threw his arms around Marcus’ neck and said, “Thank you! I will look after it I promise.”

Fighting back tears at the remembrance of his dead son the tribune could only nod. Gaius’ sons had mixed emotions; they were both joyful that their friend had such a lovely present but also jealous for they wanted one. “Well when we get back to the farm I shall have to get you two one each eh? I shall have to find out where the Tribune got such a fine weapon.” All jealousy forgotten the two boys rushed to their father and each grabbed a leg.

“I think we had better make the fire a little bigger it is almost dark now.” He had already collected dry driftwood and pine needles and soon the fire blazed away. "If we sit on the forest side its glow will be harder to see from the land."

Suddenly the sharp eyes of Ailis picked out something. "There a splash of white on the pink sea."

They all looked each desperately hoping to confirm what Ailis had seen. "I see it too. It is about a mile away."

Marcus stood, "I will go and tell the others."

Before he could move Gaelwyn raced in gesticulating behind him. "Caledonii and close! Where is the boat?" They pointed out to sea and Gaelwyn shook his head. They will be on us before it can beach."

They were trapped.

Julius saw the Brigante camp as he and Livius scrambled up the bank. They had found a cliff, south of the settlement which overlooked both the fort and the Brigante camp. "It is as I remember it. It looks as though Atticus has decided to fight. Good for him."

"Who is Atticus?"

"The headman of the village and a good man. This works in our favour. We will send a single turma in to attack and then withdraw to the bank here where our archers can thin them as they follow and then our dismounted warriors can use javelins lower down."

"Fight on foot?" asked Livius doubtfully.

"The horses are exhausted and you may not have noticed but the ground does not suit them. Come on let us tell the Decurion Princeps what we intend."

Salvius was not happy when the Prefect told him that he would be leading the attack. "But sir you should be on the ridge directing the men."

"No Salvius you know how to use archers more effectively and I want Livius with the men on foot. When we come you must open ranks to let us through and I will wait on the left flank in case we need to do something dramatic"

"Very well sir but I am not happy."
Grinning Julius said, "That will teach you to join up."
As he rode away Salvius turned to Livius, "I am worried about the Prefect. Since we killed Modius and Macro deserted he has not been himself. I worry that he is seeking his death in battle."
Livius looked at the back of the departing Prefect anxiously. "I hadn't thought of that but he has been putting himself in harm's way lately."
"The good news is that he will not put his men in jeopardy but we need to watch him carefully young Livius and Livius?"
"Yes?"
"Watch yourself as well. You are a good officer. Don't be foolhardy." Livius went to his men feeling as tall as Macro. He had been called a good officer by the Decurion Princeps.
Atticus was not overly concerned when he saw Ownie's men line up in four ranks as they prepared to attack. The ditch had been copied from the Roman one he had seen at Derventio and it was littered with spikes and had a steep glacis. He had enough men on the wall to pick off any survivors. Atticus would become worried if they assault the gate at the same time. He smiled to himself; for that to work they would need to know the tides and tide times.
"Sir look!"
One of his sentries pointed to the ridgeline where a line of horsemen appeared. From the slight panic in his voice the man obviously thought they were Brigante. Atticus had seen these horsemen before and he knew who they were. "Don't worry they are friends. It is the Roman cavalry."
"There look to be too few to make a difference."
Atticus had to agree that the small group could do little against the huge number but it increased the likelihood that they would survive. "They will not like to have an enemy so close to their rear ranks. See how many of these rebels we can hit with our arrows; perhaps we can annoy them a little." Although the range

was not perfect it might distract them from the Roman cavalry which was about to hit them.

The first that Ownie knew of the attack was the thunder of the hooves coming down the ridge. He almost laughed when he saw the pathetically small number of horsemen. His war band was both well armed and well armoured. "Rear rank, cavalry behind you!" Those at the rear turned and faced the charging horses. The rear rank alone outnumbered the advancing cavalry by at least four to one and they were confident of victory.

Ownie turned to his lieutenant. "Looks like they have stumbled on something they didn't expect. We will have the rear ranks turn and halt them. It will give the men confidence to defeat the famous Roman cavalry. "

The rear rank placed spears on the ground and braced their shields. They were confident that the horsemen would ride into them but instead the line halted twenty paces from the Brigante spears and they hurled their javelins at the waiting spearmen. The missiles were well aimed and every one, at such short range found a victim. Before they could recover, they had launched another volley and then they turned and ran.

Atticus' bowmen were hitting enough warriors to be annoying Ownie. He decided he would take the stockade with half his men and let the other half destroy the Roman cavalry. "Rear ranks eliminate the cavalry. First two ranks charge!"

All of the Brigante were angry having taken casualties and inflicted none. The ones at the rear ran in two haphazard lines. They were so intent on pursuit that they did not notice the cavalry slowing up effectively blocking their view of the ridge ahead. Suddenly the cavalry seemed to disappear in a rains storm of arrows. Even though many men fell to the deadly barbs enough carried on, desperate to get to grips with the annoying horse men. As they started up the slope the arrows were replaced by javelins as the arrows hit the second line. The first line was so depleted by the time it reached the dismounted horsemen that they were easily disposed of. The second line was a stronger one and its leader,

Donncha ordered his men to lock the looted Roman shields and protect themselves from the missiles. He had seen the Roman infantry use such tactics and he knew it was effective. When the line hit Livius and his men the force was such that the Roman line buckled. The Decurion Princeps could see that his arrows were doing no damage. "Swords, follow me!" As soon as the second line joined their comrades the line stiffened but the superior numbers of Brigante meant that, eventually, they would break through.

The Prefect had reformed his horses on the enemy right. "We have no javelins left so we us our swords. Force them towards the cliff." The cavalry hit the exposed flank of the Brigante line. On the right the warriors had no shield to protect them and the cavalry could pick their targets with impunity. Some of those armed with axes chopped at the legs of the horses but, in the main, it was the Brigante who were dying as the well disciplined Romans moved inexorably forward.

Slowly the right flank of the line turned in on itself as it was attacked from two sides and Livius was able to shout orders to his beleaguered men. "Push them towards the cliff."

The right flank of the Roman line plunged down to a cliff and the Brigante were fighting a foe which was uphill. The warriors on the left of the Brigante line found themselves using their shields in their left hands to block the increasingly fierce attacks and as they did so they inevitably edged closer to the cliff. The horses began rearing on the right of the line and warriors pushed back to their comrades. It was like a finely balanced scale and suddenly it tipped, scores of men plunged down the cliff, while those who could, raced down the slope to the safety of the other lines.

Ownie was not finding the settlement an easy one to defeat. The slope on the ditch was steeper than he had expected and the arrows of the defenders were being augmented by stones accurately slung by boys eager to join the fray and aid their elders. The withering onslaught slowed up the attack and prevented the Brigante from actually climbing the walls. As he glanced over his shoulder Ownie saw, with horror that his two rear lines had broken and the force bearing down on him was not a handful of cavalry but at least a hundred Roman soldiers. This was not the walkover he had assumed; it was assuming the proportions of a minor and the only way to avoid a major disaster was to retreat and fight another day.

"Brigante retreat!" There was only one avenue of escape, down the gully and down the path which was still partly under the sea. Ownie's cunning brain had worked out that the roman horse could not climb down the gully whilst his men could. If they had to swim at the bottom then so be it.

The Prefect halted his men when they came to the gully. There was little point in damaging horses and men when the threat had gone. He could see from the Brigante bodies that the band was much smaller now having suffered heavy casualties in the attack. In the morning the fully mounted and rested ala could easily catch them.

Atticus came out of the settlement and hugged Julius who had dismounted. "Thank you, Prefect. It has been many years since we have met."

Julius looked at him curiously, "How did you know I had been promoted to Prefect."

"I am a Roman remember. I recognise the insignia. Please bring your men inside and we will feed you and see to your wounds."

"Very well but first I want to secure the prisoners."

Although there were not many prisoners, there were enough to warrant a guard. And as Decurion Princeps Cilo said, "Every captive is worth a few denari. Better in our pocket."

Chapter 12

"Where is Macro?"

"He will ambush them and then join us." Looking desperately around the old man suddenly said, "I have an idea. I will take the horses and ride down the beach, south. Gaius, Marcus bunch up your cloaks on the backs of two of the horses. They will follow me. When I have gone a mile I will wade into the water where you can pick me up."

"That is madness old man."

"Can you swim?" Gaius shook his head. "Can any of you swim?" They shook their heads. "Then it is the only plan. Go out as far as you dare in the water. I will tell Macro and he will join you." He looked at their faces and ruffled young Decius' head. "I am not going to my death. I will see you again." Springing on the back of his horse Gaelwyn led the string towards the waiting Macro in the woods.

"Come on let us do as he says or it will be a sacrifice in vain."

"Where is my father?"

"Picking up Decius Marcus said, "He will join us. Don't worry." The three of them each picked up a child and waited until the water was chest deep. They could see the boat tacking towards them but it seemed to be taking an age against the off shore wind. The surf disguised any noise from the shore and, with the woods in darkness; the three of them were effectively blind and deaf to any impending attack.

Gaelwyn rode next to Macro, "Go to the boat and I will lead them south."

"Very well old man. Thank you for all the times we have fought together and thank you for this quest to save my child."

Snorting the old man said, as he galloped through the woods, "Thank me after. I go no to my death."

"No but I do." Macro planted some arrows in the soft soil and then walked forward to do the same. When he had four places marked out he waited patiently for the warriors he knew would be hurtling up the path.

Gaelwyn made as much noise as he could as he peered down the darkening gloom of the forest trail. Even so he barely had time to react when the arrow came out of the darkness; he leaned to one side and it thudded into a tree behind him. He jerked the reins of his mount to the right and headed for the lighter area nearer to the beach. The shouts behind told him that some, at least of the warriors had taken the bait.

Lulach was in the second group of warriors. One of his scouts waited with him where he had seen Gaelwyn. "They rode west, towards the sea."

"Eoin, take your men and cut south and west in case they outrun our men. The rest of you come with me we will head along the trail in case this cunning group of Romans double backs upon itself." Lulach's warriors were his elite; he wanted them with him for he was not convinced by the noisy horses. It was not in keeping with the escape so far. Whoever had led his men astray would, he thought double back otherwise he would be easily taken on the open beach. As he had trekked north Lulach had become increasingly persuaded that the escapees intended to wait in the coastal forests until the hunt had died down and then would head south. It was what he would do. The Romans were many miles from home and were surrounded by enemies looking for them, better to wait for a quieter time.

Macro had made peace with himself. If he could escape then he would do so but he would only do so once he knew his son and Ailis were safe. His son's future was paramount and Ailis and Gaius were the guarantee that he would have a future. He knew he had had a good life, he had hoped for a longer life but at least this way he would have a glorious end. The first warrior up the trail was so intent on the path that the arrow hit him without him seeing it or being aware of the danger. The second man had a moment's notice as the warrior in front fell and then he too hit the ground, dead. Macro shot the remaining two arrows vaguely in the direction of the warriors and then silently slipped back to his next cache of arrows. He no longer watched the path for he knew they would try to surround him. He hit one pursuer in the thigh and another in the chest before they hit the ground. Once again he shot two arrows down the trail. The grunt told him that one at least had struck home. He then crept back to his last stash, close to the edge of the trees and waited while Lulach's men exercised even more caution now that eight of their comrades lay dead, dying or wounded.

Gaelwyn risked a glance over his shoulder. The horsemen behind were gaining on him. He pulled the next horse towards him and, as he leapt on its back he let his first horse go. Gaelwyn knew that the Allfather was with him when it veered back to the woods and four warriors followed hearing only its hooves and glimpsing the movement. With a fresher mount Gaelwyn was able to maintain his lead and even increase it a little.

Marcus and Gaius were now close enough to the boat to be able to see the old man steering. "Hurry! They are upon us."

"Would that the wind was. Can you not swim out to me?"

"None of us can swim."

"Then you will have to be patient."

Macro glanced towards the sea and he could see that the boat was closer to his family. Four more arrows and he would join them. Three warriors fell dead to the unerringly accurate Decurion but then there were too many of them for him to control with the couple of arrows he had left. He could see that the boat was but ten paces from Ailis and he took his last arrows and shot them at the warriors he could see. It was a good two hundred paces to the shore and Macro ran swiftly through the soft sand.

Lulach had edged around the side of the forest and he emerged less than a hundred paces from Macro. At the same time he saw the boat and he yelled to his remaining men. "They are in a boat get them."

The three children had been hurled into the boat and Marcus and Gaius pushed Ailis in. The old man said urgently," The wind is blowing us off shore hurry or you will not get on board."
As Marcus was helped over the side of the ship Gaius said, "But our friend…"
"Your friend is a dead man," and he pointed to the shore where Macro had just reached the water.
Even as he began to wade in the shallow surf the Caledonii archer shot the arrow which plunged into his calf. Although he did not fall Macro felt the weakness and knew that he would survive another. He sadly looked at the boat and raised his hand in farewell. Gaius had just rolled into the bottom of the boat when he saw Macro's wave and he roared,"No!"
Decius saw that his father was not coming and he began to cry screaming, "Father!"
Macro turned on his pursuers with his sword in his right hand and a dagger in his left. The sea behind him was but ankle deep and he wanted to get at the warriors before they could use their bows. Even at this point, with death facing him he was thinking of his son. He did not want a stray arrow making his sacrifice futile. He raced towards the two archers who were notching arrows hurriedly into bows. The sword sliced through the bow and the man's neck whilst the dagger sliced the other open from the crotch to the neck. Macro found himself grinning as he faced the finest warriors left to Lulach. "Come on then you Caledonii bastards! You have shown that you can fight women and children now face a man. Face Decurion Macro Curius Culleo the finest warrior in Marcus' Horse!"
His sudden onslaught took the men of Lulach's band by surprise. He charged at them rather than fleeing them. They did not know that this was how he practised and how he trained his recruits. He was even more reckless than usual for he knew he could not survive and he relished the combat. Using his dagger to fend off blows and inflict deep wounds while his wicked blade,

razor sharp sliced through arms and legs unencumbered with armour.

For Gaius and Marcus, slowly drifting from the shore it was almost like watching a spirit or a ghost fight for he seemed to have a charmed life. Each warrior, or pair of warriors who faced him fell and he remained wound free. "Get us ashore we can help him!"

The old man sadly shook his head and pointed, "No, for their leader has had enough."

With a sickening horror they saw Lulach's remaining bowmen draw back their bows and six arrows plunged into Macro's arms, legs and neck. Even though he was mortally wounded he continued to defy them. "You cowardly bastards!" Throwing his knife into one archer's neck with his dying stroke he sliced the head from a second. As he fell to the ground the handful of warriors who remained hacked and chopped his body to make sure that the mightiest warrior they had ever seen was dead.

Sadly looking at the old man while Ailis comforted the children Marcus said, "One of our number is waiting for us south of here. Can you sail as close to the shore as possible?"

"Aye. "Almost as an afterthought he added, "I have never seen such courage or such skill. Truly he will be with the Allfather now."

"That he will, old man and the Allfather had better watch out for I think our friend was just getting warmed up."

Gaius took Decius Curius Culleo in his arms and said, very quietly, "Your father has now gone to the Allfather. Do not cry tears for he is with his lost comrades and even now they are telling tales of great deeds and the greatest will be your father's tale for never has one warrior achieved so much, not even the mighty Ulpius Felix. And know this you are now my son and I will do for you as I would for Decius and Marcus in honour of the bravest man I ever knew."

Lulach looked at the desecrated and butchered body lying at his feet and noticed the smile on the Roman's face. This truly was a warrior. If he had a hundred such men he would be able to conquer the world. He saw, with regret, the boat sailing away, beyond his reach. He would meet them again these impudent warriors who had dared to steal from him in the heart of his own kingdom. When the snow thawed in the spring he would return and the next visit would be more terrible and more lasting.

Gaelwyn released his mounts one by one. Glancing over his shoulder he could see that they were gaining. He had two mounts still tied to his own and they contained the cloaks of Gaius and Marcus. He ripped them from the backs of the horses and threw them in the air. Letting one of the horses go he took the other one towards the tree line. As he had expected the loose horse ran away from Gaelwyn towards the sea at the same time the cloaks fluttered to the ground before the pursuing horses making them check and veer to the side. A small gap opened and the furious Caledonii whipped their horses angry with themselves for following the horse towards the sea. The man they were chasing would go into the woods to evade them. Gradually Gaelwyn edged towards the sea. He removed his own cloak and lay flat on his mount's back. In the darkness it was hard to see which horse had a rider. Throwing his own cloak in the air he kicked the spare horse so that it reared and traced away from the pain towards the woods. Gaelwyn went straight into the sea galloping as hard as his horse could manage. As expected the warriors chased the spare ignoring what they perceived to be the loose horse. The loose horse stopped quite quickly and the warriors drew their swords ready to kill the elusive warrior. When they saw the horse had no rider they looked back to the sea where they could see Gaelwyn and his mount both swimming strongly away from the shore.

The water seemed like ice to Gaelwyn and he lay on the back of his horse, his hand gripped around the mane. Although he was not moved swiftly the current and the tide were taking him to sea. He had done his part and he hoped that the others had done theirs. Whatever happened, it was in the hands of the Allfather now. He felt his feet turn to stone and his horse began to weaken. He peered through salt encrusted eyes out to sea but all he could spy was a black and stormy sky and whitecaps growing larger. Quite calmly he reflected that this was a strange way for a warrior from the high country to die, swept out to sea but he had done his duty and his honour was intact. When he met the Allfather he would be able to hold his head up.

"Gaelwyn!"

He heard the voice but where was it coming from? He looked towards the horizon but could see nothing. Perhaps he was dreaming or perhaps he was dead already and did not know it.

"Gaelwyn! You soft old bugger! Behind you!"

Turning he saw that he had swum so far out to sea that the boat was behind him. He jerked his horse's head around and it began to swim towards the boat. He was more exhausted than he knew and it took all the efforts of Marcus and Gaius to pull him aboard. As the boat slipped by Marcus smacked the horse on its rump, "Keep swimming noble beast and you will reach the shore." The wild, white eyes of the horse showed its terror but it was swimming in the right direction and, without the dead weight that was Gaelwyn was moving more quickly.

"What were you doing you old fool? Trying to swim to Ireland?"

"Hah! It is not impossible for a warrior such as me eh Macro?" The sudden silence made the old man open his eyes and glance around the huddled group sheltering in the bottom of the boat. Nodding he looked heavenward, "So he has gone to the Allfather. Was it a noble death?"

"You have never seen one as noble." As the boat tacked south to safety Gaius told the tale to Gaelwyn and Decius sat with open eyes hearing for the first time the famous tale of Macro's last stand; a story which would be passed down and told around fires in the land of the Brigante until it became a legend, disbelieved by many but cherished by true warriors everywhere.

Ownie headed north when he left Streonshal. He knew Morwenna was less likely to have encountered Romans; until he reorganised he did not want to meet any. He pushed his men harder than they had ever been pushed before. He felt sure that they still outnumbered the Romans but, in the open, his men were no match for them. For the first time since the revolt had started he was regretting joining. The enemy were not as easy to defeat as he had thought. The initial victory had been gained by deception; it was not a trick which could be tried twice.

Once they reached the top of the moors they made good time. When his men questioned the wisdom of running along the skyline he scornfully pointed eastwards. "If they can see us then we can see them for they are on horses. We will push on and cross the Dunum at the narrow place."

"Not Morbium then?"

"No Jared for even if the Queen managed to cross against the Romans there we are too few in number now. We need to join forces with the Queen. Once we cross the Dunum we will rest and I will send out scouts to make contact with the rest of the army."

Knowing that they only had thirty or so miles to travel gave them impetus and they half walked half ran until, when evening fell they could go no more. They found themselves close to a conical shaped hill with a dell to the north. "Here we will rest for the night and travel again tomorrow. Jared take two men to the top of this hill; and watch for our pursuers. Kai, find us food."

Ownie needed time to think, to plan his strategy. He still wished to be the leader of the Brigante but, perhaps, the time was not right yet. When he met the Queen he would decide then if her plans had a chance of success if not then he would melt back to the high moors and wait there for the snows to melt and then see which way the wind was blowing."

"You have forty horses."

The Prefect looked at a stern faced Sergeant Cato. It was often said that Cato loved horses more than the men who rode them and

Julius was beginning to understand that idea. "You mean forty horses that are fully fit?"

"No, sir, I mean there are forty horses which are available for gentle use. If they are pushed we will have less than twenty." The sergeant softened his voice, it was as though talking to a child. When the Tribune had been Prefect then they had a leader who understood how to husband horses, how to care for them and protect them. The officers in the ala now saw them as a weapon to be honed and sharpened. "We have raced these beasts from the Lands of the lakes to Cataractonium to Eboracum to here without a rest or a stop. They have fought in more battles than I care to count and there is a limit to what they can do." He raised himself upright and looked the Prefect straight in the eye. "You can use forty horses for a walking patrol and that is all. The rest need, grazing attention and most of all care for at least seven days and then, after another week or so of walking patrol they will be able to function as you wish them to."

The Decurion Princeps hid his smile behind his hand. The Sergeant was the shortest trooper in the ala but at that moment he looked like a parent admonishing a small child. Salvius found himself agreeing with Cato and not just about the horses. The men and their equipment were a shambles. Armour needed repairs. Weapons needed replacing and sharpening and most of all the men needed feeding up.

Julius felt all eyes upon him and he knew that he had started this whole debacle with his ridiculous quest for revenge. He had demanded justice for his dead brother but the horses and men of the ala had paid the price. Looking at the three officers and one sergeant he had left he could see that they were right. They would obey him if he ordered a chase but they would never trust him again. "Very well. In that case Salvius I need the fittest officer and the thirty fittest troopers to trail, at walking pace, the Brigante who have just headed north."

Grinning Salvius said, "Well the officer is easy; that would be me and I will find the rest of the troopers now sir."

“And you Sergeant Cato. Don’t just stand there. Get the horses fed and cared for and Livius close your mouth, you look like a fish, and arrange with Atticus for a place to erect the tents. Apparently we are here for a week.”

Salvius had no trouble locating their trail for some of the severely wounded had died along the way and been hastily buried beneath whatever stones and rocks had been available. Once they saw that the Brigante were heading for the high moors their task became so much easier. “Remember what the sergeant said lads, keep a gentle hand on your reins.” The fact that the men laughed showed that, despite what he had said they were still in good heart. He knew, in his own heart, that the loss of Macro, a deserter, had been the biggest blow to both morale and confidence. They would need to work hard over the winter to recover that morale. Thinking about the winter also made the Decurion Princeps acknowledge that when they managed to get their hands on some new recruits, unless Macro had been recaptured then they would not have a training officer. Indeed even if Macro were returned to them it was unlikely that he would be allowed to continue as an officer. It was a great shame that a good officer could have his whole career ruined; the Parcae were indeed fickle.

It was drawing on towards evening and yet Salvius was loath to camp. He would at least like to be over the moors. The thought of building a camp on such an exposed ridge went against all of his training. They dropped over a small hogback and found a dell. While the men were building the camp Salvius decided to satisfy his curiosity and explore a little. Later he was glad that he did for; off to their left in the lee of a conical shaped hill he could see half a dozen fires. It could mean only one thing, Brigante. He had found them.

Chapter 13

The next morning as Ownie led his men north west to the shallow bend of the Dunum he little realised that, close behind and watching his every move, was Decurion Princeps Salvius Cilo and a turma of cavalry. It was easy to follow the large band of men who left a swathe of land behind them. Once they were across the river Ownie set about building a camp on the steep escarpment of the river. Salvius took the opportunity of sending a report back to the Prefect of the situation. It was obvious to the Decurion that the Brigante were going nowhere for the moment and as this fitted in with Sergeant Cato's desire for rest and recuperation he would happily wait until they moved.

Ownie sent out his ten horsemen in an arc northwards to ascertain the whereabouts of his Queen. It would do no harm for his warriors to rest; the encounter with the cavalry at Streonshal had proved at best disquieting and at worst terrifying for his men. He wondered how Parthalan had fared.

His erstwhile rival had suffered even greater casualties and he would have been pleased to have only lost half his men for Parthalan had run into two cohorts of the Twentieth hurrying north to put down the Brigante rebellion. The experienced legion, which had fought Silures, Ordovices and every other tribe in Britannia made short work of the unruly and disorganised Brigante. Had they had cavalry there would have been no survivors but, as it was, enough Brigante returned north to tell the tale of the terror that was the legion and spread the word that rebellion was not as simple as their leaders had suggested. Those who escaped buried their swords and shields and became fervently dedicated farmers for they did not want to face the scything machine that was a Roman legion intent on revenge.

When his scouts returned Ownie discovered that his queen had taken refuge on the coast in a secret settlement only threatened by rising tides and eroding beaches. He took down his defences and headed north east. The scout watching the Brigante reported back to his leader. Pausing only to send another messenger to the Prefect Cilo continued his pursuit. This land was unfamiliar to the Decurion Princeps and he rode warily. He was always within sight of the Brigante for they took a clear path to the coast but he was careful to scout for ambushes. His enemy seemed blissfully unaware of his pursuit and did not deviate an uncia from a straight line- almost Roman thought the Decurion Princeps.

Ownie was amazed at the settlement and the way it was hidden from the rest of the world. He realised as he was led around the edge of the woods that it was precariously placed. Already the sea was lapping around the trunks of the trees some of which were already dying and he could see, beneath the relentless waves, the stumps of trees killed by the sea and taken out. This might be a secret and hidden settlement but within a few years it would be too small to contain even half the numbers it did but he could see that, at the moment, it served its purpose well.

The Queen took the losses well. “But you killed many of the cavalry?”

“At least half their horses were left on the field.”

“Good for that is the one force which can hurt us.” Had she known of the Parthalan disaster she may have changed her views. “We will soon head north west and, even now, I am spreading my power in those lands. As soon as your men are rested, we will join with Cruatha’s people and drive north.”

Salvius was astounded when he saw the warband disappear into the forest. During the night his two best scouts skirted the wood and creeping close to its wooden walls, closely observed the settlement. When they reported back Salvius could scarcely believe their report but he was forced to acknowledge that Queen Morwenna had a new base and almost as many warriors as had escaped from Eboracum. He awaited the Prefect’s message for it would have done little good to send a message the fifty miles south. He would wait. His messengers knew where he was and he was in a good position to observe. He had found a sand dune filled bay which looked towards the settlement. Just behind it was a headland which looked, at the moment to be unoccupied. When the Prefect arrived he would suggest placing a patrol there for they would be able to observe the settlement and follow should they leave northwards. All he had to do was wait.

Twenty miles away in the stronghold above the bend of the river Vedra, Maban and Anchorat were busily sowing the seeds both of discord and preparing the way for the arrival of their leader. Using Morwenna's trick of pretending to be an orphan following the Caledonii raid they insinuated themselves into the household of the headman Daire. They did this through the offices of his wife, Muirne. The kind woman felt sorry for the girls and when they saw the altar in her kitchen to the Mother they knew they had an ally. When they explained to her that they had been acolytes of the sorceress she took them in and risked the wrath of her husband. Each night after the meal they would explain to her the mysteries and power of the religion. Through her influence they met other similar minded women and, while the men sat in their hall drinking and telling tales of long dead heroes, the women of the village were learning about the woman who would change their future and their lives. Muirne had not realised how much power she and the other women of the stronghold held. Maban showed them how to read the bones and foretell the future. Anchorat spent her time bemoaning the lack of control of the Romans who had promised safety but left them helpless. The nearby deserted fort of Vinovia was testimony to that neglect. After five days of their work the women of the stronghold were eagerly anticipating the arrival of Morwenna. The two acolytes had been deliberately vague about Morwenna's precise arrival but the longer they spent with the women the more powerful this mysterious Queen became. Dun Holme would fall without a blow being struck when Morwenna finally arrived.

The Prefect took his time riding north to Seton. There was no rush for the Decurion Princeps had said that the Queen was fortifying the settlement. Until the Legate had sufficient forces the campaign would be one of containment. The latest orders received by the ala were for them to report the whereabouts of the Brigante rebels. Once the Prefect had time to assess the situation he would send off turma to discover the rest of the rebels. The Ninth had destroyed one army; the ala badly damaged a second. That left Morwenna's and the second which appeared to have disappeared north west.

As with Salvius the Prefect was surprised by the size and strength of this hitherto unknown town for it was a large place. He could see why it was so large for its resources were ample. Unlike Streonshal with its high cliffs this town was on the beach. "Well Salvius what is your assessment?"

"She looks to have about two thousand warriors under her command. They have spent the time, so far, improving the defences and I assume that she will be using this as her new base."

"It looks likely. We are to scout at the moment. Your mounts have had a good rest, take Livius and his turma and scout west. We need to find the last band and report to the Legate. Once Eboracum has been repaired he will be heading north with the Ninth to, finally, crush this rebellion. Cassius and I will stay here and monitor the Queen."

"Who do we report to, you or the Legate?"

"Both. He will need the bigger picture and I need to know if you are going to require help."

Shaking his head the Decurion Princeps complained, "That is a lot of riding just to give the same message twice."

"I know but, at the moment that is our role."

"Come on then Livius, mount your men we are going west again."

"Look on the bright side Salvius; at least we know that area well."

They took the northern bank of the Dunum. It gave them the opportunity of visiting Morbium. The Camp Prefect told them that no Brigante had passed the fort. "They must have headed further west Decurion Princeps."

"It makes sense. There would have been little point trying to cross the bridge they would have lost too many men. I suspect they have headed to the land of the lakes to cause mischief there. I cannot understand why we abandoned the fort at Glanibanta. It was perfectly placed to control movements over there. We are blind at the moment and I do not look forward to making the journey when the snows are upon us. Once we reach Brocauum we will separate. I will head north and you can head south."

The first signs of the rebel army occurred twenty miles from Morbium. They found a series of mounds and freshly turned earth marked by inverted spears and a small pile of stones. "Looks like some of their wounded died here."

"Or more likely they waited until here to bury their dead for they must have feared pursuit. They did not know which of the four warbands we would follow." Turning to his men he shouted, "Keep a sharp eye out. Remember this is the country where Decurion Drusus and his turma were wiped out in an ambush." The admonition and warning were gratefully received by the young troopers. The story of the slaughter had been told many times for it was the action which first brought the Prefect his phalerae. "Livius take half your turma and ride to the north, but keep close enough to see the rest of the troopers."

That night as they camped on the high moors the troopers were quite anxious. Having lost so many comrades in the past few months their confidence was not as high as it should have been. "The trouble is Salvius that Macros' departure has had a huge effect on the men. He is more than a Decurion and training officer he is their talisman. To the troopers he is all that they might aspire to, the perfect warrior."

"I know Livius. As with you, he was the salvation of poor Galeo and me. He made us the warriors we are. I have forgotten how many lumps of clay he has moulded into fine warriors."

"And officers."

“True and we are living examples are we not? I do not doubt that he will return from the quest he is on , face his punishment and the men will, one more, have their talisman.”

Livius looked at the Decurion Princeps doubtfully, “Would he not have to be punished by the Prefect?”

“Obviously but there is not necessarily a set punishment for what he did. He escaped from his cell. He had already been stripped of office and was suspended so technically he did not refuse to obey an order.”

“Isn’t that just playing with words?”

“Yes but the Prefect feels badly about Macro and blames himself for his action. I am the last of the old Decurions now and I know that the old Julius would not have led us away from our patrol area to seek out this Modius if he had known the Caledonii were raiding.”

“I hope you are right, for Macro’s sake as well as the men.”

The next day was a foul day with driving, unseasonable rain hurling itself into the men’s faces. They had to draw their cloaks around them as they faced the worst that nature could throw at them. The rain felt like needles being driven into their exposed faces and the biting wind found every opening and crevice in their armour. They were soaked to the skin and raw, red skin began to chafe and blister. They were so intent on protecting themselves that it was with some surprise that they found themselves outside Brocauum for the rain was so strong it was almost like a fog and had made the stockaded town almost invisible..

“The gates are closed. Does that mean we are welcome or not?”

“Only one way to find out sir. With your permission?”

“Just take two men with you and be prepared to ride for your life if it looks dangerous.”

Livius felt a thrill of nervous excitement as he walked his mount towards the gates of the stockaded settlement. There were guards on the ramparts but so far they had shown no sign of aggression. Perhaps they were waiting for the two turmae to ride up and then unleash their weapons. He stopped below the gates and shouted up, "Decurion Princeps Cilo and Decurion Lucullus of Marcus' Horse. In the name of the Legate open the gates."

There was silence. The two sentries looked at each other and then one of them disappeared. Livius felt vaguely exposed. Were the Brigante waiting out of sight to launch an ambush? It was one of their favoured tactics. The survivors of Cataractonium had told them how the rebels had hidden in the fog and used nature to destroy the garrison. This was a similar day with the driving rain and poor visibility. Suddenly the gate slowly opened. Livius was in a dilemma; should he wait for the Decurion Princeps? If he did and it was a trap then two turmae would be destroyed. On the other hand if he and his two men entered and the gates were shut then they would be hostages. Glancing behind he saw the turmae moving slowly towards the open gates and Livius took a brave decision. "Right lads, hands on swords were going in. Watch out for traps." The two troopers were from Livius' own turma and both of them would willingly have given their lives for the likeable young officer. If this were a trap then the Brigante would pay dearly for their deception.

To Livius' relief there were no armed warriors awaiting them but unarmed elders with a bound Brigante warrior. The three men waited just inside the gate until Decurion Princeps Cilo arrived. As he rode next to Livius he murmured, "Bravely done Livius, bravely done."

The elders stepped forward. The man who stepped forward looked to be very old and Livius wondered if they had chosen him for his wisdom or as the least threat. "Welcome to our town. We have this warrior, Labraid as a prisoner for you. He and other rebels tried to ensnare us in a plot to revolt against the benevolent Roman rule. The others escaped but this one we caught and cut out his tongue as a punishment."

Salvius could now see the scars around the man's mouth. He turned to Livius and said quietly, "Very convenient it means he cannot confirm or deny their story."

"Do you think they are rebels?"

Cilo glanced around and could see some warriors with bandaged limbs. "Undoubtedly they were but it looks like they had decided to become Roman again."

"Do we ignore their revolt?"

Shrugging Salvius said, "It is for the Legate to punish. We merely report. Our job is to find the rebels and tell the Legate. We can tell him that we have found some reformed rebels." He looked at the elders and said in a much louder voice. "It is good that you have captured this rebel." Livius was sure that he saw the whole council breathe a collective sigh of relief. "We need to know where the rebels have gone and who their leader is."

The elders looked at each other and then the eldest said, "West. They went west. The leader was a warrior named Tole."

"Very well we will stay the night here."

"You are welcome Romans and we thank you for your protection."

As Livius and Salvius headed to the stables provided for them Livius said to his leader, "They are lying."

"What about the direction they took or the name of their leader?"

"The name of their leader for Tole in their language means… leader. And I recognised two of the elders as men who were in the forefront of the battle. Their leaders are here."

"Well done. Tell the men to be on their guard tonight. I do not think they will try anything but if they do I want us to be ready. I will send this news to Julius and the Legate. Try to engage the two leaders in conversation and we will try to discover their names."

The same rainstorm which battered Livius and Salvius also battered Seton. The difference was that Morwenna had predicted the rain. She had gathered all the warriors and women in the centre of the settlement. "Tomorrow I will summon such a rainstorm that the sky will be black and the rain so thick that it will be as fog. We will use this power to attack those Romans who are spying on us while we attack them I will lead the rest of the warriors to Dun Holme for the Carvetii there are going to join us."

"One warrior, braver than the rest had ventured, "How do you know?"

Turning her fierce green eyes and even fiercer look she had said menacingly, "I am Morwenna servant of the Mother and a sorceress with immense and limitless power." After that no one had ventured a word.

So it was that when the rain began to hurl its icy barbs and the wild wind whipped up the sea sending droplets of savage salt encrusted spray over the sand dunes that the troopers retreated, gratefully, into their tents and leaving a skeletal team of guards to watch for any enemy foolish and brave enough to challenge the elements. "I tell you Cassius this country has the strangest climate of any I have ever visited. One day bright sunshine and the next, a day like this where one cannot see a hand in front of your face."

"At least we know that they will not be going anywhere today."

His misplaced confidence was shattered when the two guards on the gate to the camp fell, struck by arrows. The well trained turmae reacted quickly and men rushed from their tents to get to the ramparts. They could see little but there, just off the beach was a fleet of ten ships and each contained archers who were firing arrows blindly in the air, those same arrows were falling with the rain striking men and horses.

"Sir look!" The trooper attracted Julius' attention and there, in the dunes was another warband racing towards them. Julius could see that he was outnumbered and surrounded. He reminded himself that they were a scouting force not a punitive one. "Sound retreat!"

Each trooper grabbed his weapons and mounted his horse. Those who were wounded were manhandled on to horses and the dead left where they lay. The turmae raced out of the Porta Decumana with Cassius and Julius the last to leave. They rode hard for a mile and stopped amidst the low marshy ground close to the Dunum estuary. The wild birds screaming as the quiet desolation was disturbed by the men and horses. "Where did that come from? And how did they know we were there?"

"We were over confident Cassius. I should have realised that we could not hide ourselves as close as that to the enemy without them being aware of our presence but what concerns me is why attack us at that moment and why in such small numbers. Had they wanted to destroy us they could have surrounded us and killed us all for they had total surprise and it was a stroke of genius to attack from the sea and the dunes at the same time. No there is some clever, well thought out plan here. This Morwenna is as cunning as her mother." He pondered for a moment or two and then decided. "We rest for a while and then tonight we return and we will spy out the settlement."

The Brigante and their allies had destroyed the camp and desecrated the handful of bodies that they had found. While Cassius arranged the burial of the slain men Julius led the rest of his troopers to check the vicinity for any ambushes and signs of the enemy. When they returned to Cassius the bodies had been buried and the grim faced men waited for their orders. "They think we have gone back to Morbium with our tails between our legs. They do not know Marcus' Horse. "The smiles on his men's faces told him that they were still eager to fight. "We will do what they do not expect we will go and pay them a visit, perhaps give them a taste of a raid in the dark."

Leaving their horses with four horse holders the two turmae crept through the woods to the stockaded Seton. Two guards lounged by the locked gates and they could see no guards on the walls. Inside they could hear the noise of a celebration and firelight flickered and gave a glow to the buildings within. Nodding to the two scouts Julius watched as they covered the ground towards the two unsuspecting guards. The noise from inside helped to mask any noise they might have made and Julius could see from the beakers by their feet that they had been celebrating the defeat of Marcus' Horse. The two guards made not a sound as their throats were slit and they were dragged away. The troopers ran swiftly and quietly to the walls. In groups of three two men boosted a third over the ramparts. Within moments the gate had been opened and the turmae entered. In the distance a huge fire had been lit and the warriors were sat around drinking heavily.

Julius turned to Cassius, "These are just the men who attacked us today." Cassius looked at his men, confused. "There should be ten times the number! The rest have gone." Tell your men to fire the buildings on this side and then bring the horses. We will pay them back a little for their attack on us" As Cassius gave his orders Julius led his men closer to the fire. He pointed to the bows the men carried and they all notched an arrow; their targets were obvious. There were so many warriors around the fire that any arrows sent in their direction would have found their mark. Julius glanced over his shoulder and when he saw the first flicker of fire from Cassius' fire starters, dropped his hand. The arrows flew towards the conflagration and the mass of men drunkenly cavorting on its periphery. He dropped his arm a second time and, even as the volley flew, led his men as quickly as they could manage it out of the village. Their horses were waiting and they mounted swiftly. The enraged warriors of Seton charged towards them eager to wreak revenge for the slain men and the burning buildings, a volley of arrows and javelins halted them like a slap in the face and Julius saw, with some satisfaction, the whole town burning from within and without. There would be no pursuit from the dazed and half-drunk warriors for they were too busy putting the fire out.

"Back to our camp but in the morrow we need to find where Morwenna has gone. It does not bode well for she is an evil woman with a mind as intricate as a bag full of venomous snakes."

They left before dawn and headed west. As Julius had said to Cassius, if it had been south we would have seen them and there are rocks to the north. If we cut west we may pick up their trail."

Once they found the main trail and saw that it headed west by north he despatched a trooper with a message for the Legate. "When you return look for us in the north west of here."

"You were right sir. They must have emptied the settlement for look at how wide the trail is."

"Worrying Cassius for the Carvetii and the Votadini are barely pacificd. If she gets their aid then we will need all of the legions again."

It was just before midday when the shout came from the rear. "Riders approaching."

Julius was surprised to see his own messenger riding with a trooper from Livius' turma. "Did you get lost Metellus or did you miss us?"

Sheepishly grinning Julius' messenger said, "No sir but I met the Decurion Princeps messenger and thought that his message may have a bearing on mine."

"Good thinking lad. Here give me the Decurion Princeps' message. Well Cassius some good news at last. It looks like the rebels in the west have largely given up. Certainly the Decurion Princeps can handle them. Return to the Decurion Cilo and tell him to continue to patrol around Brocauum until he hears from me. Tell him we have found Morwenna and she is heading from here towards north west and he may need to watch for her." As the tired messenger rode away Julius finished adding his note on his message to the Legate." Metellus impress upon the Legate that the danger is here with Morwenna and he should send up reinforcements to Morbium as soon as possible."

Chapter 14

Morwenna used nature to make her arrival even more impressive than it was with an army of two thousand well armed warriors behind her. She timed it so that, as the sun was setting in the west it lit up her face and body. The pure white shift and the white horse seemed to glow like fire and her already red hair seemed to burn like a magical bush. Although the gates were barred she rode up to them without a trace of fear or hesitation. "I am Queen Morwenna of the Brigante and I am here to help my Carvetii brothers and sisters throw off this Roman yoke." The river rushed beneath the bridge and the gate giving the only sound to disturb the tense stand-off.

Behind her Aodh, Ownie and the other leaders waited with bated breath. It was such an audacious move and so reliant on two young girls that even the ever confident Aodh began to ease his sword from its scabbard. Morwenna half turned and flashed a fearsome look. "Do not begin to doubt now. You will not need your sword." Reluctantly he returned his sword to its scabbard and silence reigned once more.

From behind the gates they could hear raised voices and suddenly the more strident and higher pitched female voices became more dominant. Without warning the huge doors swung open and Maban and Anchorat stood there with a group of triumphant looking women and some red faced men. As they entered through the gate and across the bridge Morwenna half turned to Aodh and said quietly, "You need not doubt my powers for the Mother is with us."

In that moment both Ownie and Aodh realised that this phenomenon was getting bigger than they had ever realised. Now she was winning battles without weapons, at least not weapons which they understood and gaining recruits almost without trying. She was more than a woman she appeared to have an insight into the world of the gods and that was truly terrifying.

The boat seemed to take an age to cover the smallest distance. None of the occupants of the boat apart from Gaelwyn and the old man appeared to be able to come to terms with what had happened. "He was indestructible."

"No Gaius, no man is indestructible. He was a brave and worthy warrior but the Allfather gives us all a weakness. For Macro it was never knowing when to withdraw, always believing that he would win."

"But he nearly did win," said Marcus quietly. "If they had not used arrows then he would have defeated them all."

Gaelwyn laughed. "What a noble idea! Whoever their chief was he did what you would have done when you were a leader Marcus, he used the best tools to get the result. It is not a game with a set of rules. You know Tribune that you do whatever you can to win."

The three boys had long ago fallen asleep."I wish they had not witnessed his death Gaius."

"No, I am glad."

"But why Gaelwyn?"

"What better lesson could they have? No matter how good a warrior you are eventually there will be too many foes for you to face. Had Macro had that lesson he might have left before it was o survive and lived. Think on that."

"You are quiet Marcus."

"I am thinking that I have lived too long. Gaius is the last of my comrades, all the others, Ulpius, Decius, Drusus, Lentius, Metellus and now Macro have all died. I have seen enough of death."

There was a silence only broken by the slapping of the ropes and the water breaking at the bow. The old man steering the ship spoke quietly and thoughtfully, weighing each word for its worth and value. "It seems to me that how we live and how we treat those that we live with is a measure the Allfather uses. We know not when our time will come. Your friend's time was right. His son will miss him and you will miss him but the Allfather and the Parcae decided it was his time. I have lived long, my wife and sons are dead, my daughter is dead, my grandchildren are dead but I am still alive. Perhaps the Allfather kept me alive so that I might help you. Tribunes do not bemoan your life. The Allfather has not done with you yet and he has, perhaps, something else he needs you to do. When it is your time he will take you."

Gaelwyn nodded and then lay down in the bottom of the boat. "Wise words old man. Wake me when we land."

"For me the sea is the place I want to spend my last days. It is the place where I find the most peace. I have lived long enough. This has been my last adventure. I w ill go back to the village and the young men will ask me of the sea and I will raise sheep." He shook his head as though to clear a memory, his eyes suddenly bright and clear. "You did not say where you wished to land Tribune."

"No I did not, did I? Somewhere near the land of the lakes for then we could purchase horses and travel home by the shortest route."

"I know a place where we can land but winter grows closer. You will need to move swiftly if you are to avoid an icy death on the mountain tops."

Smiling wryly, for the rest were asleep Marcus said, "If the Allfather wills it old man…"

When legate Camillus received the reports from the Prefect he almost, audibly, breathed a sigh of relief. The cohort of the Ninth had done half the job and stopped the privations of the rebels towards the vulnerable south and the actions of the ala had forced, apparently, the rebels north of the Dunum. He turned to the Camp Prefect. "How go the repairs on the fortress?"

"The important part, the walls have been repaired and the ditches cleared. Another week and we will be back to normal."

“Good then I will take the First second and third cohorts north along with those Tungrian auxiliaries. You can continue the work with the garrisons who sought refuge here and the fourth cohort.”

“That will mean the work will take longer.”

“Work them harder for when I return I expect to find the fortress in a better condition than when I came.” He turned to the sentry at the door, “Send for Tribune Blaesus.”

Scaeva looked at the Legate curiously, “Tribune Blaesus has but recently arrived from Rome. Is it not a little soon to be blooding him?”

“I know young Titus. His father and I served together as Tribunes. The problem with Britannia is that the Governor used auxiliaries as Tribunes when he should have used Romans. Titus will need to learn quickly. Had we more Tribunes in the north then this debacle might not have occurred.”

“I do not think you can blame Prefect Demetrius.”

“Indeed I do not. His father, Senator Demetrius, is a fine man and a fine Roman. No I do not blame the Prefect I blame those who neglected this land for so long.”He held out a tablet. “Look here. The previous governor and his nephew were so busy siphoning off gold and building up private armies that they failed to stop the invasion from the north and even worse, the nephew is still loose somewhere. Once this little uprising has been sorted out I intend to head to Deva and find out where the gold and the thief went.”

Just then there was a cough and a young officer stood there. “You sent for me sir?”

“Yes I did come in Titus. You know Vibius I take it?” The two officers one young and one far older nodded at each other. The camp Prefect resented young Romans like Titus who came for a short season to make a reputation and then return, a war hero, to Rome where they would become fat, lazy senators. Vibius had come up through the ranks and fought his way, quite literally, to his present position. He started to go but the Legate called him back. “No Vibius, your knowledge would be invaluable. Titus and

I are new to the province. So Titus the rebels have escaped north of the Dunum. In the west they have gone back to their ordinary lives. Those we shall leave for the moment; their punishment will come later. The more worrying group is this one. " He stabbed a bony finger at the map. "This Queen Morwenna, who, incidentally, you do not want to underestimate, for while she is a woman, she has the mind of a man. She could be another Boudicca."

Vibius shook his head, "Boudicca did not have the subtlety of this one. Morwenna is far more dangerous."

"Quite so. They have moved into the lands of the Carvetii and they have always been a troublesome people. The cavalry is watching them at the moment. What are your thoughts Titus? You have eyes and mind fresh from Rome. What do you see that the old eyes of two aged soldiers do not?"

The young man felt the two older men watching him. He suddenly felt hot, even though, in this miserable climate it was hard to feel hot even with a brazier burning. "What are our forces?"

"I have earmarked three cohorts of the Ninth and a cohort of the Tungrian auxiliary and there is a depleted ala of cavalry. A small garrison at Morbium and that is the total forces at our disposal."

"And the enemy?"

"Ah that is the problem Titus. In Britannia they fight loosely in warbands. Numbers are notoriously hard to assess. There could be anything from two thousand to ten thousand, we just don't know and if the Carvetii join the Brigante then there will be tens of thousands available."

"And do not forget the Caledonii."

Titus looked at the camp Prefect who was trying to keep the smug smile from showing on his face. "The Caledonii?"

"Yes this rebellion appears to have been sparked because the Caledonii raided the Brigante land and took many captives. Even if we stop the rebellion we have to bolster the north to prevent future raids."

Titus looked up helplessly. “But we do not have enough men. Why does Rome not send more?”
Smiling the Legate said, “Because the Emperor has not looked west yet he is still looking towards Dacia where the Emperor Domitian sent so many legions, legions which had been based in Britannia.” Seeing the crestfallen look on the face of the young Tribune, Camillus patted him, paternally, on the shoulder, “That was unfair of me but I have my answer. You see the same problems that I do.” He leaned over the map, in a far more business like manner. “Here is the problem. We need to get to Dun Holme as soon as possible and make the rebels fight us on a field of our choosing. They will outnumber us and we will need to use every tactic and strategy we can. I am involving you because I want you to take charge of the artillery. It is the one thing the barbarians fear, apart from the legions of course but with only three cohorts we will be using the legion as a barrier to prevent them getting to your artillery.”
The camp Prefect suddenly realised the implication of the Legate’s plan. “But that means you are stripping Eboracum of its artillery and those trained to use it.”
“Of course I am. You can build and train others, we cannot. So Titus how does that seem to you?”
Titus was a little worried about such a responsibility but his father had warned him that in the provinces you took your opportunities when they came. You grabbed them with both hands and then worried later on about how you would use them. “Excellent sir. I look forward to meeting the centurion in charge of the artillery to discuss strategy and logistics.” In his mind Titus meant how he would find out how to use the artillery.
“Good. You will need to be speedy then for we leave tomorrow. We have almost a hundred miles to cover. My only concern is that the rebels strike sooner rather than later.”

The Prefect was a happier man once he knew where the Brigante had gone. Dun Holme was a frightening stronghold on the ox bow of the river but at least it was close to the main road to Coriosopitum and Morbium which meant the reinforcements promised by the Legate would be able to get there swiftly. There had been a garrison north of Dun Holme and Julius wondered if any had survived the Caledonii raid. The fact that Morwenna had seemed happy to camp at Dun Holme meant that both men and horses of the ala could rest and recuperate; much to the delight of Sergeant Cato. "Cassius."

"Yes Prefect?"

"Take half your turma and head north. See if any of the garrison at Longovicium survived the Caledonii. You should be able to get there and back in half a day."

"And if I find any?"

"Tell the garrison commander of the situation. I think it is important that we give the Legate as much information as we can. Even if there is only a century left there at least it narrows Morwenna's options." Cassius looked curiously at Julius. "If she goes east, excellent for she will be against the sea and we can summon the fleet. She cannot go south for there lies Morbium and the Legate. If the road north is barred, however weakly it means she must go west and there the Decurion Princeps is watching. The danger with Morwenna is that we do not know where she will go next. Your information will determine if she goes north, towards the Caledonii or west."

Inside the stronghold Morwenna was finding the leaders and chiefs difficult to persuade. They had been left largely alone by the Romans and the Caledonii had decided that Dun Holme was just too difficult a place to assault when there were easier pickings further south. As their leaders told her there was little advantage to be gained from a war with an enemy who, thus far, had defeated them at every turn.

"I cannot believe that the Carvetii who fought alongside my father and almost defeated the Romans would not take the chance of one final chance to rid this land of their pestilence."

Broc, one of the grey haired warrior chiefs spoke. He was obviously a respected warrior as well as a brace one for he wore his amulets and his torc with pride. His arms and face bore the scars of battle and, when he spoke, the other chiefs and leaders showed him total respect. "You speak of your father and he was a brave man for I fought with him in the west when we came so close to destroying the enemy but we failed and our finest warriors also fell. We have not fought the Romans for many years. Where are the warriors who will fight with you? Where are all the Brigante who left the north to destroy Eboracum? Is this the total force you have?"

Ownie exchanged a look with Aodh. This was always going to be the sticking point. How many men could Morwenna lead? Her army of women was numerous but they were not fighters and, whilst they might cow their men, the Romans would sweep them away.

"There are more Brigante, they are waiting on the coast at Seton. I did not bring the whole army for I came here no to fight the Carvetii but to join with them."

Broc was not convinced. "Winter comes soon in this land. Would you have us fight now in the winter? If we were to join you then the spring would be the better time when we have prepared and when we have trained."

Ownie could see that the wily warrior was stalling for time. He had no intention of fighting for a young woman and no intention of hurling his men at a shield wall of Romans which he knew would end in disaster. "If we strike south now we can destroy Morbium and then rest for the winter. With Morbium destroyed they would have to wait south of the Dunum."

For the first time Aodh could see a glimmer of hope for the younger chiefs saw a chance to gains some quick glory and then spend the winter lavishing in the tales of their heroic deeds. "It may be that such a victory might halt the Romans but would you need all the might of the Carvetii to achieve such a victory? Could you not do so with your Brigante and those," he glanced at the young bucks eager for blood, "who wished to join you?"

Morwenna could see that she had been outfoxed by the wily warrior. She took the small victory as it opened the door for a larger rebellion in the spring. In her mind she was planning to send a message to Lulach to enable a joint invasion when the snows melted. Until then she would have to make do with what she had achieved. "If it is the Carvetii will that they send their best warriors with me and prepare the rest for a war in the spring then I thank you." The young warriors immediately fell under the sway of the persuasive young queen, they were the best.

Broc smiled a wry smile. They were young and keen but they were not the best. "We will have to discuss it at length but," Broc looked at the other elders who nodded, "in principle the Carvetii will support you."

Morwenna immediately turned around and gestured for Ownie and Aodh to follow her. "Damn the old man. Still we have their agreement and we should be able to take Morbium from the north. Ownie ride to Seton and bring the rest of our warriors. Aodh take your men and scout Morbium."

"Sir. The scouts watching Dun Holme report two groups of horsemen have left the stronghold."

"How many?"

"Thirty in each group. One headed east and one south."

"Is the Decurion back yet?"

"No sir."

The Prefect was in a dilemma. The main force was still in Dun Holme and he could not leave his post. If only he had more men but, as it was, he needed to keep the bulk of the force in one piece. "Send for Metellus and Lentius." The two chosen men were the obvious choice for the next Decurion post and they were highly experience. He would have to take a chance. This was where Macro would have been the first choice but the mighty Decurion was in the north, would that he was at Dun Holme.

When the two men arrived he noted that they were ready to ride, anticipating his command. "Each of you choose a trooper to ride with you. Metellus a band is heading south follow them and find out where they go. Lentius there is another heading east, I suspect they are going to Seton, follow. Do not be seen. I would rather you lose them than your lives, we cannot afford any losses."

"Sir."

By the time Cassius rode in Julius had worked out what the likely scenario was; the Queen was finding out where the ala was and, probably gathering all her men together. He smiled to himself. They would get a shock when they found the burned settlement and the dead Brigante. He just hoped that the Legate would move a little quicker. Things looked like they were coming to a head.

"Decurion to see you sir."

"Ah Cassius well what did you find?"

"There is a garrison. It seems they had prepared for such an attack when a couple of survivors from Coriosopitum arrived. They took losses but beat of the attacks. They are short of rations but there are still four centuries left. I informed the centurion of the events down here and he said he would improve the defences."

"Excellent, so we now await the Legate."

Chapter 15

Marcus was awoken by the sound of the gulls screaming overhead. As he came to and his eyes adjusted to the bright blue sky which had replaced the driving rain of the previous night Gaelwyn also awoke. "I am not a man of the sea Tribune."

"Me neither."

Hearing their voices Gaius and Ailis came to whilst the three boys snuggled closer together deep in sleep. "How far then old man?" Marcus looked over at the old man who was dropped over the tiller. He noticed that the sail was not catching the wind but idly flapping.

Gaelwyn leaned over to touch him awake. "Come on old man or we will be in Ireland ere long." As he touched him the old man fell forwards and Ailis gave a gasp of shock.

"Gaelwyn, he is dead!"

The old man's sightless eyes stared up at the blue sky and the creaming gulls, a half smile on his dead face. Gaelwyn gently closed the old man's eyes. "May you find the Allfather and peace old man and may your family be waiting for you."

Marcus peered over the bow. "It looks like we are drifting out to sea. Can you steer this Gaelwyn?"

"Do I look liker a sailor?"

Ailis went to the tiller. "I watched him last night. Gaius Marcus pull the ropes tight." As the sail filled with the wind hitherto spilled Ailis leaned on the tiller and the boar headed slowly towards the beach some way in the distance.

"Where are we Gaelwyn? Can you tell?"

Shaking his head the old scout said, "I am not sure. Those mountains look like the mountains of the land of the lakes but I am not sure. It matters not Tribune. We land where we can for we are no sailors."

Without the old man's skill the small boat took an age to reach land but eventually they felt its bottom scrape along the sandy beach. Gaius leapt out and held the bow against the tide which wanted to take it out to sea. Gaelwyn, Ailis and Marcus lifted the children from the bottom of the boat and carried them up the beach. When they returned to Gaius they looked at each other. Gaius spoke for them all. “Well what do we do? Do we bury him or burn him? I do not know the customs of his people?”

Marcus took Gaius’ hand and released it from the boat. The tide and wind immediately turned it towards the open sea. “This is what the old man would have wished. He is not at one with the sea. His only possession will take him across the undying seas to the Allfather and his family.” All four of them bowed their heads as, with the gulls crying above, the old man of the Novontae went on his last journey westwards towards the ends of the world.

“What now then Marcus?”

“We need to know where we are but we will need to head east.”

“There is a pass there between those mountains in the distance. We still have two bows and arrows and your cloaks. We may find a settlement, if not we hunt for food and shelter but thank the Allfather that we have escaped the clutches of Lulach and the Caledonii.”

“We have Gaelwyn and it is thanks to Macro. We owe our lives to him.”

“Aye and an old man who wanted to help a family.”

“We never even knew his name.”

“The important thing is that we remember him and his deed. Let us go. Come on boys you need to work those legs today we have a long way to go. Are you ready? Will you be warriors?”

Gaius’ son Decius thrust out his chest and said, “I am ready father.”

Macro’s son heard the word, father, and looked like he was becoming tearful. Young Marcus put his arm around him and said, “Decius and I may be the smallest but we are ready, are we not brother?”

Biting back the tears he said, “I am and I will be a warrior, like my father.”

At first the path they took was gentle and undulating through dunes and thin scrubby trees but then it began to climb. Gaelwyn looked at the boys. “I will scout ahead and try to find some food and shelter for we will need it ere long. Stay on this path and do not deviate from it. If you see my sign obey it.” Suddenly he was gone.

Ailis said, “Sign?”

“Yes when he was a scout he would leave markings to tell us which way we ought to go. I am glad that the old man is still with us Gaius.”

“If he were not my love we would now be dead.”

They took it steadily as they climbed up the pass. Ailis kept looking at Gaius and Marcus for confirmation that they were on the right track but each time they smiled and nodded. This was where they were confident; it was like being back in the ala with Gaelwyn sniffing out the enemy. When Marcus sneaked a glance at Gaius the warrior was once again a young man. Finally they turned a corner in the pass and there was Gaelwyn with a small fire burning and two hares on a spit. “Had I known that you would take as long I would have hunted a deer.”

“Old man, we did not wish to push harder in case you could not cope with the pace.”

“Pah! Make a shelter while I finish the food.”

When the shelter was finished and the boys asleep Gaelwyn pointed east. There is a high pass and then the land drops down. I recognised it; once we cross the col we will be but twenty miles from Glanibanta.”

“Glanibanta,” murmured Marcus. “We never seem to get too far from Glanibanta. Well at least we know we can find food and horse there and we still have the funds to pay for it.”

Gaius looked westwards. “I think the Allfather sent the old man. “The others looked at him with unspoken questions written on their faces. “He came when we needed him and stayed until we did not. He came just in time to save us and out of time so that Macro could achieve the honour he wished.”

"Do you not think Macro would have wished him to arrive earlier?"
"No Ailis. Macro always wished for an heroic death, perhaps not one witnessed by his son, or then again perhaps. Are you not certain that the wind and tide which kept the boat from landing was not directed by the Allfather? No I believe that the old man lived long enough to save us and no more."
"Which means the Allfather is not finished with us yet."
"True Gaius. I think that the Sword of Cartimandua and the sons of Gaius and Macro still have much work to do in the land of Britannia long after we have joined Macro."

Morwenna led her band of warriors, Carvetii and Brigante, south to Morbium. Ownie had not returned but she doubted not that he would bring his forces to Morbium in time. Aodh had assured her that they had more than enough warriors to complete the task. Morbium had been attacked and assaulted so many times that one more determined attack, from a strong force such as she commanded, would cause the walls to fall quickly. The army took a leisurely pace south allowing Morwenna to garner as many warriors as possible and to glean as much adulation as she could from those who came to view the royal progress. Encouraged by their women folk many men joined the ever growing column. The men found themselves behind the women who had joined, desperate to be close to the woman who appeared to be at one with the Mother. Aodh and his men guarded the Queen like a metal cloak.
For Prefect Demetrius it was a simple task to keep the column in sight. There were so many warriors and women cutting a huge swathe through the land that even one eyed Ulpius could have followed them with his good eye closed. Julius had been close to the force and knew that it was just numbers rather than quality. He had counted the warriors with full armour and helms. He had seen how few of them had good swords and axes. He had observed the lack of organisation. This was not a Caledonii

warband, with chiefs and order, with roles and responsibilities. This was a mob intent upon taking plunder. They would not have stood a charge for a full ala let alone the might of the legion which was about to be unleashed upon them.

"Cassius, take your turma to the west of the column. When the Legate destroys them follow them west. If they go east or north, which I think is unlikely then I will pursue."

"You are confident, Prefect, that the Legate will destroy them?"

"I have seen the legions at work many times. There are some foes who might cause them problems but this rag tag army will not. If they head west send a rider to the Decurion Princeps to join you. We do not let this witch escape to cause more mayhem with her magic. We end it now."

Metellus had soon come back to tell the Prefect that the warband sent south had scouted the fort and was now waiting in the woods to the north. Lentius had still not returned and the Prefect was becoming concerned when two tired, and weary troopers rode in. "It is Lentius!!

"Sir the warband went to Seton and they are returning with the warriors who survived our roasting!"

"Good. Cassius send a couple of riders across the Dunum. Find the Legate and give him the information we have gathered; a smaller warband approaching from the east and the large one travelling towards Morbium. We will have to wait to find out what role he has in mind for us."

The Legate was pleased with the condition of the roads for he had expected, with the privations of the rebellions and raids that they would have suffered damage but he and his legionaries made Morbium in three days. As the auxiliaries took down the barriers hastily erected by the doughty defenders the Legate met with the centurion in command.

"I am glad to see you sir. The Brigante scouts arrived yesterday and have been busy in the woods north of us. I think it means the main army is heading here."

"I agree and the reports from Prefect Demetrius would confirm that information. You have done well centurion. Lesser leaders would have fled to the safety of Eboracum."

"When the Prefect told me what had happened at Cataractonium I was just pleased that we were still alive."

"How many men do you have in the fort at the moment? I mean how many are fit for duty?"

The adjutant handed him a wax tablet. We have six centuries who are fit and two with either wounded or injured men."

"Good. Leave the injured and wounded to man the walls and you command the rest. We have a small enough force as it is."

"With due respect sir isn't that a little risky? If they get by us then…" the question hung in the air like the sword of Damocles.

"Thank you for your honesty centurion but if they, as you say, get by us then it means we have been defeated and I do not think that even with a cohort you could hold the damaged fort against a barbarian horde. But I do not think we will be defeated. My Tribune assures me his artillery will see off the rebel rabble. Isn't that so Titus?"

Titus looked up at the Legate. Those were the words of the Legate, not his. He could see that the Legate was a political creature; failure would see the blame heaped squarely on the Tribune's shoulders. "Yes Legate as long as we have a field of battle which suits us."

"Good point Tribune. Centurion you know the area north of us where would be a good place to stop them? We need height to enable our bolt throwers to cause maximum casualties and we need some sort of narrow shallow valley to funnel them into the legion."

The centurion went to the map on the wall and then returned to the Legate. "The other side of that ridge would be the best for there is a quarry to the east which would force them west and the river takes a bend to the other side. The ridge is wooded which would allow the bolt throwers to stay hidden and not impede their rate of fire.

"Excellent centurion! We have finished our march and we get to sleep under a roof. Excellent! Titus, coordinate with the centurion of the Ninth and build our camp on the field of battle. When the Prefect tells us where they are will end this rebellion. Oh and Titus, get the Tungrians to get rid of those scouts from the woods. It wouldn't do to let our enemies know we have arrived eh?"

Ownie and his warband joined up with the Queen as she camped five miles north of Morbium. Aodh was angry at the depleted numbers. "What happened? Where are the rest?"

"After we left Seton, the cavalry returned and burned the settlement and killed many warriors. Some took the attack as a sign that things would not go well and they left to return to their homes."

Morwenna was not happy but she appeared philosophical about it. "We have more than enough to destroy Morbium on the morrow and, once we have captured it the rest of the land will flock to us. Only Eboracum will still remain as a symbol of Rome and it was so badly damaged the last time we attacked that the next time it will crumble like a piece of sheep's cheese."

Ownie was not convinced but said nothing. He was beginning to realise that the Roman war machine was not as easy to destroy as the Queen and her advisors thought. He watched the wild women adoring her and shook his head. She was beginning to believe all that she preached. Ownie would prefer armoured men to a wild rabble of women if he were to attack a shield wall. He knew from speaking to the men he had brought from Seton that the attack by the Roman cavalry had severely damaged their confidence. They had seen how few cavalry there were and yet they had destroyed a strong settlement.

Aodh called Ownie over. "Our scouts have not reported for a while. Send a few scouts out and find out the state of the fort."

"Aodh, you are a warrior. Can we still win?"

"We can win but we need the legions to stay in Eboracum. This is a large army but it needs more training and preparation before we take on the best that Rome has. Were these Caledonii... but they are well trained and have never stopped fighting. Do not get upset Ownie, for I know you to be brave, but the Brigante did not fight for many years. You do not pick up the skills as quickly as that."

"I know. If I had Colla here I would strangle him with my own hands. I will send out the scouts."

Morwenna and her leaders, men and women were planning the battle when the scouts returned. "Well where are the scouts?"

"We never got as far as the woods. There is a legion at the fort."

Even Morwenna looked surprised. "A legion; are you sure? How many men?" The scouts could not use numbers and had not counted. They shrugged.

Aodh understood their confusion. "You say a legion because they had the armour, square shields and red crests." Eager to be able to give an answer they nodded. "Could you see into their camp?"

"Yes for the walls were not high."

"Did you see an eagle?" They looked at each other in confusion and Aodh drew the eagle standard in the soil. They shook their heads.

"They had a standard but it looked like this." The scout drew a boar.

"You are sure there was no eagle?" They shook their heads. As they were dismissed Aodh turned to the others. "It is legionaries not the legion. I did not think they would send a whole legion north. It is probably a few cohorts, probably two thousand men at most."

Ownie spoke up, "A legion or even part of a legion does change our plans does it not?"

Morwenna nodded, "You are wise Ownie. It means that our warriors will not have to worry about the bolt throwers they had at Eboracum. Aodh you have fought the legions before, how will they fight?"

"They will be in the centre with the auxiliaries, however many they have, on the flanks. They will have lines of three in blocks of three. If they have two cohorts then they will probably have six blocks altogether."

"Then we attack the weaker warriors on the flanks. If the legion pushes then let them. We can allow our centre to fall back and fall on their sides. The sign of the boar was a good omen for we will be the boar and the warriors in the middle will be the head."

Ownie was doubtful that there was enough discipline for such a manoeuvre but at least it was not the suicidal frontal attack he had expected. "I will take the right my queen."

"Excellent Ownie for that is the place of honour."

The Brigante chief wanted the right because that afforded him an escape route should the battle go, as he expected, ill and he wanted to be able to get back to his hills as swiftly as possible.

"Sir the enemy are camped over the rise, about five miles from Morbium."

Julius was on the horns of a dilemma. Cassius was to the west and in a perfect position to observe the westward movements of the horde. If they were to turn north or east then Julius had the only force which could scout and trail them but he needed to meet with the garrison commander to coordinate his own movements. "Sergeant Cato."

"Sir. "The Sergeant was on the Prefect's shoulder.

"Detach four men and shadow the army. If they retreat stay in touch with them. If they deviate from a southerly or westerly direction then let me know."

The phlegmatic sergeant absent mindedly ruffled the main of his horse, "And where will you be sir?"

"In Morbium."

"Don't forget that quarry sir, you will have to go a long way around to get to the fort."

"Thank you sergeant, good advice."

"As he rode away with his four men he shouted over his shoulder, "Wouldn't want any horses getting injured."

It was dark by the time the weary troopers approached the fort from the east. "Halt! Who goes there?"

"Prefect Demetrius of Marcus' Horse." Julius could feel the arrows being aimed at them and it was with some relief that he saw the light from the fort as the gates opened to allow them entry.

The Legate strode towards him. "Well done Prefect you and your men have done all that was asked." Suddenly he saw how few men there were. "Is this all that is left of the ala?"

Dismounting Julius shook his head, "No sir. I have detached four turmae. One and a half are to the west of the horde and two and a half are at Brocauum watching the rebels who, apparently are at peace."

The Legate looked at the young patrician with new respect. He had used the limited forces he had well. "Excellent. We have a surprise for our young rebellious queen. I have brought some of the Ninth north. When she attacks this time we will be prepared. Come meet my new staff and have some food you look exhausted."

"I will just see to my men sir and then I will join you."

When Julius finally joined the Legate, his Tribune and the three centurions he was ready for bed but the Legate had other plans. "Have something to eat and drink while my Tribune, young Titus explains the battle orders."

Julius smiled at the discomfort of the blushing and uncomfortable young Tribune. "We will have two cohorts of the Ninth in three lines with the First as a reserve. The Tungrians will be on the right and the four centuries of the garrison on the left in front of my force. I will be in the woods with the artillery." He leaned back pleased that the ordeal was over.

Wiping his mouth Julius said, "And where will the cavalry be?"

The Legate hid a smile as Titus looked around in confusion. "But you have less than thirty men Prefect. What can you do?"

"Queen Cartimandua was rescued by less than thirty men. They fought off a warband as big as the one we face. They only emerged with a handful of troopers but they did their job."

Titus looked at the legate for advice but the old soldier was enjoying watching the young puppy squirm. "Well Prefect, where would you place your cavalry?"

The Legate smiled, young Titus was a politician. He had adroitly taken the initiative. "Cavalry can either be used as a shock force or a pursuing force. Obviously we are too few for the former but we need to be in a position to catch this queen when she flees."

"How do you know she will run Prefect?"

"I know Legate because we knew her mother and we know her in the ala. She is slippery and cunning. She is resourceful and resilient. The only way she will be stopped is with her death."

The passion and hatred in his voice surprised all in the room. "You seem to have a personal vendetta against this woman."

"Her family were responsible for the murder of Queen Cartimandua, the rape and murder of Tribune Maximunius' family and the death of Camp Prefect Flavius. There is not a trooper who would not give his life if it meant her death."

There was a charged silence in the room until Titus gave a small cough. "So Prefect your troopers will be where?"

"She cannot go east, she has to go north and I have men watching that direction. I do not think she will flee there because the sea is a barrier and would prevent her escape. She will head west. Decurion Cassius is watching there but she is, as I said, cunning. She has allies in Caledonia and could go north west. She has friends in Mona and she could go south west and her father lived in the west. I will keep the ala in the woods to the west, close to your artillery. It will afford us the best view and when the fox runs then we will give chase."

The Legate nodded his approval. "When they have been dispersed Prefect what can you tell us of forces to the north?"

"There is nothing. They have emptied Dun Holme. There is one Roman fort still holding the road at Vinovia. After that the land is empty. The frontier begins and ends here on the Dunum." He added sadly, "All the land won by Agricola and paid for with Roman blood has been lost."

"It is as bad as I thought it would be. Well centurion. It looks as though your Tungrians will be building a fort. I will have to send to Lindum for more troops for this rebellion needs crushing with more forces than are available to me at this moment in time and I , young Prefect, am no Julius Gnaeus Agricola."

The scouts who returned to Aodh made their report quietly to their leader. Experienced warriors all, they knew that their news would bring dismay to the rank and file of the army. "You counted them then?"

"Yes there is one cohort of auxiliaries and some of the garrison but they have brought three cohorts of the Ninth. There looked to be some artillery in the woods but their guards prevent us examining them closely."

"Thank you my brothers. Now we know what to expect."

When the news was relayed to Morwenna she was not discomfited in the least. Aodh was worried about her for, now that she surrounded herself with the women who believed in the magic and the sorceress' power, she was beginning to believe her own legend. Aodh knew she had power but he had not seen a power which could defeat a gladius and a scutum handled by the most ruthless soldiers in the world.

"It will be hard Aodh but the Romans have not met my women." Morwenna had armed the women with the weapons looted from the some of the smaller garrisons. Aodh was not convinced they would be able to use them but at least they would look like warriors from a distance.

"I will have my men prepare an escape for us should the day go against us."

Kissing him gently on the forehead she said, “You worry too much my love. We will win tomorrow.”

Chapter 16

The autumn mist masked the sun rise and the valley of the Dunum was filled with a clinging dampness which dulled sounds and hid the two armies from each other. The Legate frowned as he spoke with his commanders. “This suits our enemies more than us. The can sneak forwards in the mist.”

Julius stepped forward. “We could sow the ground before our front lines with caltrops. In my experience men cannot help but make a noise when they step on them. If will, at least, give us some warning.”

“Good idea.” He turned to an aide. “See to it. We have made our plans it is now down to the men.”

The First Spear, Gnaeus Seius Pavo grinned a lopsided grin the result of an old scar running down his cheek which made him look perpetually happy, in reality he was a dour warrior but at that moment he was grinning. “My lads are looking forward to it. I just want to get to grips with them.” He turned to Julius. “The last time I fought with your ala was when we sent the Caledonii back a few years ago. I was optio under Decius Brutus then.”

Grasping his hand Julius smiled the widest smile he had in a few weeks. “Decius Brutus! How is the old goat? Retired I take it?”

“Aye. He has a farm near to Derventio. If I get the chance I will have to go and visit him.”

“When we have seen off this witch I may join you.”

“If you could just defeat them first gentlemen?”

“Of course Legate but I feel happier knowing that Marcus’ Horse is still around. They have always been lucky for the Ninth.”

The Tungrian centurion nodded his agreement, “And the Tungrians also. The Allfather must like you.”

Almost to himself Julius added, “Lately I am not so sure.”

The women in the Brigante army were excited as were most of the warriors. Morwenna had spent the night casting a spell and dreaming the dream. When she announced that the Romans would not see their army they wondered what magic she had conjured. When the dawn broke and the grey murk and mist filled the field they knew that the mother was with them and the day would be theirs. Even Ownie and Aodh agreed that it gave them an edge they had not had the previous night.

"It means that, even if they have artillery, they will have to fire blind."

"It is our best chance."

"My warriors and my sisters." Morwenna's powerful and entrancing voice seemed to rise out of the fog. "Today we destroy the Romans. The Mother is with us and has sent this powerful mist as our ally. To make it more potent and powerful we need to make not a sound so that when we emerge the Romans will run before us."

Ownie was not convinced that the rag tag army would make the Romans run but he had to admit that they would be able to close with the soldiers without as many casualties as on a clear day.

"Go! On to victory!" Those nearest her tried to touch her shift, or her horse for luck. Aodh saw the fanatical look in their eyes and wondered if this just might be the day when the Romans lost and lost in a major battle.

Titus was nervous; this was his first battle and so much depended upon him and his bolt throwers. He peered at the mist unable to pierce the gloom. One of the optio engineers ran up to him. "Sir I see movement on our left."

Titus could see nothing but an idea came to him. "Is it within the range of the onagers?"

"Yes Tribune. We marked them out last night but we have no targets."

"We have plenty of rocks. Begin to fire it may provoke them." As the optio raced off to the onagers crews Titus turned to the messenger next to him. “Tell the Legate there is movement to our left.” Titus felt exposed and was strangely grateful for the presence, in the trees behind him, of the cavalry. He had been surprised by the affection in which the ala was held. The First Cohort of any legion was elite and felt themselves to be superior to any other but First Spear had shown genuine joy at fighting alongside the auxiliaries. He felt confident that, even if they were attacked directly, the Prefect would do all in his power to save him and that gave him less fear. Perhaps that was what bravery was, having less fear to do what you had to.

As the onagers began to hit they heard the dull thuds as they hit the ground. Suddenly they heard a harder sound as though it had hit something solid and there was a dull moan. Moments later there was a scream as a rock hit and killed some hidden warrior. Turning to a second messenger Titus ordered, “Tell the Legate they are attacking.”

All along the battlefield there were cries and screams as warriors stood on the painful and incapacitating caltrops. In the middle the Legate said, to no-one in particular, “So it begins.”

To the legionaries and auxilia waiting for the attack to materialise it was a strange, eerie time. They could hear screams and cries emanating from the mist but they could see no-one. The Ninth were stoic about the waiting; whatever came through the fog they could deal with. The auxilia were a little more nervous for they fought in a looser formation and preferred to slow the enemy down with missiles. The legate was also in a state of nervous excitement. He had confidence in his men but he did not know how many barbarians would erupt from the fog. The mist also masked the sounds and the cries of those injured by rocks and caltrops seemed to come from all over, sometimes, bizarrely from behind them.

Ownie and Aodh, leading their men were also enjoying mixed emotions. Aodh knew that they were taking far fewer casualties than if they had been in the clear morning of an autumn day but, like their enemies it was the not knowing where the enemy line was. The caltrops also negated the effect of a charge which relied on a solid line of men. They could not afford to run. Ownie was pleased that they were closer to the Roman line for the rocks were now falling further behind and killing fewer of his men. They had quickly learned to watch for caltrops and were able to keep up a solid line.

As the barbarians neared each other they could see their enemies as a vaguely indistinct blur. Titus, on the hill was able to pick out figures and was about to order his men to fire when the optio in charge of the bolt throwers did it for him. The bolts flew through the air and they could tell they were striking home but could not see the effect. To the Brigante it was even more terrifying than a normal battlefield for they could see nothing until the warrior in front of them was thrown back and the bolt hurtled through his body to strike the next man.

Aodh had seen the first bolt and knew that the time for secrecy and silence was over. "Charge!" he roared and the line hurled themselves forward. Suddenly the shadows became firm and the two armies saw each other. The legionaries and auxilia only had time for one volley of javelins and pila before the two lines met in a crunch and clash of sword on shield and man on man. For the first time Aodh felt the Brigante were fighting on an equal footing. Their numbers were not thinned and they had, for the first time, a huge weight of warriors pushing forward. Their weight of numbers began to tell.

The three Roman lines absorbed the pressure but very gradually began to be pushed backwards. The centurions roared their orders out. "Hold the line!"

The legate tut tutted in frustration. "They are forgetting their basic training. "Stepping forward from the First Cohort he placed himself behind the third line and roared. "Use your shields. Stab and thrust! Remember your training!"

The senior centurion of the second cohort, which was on the right of the line, reddened with embarrassment when he heard the Legate reprimand the cohorts. Without turning he shouted, "First century! We are going forward! Hold the line and on my command… Push!" With a mighty blow he punched one warrior in the face with the boss of his shield, head butted a second and slashed the neck of a third. On either side of him the legionaries managed to despatch their opponents and suddenly there was a slight gap. The whole of the line moved forward and the second and third lines followed quickly. The barbarians had lost their impetus and when the second century began to push forward the barbarians began to give ground. The other cohorts felt the pressure on their lines lessen and they too pushed forwards.

On the left flank the auxiliaries were being inexorably pushed back. Although their second and third lines were able to hurl javelins over the heads of the first line there were too many barbarians to make a difference. With the Second Cohort moving forward there was a danger that they could be outflanked. The Legate turned to First Spear, "Centurion Pavo, I want the First Cohort to push back these barbarians."

Eager to be in the battle Gnaeus Seius Pavo tightened his shield and drew his gladius. "First Cohort. In three lines. Forward!"

The gap was too small for the whole of the line to be accommodated and the second cohort found itself being muscled further left while the auxiliaries were just bundled out of the way. The Brigante on the Roman left had scented victory and were eagerly pushing forward to get at the weakening auxiliaries. It was with a shock that they ran into the elite cohort of the Ninth legion. The first to die were the chiefs and those brave souls who fought at the front. Their lack of armour and over confidence killed them almost as quickly as the gladii of the Ninth. Soon the whole of the First Cohort was moving forward like a giant battering ram cutting down the Brigante before them.

On the Roman left the bolt throwers were angling their bolts in front of the legionaries to cut down as many as possible. They were causing huge casualties but they were not taking out lines of men to ease the pressure nor were they touching the warband of

Ownie which was making its way towards the four centuries of the garrison spread thinly before the woods and the artillery.

Ownie turned to his warband, still almost intact. "We charge these Romans and then we will destroy the hated bolt throwers."

Ownie's band had had much success and were as confident as any. The garrison auxiliaries, by contrast had been fighting a defensive war from behind solid walls for much of the time. The sheer weight of numbers took them back. Ownie targeted the First Spear who stood in the middle of the line. He threw his throwing axe at the tall centurion and then raced in with his long sword held high. The axe nicked a piece out of the centurion's shield before angling up and catching his helmet on the cheek guard. As his head flew uncontrollably back Ownie hacked down with his sword on the suddenly bare neck of the leader of the auxiliaries. Ownie gave the man to the left of the dying centurion no chance and he backhanded his sword into his thigh slicing through to bone. The gap in the front line was suddenly filled with Brigante and the second liner found itself facing the Brigante chief. With their leader gone, much of the order went and the line fragmented which suited the barbarians. Almost unconsciously the auxiliary line began to wheel to face these enemies and retreat towards the protection of the legion on their right.

Titus suddenly saw, to his horror that there was now open space between his artillery and the warband. Even as he prayed to his household gods for the barbarians to ignore him he saw half the warband leave the auxiliaries and begin to run up the hill. The optios saw the danger and began to depress their machines. It was a race against time and Titus could see that only a few would be able to bear and the warband would be amongst his lightly armed artillerymen. He turned to look for aid and suddenly heard the sound of the buccina.

Julius had seen the disaster unfold before him. He had less than fifty men with him, the men of the turma and the twelve legionary cavalry who had accompanied the Ninth. "We need them to think we are an ala. Sound the buccina and then make as much noise as you can. We need to give the lads a chance. Marcus' Horse!"

The rallying call was repeated throughout the ala and rolled around the woods and over the fog making it like eerie call of a banshee. The Brigante making their way towards the Tribune and his machines paused as they heard the buccina followed by the shout and then heard the thunder of the hooves. They could see nothing at first but they could hear the sound growing closer and closer. They heard the words Marcus' Horse and they began to fear. Many of Ownie's warband had been at Seton and were there when they had the settlement burned. To those warriors these were not cavalrymen they were wraiths and spectres from beyond the grave. Those warriors were not going to face phantoms and they turned and ran. Their comrades wondered why they were running and halted to look for the danger. That was their death knell for the thin line of horses hit them in open order as they stood at the bottom of the hill. Even as Julius and his men hurtled through them Titus had depressed the bolt throwers and they began to decimate the ranks of Ownie's men still fighting the auxiliaries.

By this time the effect of the First Cohorts charge was taking its effect and the line rippled forward pushing Brigante and Carvetii alike back. The legionaries nearest Ownie's men spilled out at an oblique angle to take the warband in the flank and like the fog which had until recently been surrounding them, dissipated and disappeared. Ownie and his oath brothers saw that they had lost and ran up the hill from whence the cavalry had come. The Tribune could do nothing about their departure for he was busy slaughtering lines of warriors. Ownie merely paused at the top of the hill to take one last look before he disappeared west with his handful of warriors.

Julius had to stop his charge when they ran into the main line of Brigante. Over the screaming roaring mass of barbarians he caught a glimpse of Morwenna sat astride her horse. Their eyes locked for a moment and she raised her hand and pointed at him with her first and fifth fingers. The evil smile told him she was cursing him. For the briefest of moments he contemplated charging her to end it all but one of his troopers plucked at his arm, "Come on sir. If we stay here we'll be buggered. Probably literally."

Coming to his senses he shouted, "Sound retreat!"

The buccina horn drew back the ala from their charge. There were empty saddles and dead horses but the attack on the Roman left had been defeated.

The Legate could see from the small knoll on which he was standing that the Brigante attack had broken down. They had pulled back when the cavalry charged, the name Marcus' Horse inspiring fear. He turned to an aide. "Order First Spear to return to the reserve and tell the Tungrian centurion to resume his position."To a second aide he said, "Tell the Tribune to realign his artillery, the fog is clearing and he should be able to hit their rear ranks."

The Morbium garrison had been pushed so far back that they were almost next to the Legate. He walked over to the centurion who was bleeding from a deep wound on his arm a capsarius bandaging it. The centurion tried to come to attention and almost pushed the medic out of the way.

"Sorry about that sir."

"Nonsense centurion your men fought well but were heavily outnumbered. Do let that man see to your wound. The last thing I need is for you to be incapacitated. What I want you to do is place your men at the foot of the hill and woods to protect the artillery. The third cohort has moved across to cover where you were. "

"Yes sir we will do."

On the other side of the field the retreating men might well have melted off the field like the fog which was rapidly thinning but for the wall of women placed there, cunningly, by Morwenna. She knew that the men would not run away whilst their women remained. Aodh came up his bloodied blade showing that he had been in action that morning. "Ownie and his men have been destroyed." The fog had prevented any of the Brigante leaders witnessing the desertion of the chief and all thought he had had an honourable end. "Those artillery units will start to kill us soon."

"Is there nothing we can do to stop them?" Morwenna understood numbers in battles and tricks but strategies and forces were beyond her.

Aodh scanned the field looking for anything which might be effective. Cavalry would have been perfect but he had none. The Romans had sited their machines well and they were protected by trees and a slope. Suddenly his eyes lit upon the one weapon which might help him. "There is one thing." He ran to the wagons where there were fifty boys of various ages idling. "You lads. Have you got your slingshots with you?" His answer was a forest of arms holding them aloft. They could barely speak for they were being addressed by the Queen's own champion. "Good. I want you to kill as many of those men with the machines on the hill as you can. Are you up for it?" The high pitched roar prefaced a race across the open ground towards the hill. Their small stature meant that they were still hidden by the last of the low lying fog.

As soon as they were within range they began to hurl their stones at a prodigious rate. The artillerymen found themselves being struck by the stones which were being used very accurately. Casualties began to mount.

The garrison centurion saw the danger. "Right lads. Let's chase these little buggers away."

The command was easy the action less so. The boys merely changed their target and the auxiliary shields were not as effective as those of the legionaries. Stones cracked into legs and exposed arms, the crack of the bones showing the result. When his men began to fall from head wounds the centurion wisely called them back.

Aodh smile with satisfaction. Fifty boys had done what a warband in the hundreds could not, they had negated the most powerful of the Roman weapons. Morwenna nodded her thanks and pointed her arm forward signalling the renewal of the attack. She had seen how close they had come to breaking the line for the Romans had had to use their reserves. Aodh had seen the weak part of the line, the Tungrians and he, personally, led forward the attack on the Roman right.

The Legate saw the unruly mob race swiftly across the open ground unchallenged for there were no weapons which could be brought to bear, as long as the bolt throwers were neutralised. There was however a flaw in the Brigante plan for the attack was veering away from the legions as the Brigante warriors tried to get closed to what they saw as the weaker force, the auxiliaries. In doing so their flank was more exposed. "The Ninth will advance forward." As the Legate drew his gladius he turned to an aide, "Ask the Prefect to rid us of those boys."

The line was echeloned with the Third the furthest forward. Slightly overlapping and behind was the second and finally, on the right, was the First slightly behind and overlapping. This meant that most of the Brigante had to withstand an attack from a Roman line three deep but in three crucial places it was six deep and a six deep formation of Roman legionaries was a rock to break any heart.

The Tungrian line began to sag but the First Spear still smarted over their earlier withdrawal and would not brook any such weakness. "We will hold them! Stab and slash! Look for weaknesses." He was like a beacon in the middle of the line. No matter how many warriors eager for the glory of killing a centurion and taking the standard threw themselves at him he beat them back.

On the flanks of the Brigante the Roman legionaries did what they did best, they hacked their way through an army largely devoid of armour and shields. No matter how bravely the warriors on the right fought, the heavily armoured and disciplined Romans were too numerous and the horde became a long narrow beast.

Julius did not like the order but he understood it. The battle hung in the balance. The barbarians still heavily outnumbered the

Romans and the artillery needed to be brought into play. The only way that would happen was if those boys were eliminated. As much as he disliked it he would do it. "Right men. We rid the field of those boys. And remember they can kill just as effectively as a warrior." He led his men swiftly down the slope. Titus waved at them as they passed. The artillerymen, now depleted in number, were busy aiming the remaining bolt throwers at the warriors massing for their attack.

At the bottom of the hill the garrison opened ranks to allow the horses through. To the boys this was a great game. They were able to pelt adults with impunity and no-one could do anything about it. When they saw the men on horses appear they gave a cheer for it was a bigger and therefore easier target. The feeling lasted for the length of time it took to put a fresh stone in their sling for the line leapt forward and. To their horror, the boys saw the wall of long swords aiming for them. Only one or two had the courage to throw their stones and they were the first to die. The horsemen only had a small target to aim at and leaning forward they slice down, their blades slicing through tiny necks to end young lives swiftly. Those who turned to look screamed as they saw the blood spouting and spurting from their dying and dead friends.

The first to react to the horror were the women, some of them the mothers of the youngsters now spilling their blood on the green battlefield. They raced forward to protect their children but the boys were at least fifty paces away and the were being relentlessly slaughtered by the troopers who were hating their appointed task and carrying out the offensive orders through gritted teeth. The last boy managed to fall at his mother's feet only to have the life trampled out of him by the trooper's battle hardened horse and for his mother to be impaled upon the sword already aiming for the child.

Seeing the horror of the bodies and the wall of women Julius called, "Retreat!"

The call was too late for the trooper who had killed the last boy and his mother. The cavalryman, from the Ninth was pulled from his horse by an enraged mob of women who ripped at his eyes and hair and his arms and legs. Within moments he had been torn limb from limb and his wild eyed horse ran aimlessly around the field its nostrils red with blood.

By the time the ala had reformed Julius had regained some of his composure but the sight of the women tearing at the dying trooper had made him almost vomit. He had, until that moment revoked the women as a threat. He had thought they would be an encumbrance; now he knew the danger that they posed. "Station yourselves behind the garrison I am going to see the Legate."

"Sir?"

"Yes Prefect, well done for those two charges. What is it?"

"I think you need to beware the women. I know they do not look like a threat but I just watched them tear a man into pieces."

"Thank you for the warning. How many would you say are left?"

"They still heavily outnumber us but I do not think they will stand if they suffer another loss. Their leader is a woman at the rear. Brigante fight better when led from the front by a warrior."

"I thought so myself. I think now is the time for the attack. Sound the advance. Prefect, keep your eye on that Queen of theirs I do not want her to escape. Follow her when she flees and let me know where you will be and I will bring the Ninth there to finally corner her."

"Sir." Riding back to his men he could see that the Tribune had now managed to start to fire the bolt throwers effectively and, even though there were less of them, they were more effective now and the optios were aiming them to cause the maximum casualties. The women and warriors had grabbed shields to protect themselves but they only prevented them from killing larger numbers. Even a shield was no match for a bolt.

The legionaries in the front line stood still as the second and third came through them. The warriors were now faced by fresh soldiers who were keen to show their courage. In contrast those of the Brigante had been fighting all morning and were tired. With fatigue came carelessness and suddenly the front line of the Brigante collapsed. While the front line stood still the second, freshest line moved forward and hit the Brigante even harder. This last assault was too much and the whole of the Brigante line collapsed racing back to their lines, ready to flee the battlefield.

Morwenna had seen the collapse and made her plans accordingly. If the men would not fight voluntarily they would be forced to fight. As they raced swiftly back they were faced by a solid line of very determined women and they found an impenetrable barrier. They had no option but to turn and face their tormentors again. The only thing now in their favour was the fact that the lines of women pushed against them making the wall of steel stronger.

When the two lines met there was no relief for either. The outnumbered but more skilful legionaries hacked and chopped their way through warriors reluctantly forced to fight. Every time the front line of the Romans became tired they would interchange with the other two. The auxiliaries could now use their second and third lines to hurl javelins into the mêlée. The only respite the Brigante found was that the bolt throwers could no longer fire for fear of hitting their own men. The battle had been raging for some hours and even the legionaries were becoming tired. There came a tipping point when the warriors could no longer lift their arms and they began to fall and clog the feet of the legionaries. The Legate was in the third row and when he saw that point he yelled, "Melee!" and the legionaries broke up the shield line to fight as individuals. The effect was instantaneous and more Brigante began to fall as they did gaps appeared in the sides and those who could see daylight began to disappear as quickly as they could. Soon there were very few warriors and the legionaries and auxiliaries found themselves facing a wall of women. They stopped. It was a situation they had never faced. Had they won? They knew not and looked at their officers for orders. In that instant the women decided both their own fate and legionary's action; they charged. A screaming mob of angry eyed and ferocious women raced towards the legionaries with death on their faces. The death of the boys and the desertion by their men had enraged them beyond belief. The words of the sorceress still rang in their ears and they knew that this was their time; this was the time of the Mother.

The Legate watched in horror as the first women tore, literally into his men who were standing awaiting orders. The first to react were the centurions who roared, almost simultaneously. "Shield wall!" Immediately the men disengaged, stepped back and formed a wall of wood and steel. It did not halt the women's attack but slowed it down and prevented more casualties for they were just hitting towards the Romans and most blows struck shields or helmets.

The voice of the Legate, cold and chill rang across the field, "Kill them!"

The Ninth knew how to obey orders and they went into action almost mechanically. To them the women were just another enemy they had been told to destroy and they did it with ruthless efficiency. Even though there were hundreds of women they were no match for the Roman killing machine and soon the field was littered with the dead and dying.

The Legate looked around as he heard the hooves of the cavalry racing behind him. "The Queen sir! She is escaping!"

Chapter 17

Julius had been watching the Queen and her guards whilst the attack was developing. He had glanced to the right to check on the fate of the Tungrians and when he turned back the Queen, her bodyguards and her entourage were gone. He yelled to his men, "Follow me!" and raced towards the battle line. After telling the Legate of the problem he scanned the skyline. He could see nothing but the tree line. "Spread out and find the trail. We must catch her before she can do more damage."

The line of troopers each took a twenty pace wide piece of land and walked forward steadily. Some of the troopers kept glancing over their shoulders for, two hundred paces away the women and the remaining warriors were still locked in a deadly, although ultimately doomed, resistance to the Roman war machine. Suddenly a trooper on the right called over. "Here sir!"

The whole line swept into a column of twos behind Julius and the trooper. The trail clearly led west along the edge of the tree line. "She is heading west. You," he pointed at a legionary trooper, "

Report to the Legate and return with all the troopers who are left." The Legate had kept ten legionary cavalrymen to use as messengers. Julius hoped that he would realise that his need outweighed that of the legate. If the Queen escaped this time she could stir up trouble in the relatively quiet west. She could not have had that much of a start and the Prefect unconsciously slowed down. This was a cunning opponent. She had outwitted them before. The men with her were also not the mindless warriors one sometimes met. There could be an ambush. "Watch out for tricks and ambushes; anything out of the ordinary."

He looked at the trees to the right and smiled to himself. He would be the first to discover a trap for his shield was on his left side. An enemy would always attack the unprotected side. It was that thought which made him look to his right where he saw, with some shock a bearded face peering at him from not thirty paces away. Even as he was turning and pulling his sword from his scabbard he yelled, "Ambush!" and raced into the woods. The men of the ala reacted quicker than the legionary cavalry and two of them fell to the ground with arrows sticking from their throats.

Julius' sword point caught the bearded warrior in the middle of his stomach and he over the back of his horse to die a slow and painful death. In the trees it was more difficult to discern enemies. Julius appreciated the skill of his enemy. The attack would tire out the pursuers and give the queen more time to escape. Had he more men he could have left some to deal with the ambush and continue the pursuit. His last hope as he sought his next opponent was that Cassius would have his wits about him and he would find her.

Aodh had left his smaller, more wily warriors in the woods and their orders were clear, ambush and then retreat, draw them deeper into the woods. When Julius found the woods thickening he knew he had to continue his pursuit. "Marcus' Horse! Back to the trail!" He heard with a relieved satisfaction, the sound being repeated in the woods. Even so it was still some time before the remaining members gathered. The extra troopers from the Legate were there and he gathered them together. "I don't think there will be any more ambushes but watch for any deviations from the trail. This queen is cunning and we have to catch her. Rather than chasing after her along this trail we will ride the road and try to get ahead of her. We will ride to Brocauum and meet with the Decurion Cilo." He turned to the two troopers who were wounded. "You two get to the capsarius and then tell the Legate that the Prefect will meet him at Brocauum."

The Legate was impressed with the resilience of the women on the battlefield. He could not know the promises made by Morwenna, promises of everlasting life in the afterlife with the Mother. They fought with a fanaticism which the Legate had rarely seen in men and never in women. When he called upon them to surrender they responded with missiles, curses and bared breasts. Shaking his head he turned to the Tungrian centurion. "We waste no more men. Finish them with javelins." The last few did not wait for the javelins but hurled themselves at the legionaries who had no choice but to kill them.

Titus joined the Legate. "Are all battles like that?"

"As bloody and unpredictable? Yes. The women and the boys? No. I think the Prefect is right about the Queen I hope he can catch her." He looked at the young Tribune, "You did well Titus. Was it all you expected, the battle?"

Titus shook his head, "It all happened so quickly." He paused and looked at the ground, "If it were not for the cavalry…"

"They were doing their job as you did yours."

"But my feet felt frozen to the ground and I couldn't move."

The Legate smiled, "It is called fear and believe me it happens to every soldier. It never goes away, it just becomes less important."

Cassius saw the warband leave the battle and spread out like a stain on the riverside. He could see them from his position on the ridge. There were too many for him to attack but he decided to follow them. They were too far away to identify. His chosen man rode next to him, "Is the Queen with them?"

"I cannot see her." The chosen man, Aulus, looked at him askance. "I know, Aulus, I know we are supposed to follow her but we will pursue these for a while. I cannot let them cause mischief." The warband was moving quickly but the ridge and the horses meant that there was no problem following them. He had a nagging feeling that he should have remained where he was but the soldier in him told him to follow. So it was that the Queen, Aodh and her entourage slipped through the line which Julius had placed around the battlefield.

"Where do we go my Queen? Do we head to Brocauum and Colla?"

"I think we will head that way but we will be wary." Aodh looked at Morwenna wondering what complex and convoluted thoughts were racing through her mind. She smiled at the confused look on his face. "We have heard not a word from Colla since Eboracum and that worries me. He seemed less committed after the battle."

"If we do not go to Brocauum then where?" Aodh had thought that the Carvetii town would have provided winter quarters for the refugees and given them time to build up their forces again.

"I have thought we could head north to Lulach. We would have sanctuary there and perhaps join forces."

"I am not sure that I will be welcome. "

"I am now a queen I think he would overlook your desertion for the Queen of the Brigantes give him more chance of defeating the Romans." She glanced over her shoulder. "Do you think your warriors ambushed our pursuers?"

"They must have slowed them up with their attack for I cannot see them but we must move swiftly. We have the advantage that their mounts were used in the battle and will not be as fresh as ours."

Riding long into the night Morwenna and her men rode to the hills overlooking the Carvetii stronghold. Even the young energetic queen and her acolytes looked tired whilst the warriors were almost falling off their horses with exhaustion. "The town looks safe enough and it would be better sleeping where it is safe."

"We will sleep here in the trees and see what the dawn brings."

The Prefect had arrived at Brocauum before dusk and Decurion Cilo greeted him with a bear hug. "We thought we had been forgotten stuck out here at the edge of nowhere." He looked at the legionary troopers. "I see you have found new ways to gain recruits."

"Let us see to the mounts before Sergeant Cato chastises me and then we can eat." He looked around at the surly looking inhabitants of the stronghold. "From the looks of these people I take it we are not welcome?"

Laughing the Decurion Princeps said, "No I think our remaining here like a garrison has stopped them from being as anti-Roman as they might like." He lowered his voice. "I think many of them still harbour thoughts of rebellion."

"Is there an alehouse here?"

"There is an old woman sells some horse's piss she passes as beer. Some of the troopers say it is water she has passed."

"Do any of the locals go there?"

"A few."

"Good then we will go there when the horses are stabled."

Cato took the reins from the Prefect's hands. "I will take him and that way I know he will be looked after."

"Sergeant, you are like the wife I never had."

Once in the dim hut with the two beakers of weak beer Julius looked around and saw a handful of the village elders scowling over their beer at him. "We have defeated Morwenna Salvius. She brought an army down to Morbium and the Legate brought the Ninth up and she was defeated. We are here chasing the refugees who will be crucified."

"Our losses?"

"Not as many as in the Caledonii wars but then we had fewer to lose. Has Cassius arrived?"

"No. Should I have been expecting him?"

Julius smiled when some of the elders finished their beer and left."I had him patrolling to the east of you. He may have followed the queen. I hope he did for I lost her in the woods." He nodded to the elders and then dropped his voice. "I thought that the best way to persuade them that rebellion was no longer an option was to tell them what actually happened. I believe our friends will be spreading the word even now."

Livius spoke for the first time. "Tell me that we no longer need to remain here sir! I am bored beyond belief."

"We will be leaving tomorrow to find the queen for I am sure she will still cause problems for us. I will leave the cavalry troopers here to guard the settlement until the Legate can follow."

"When Cassius arrives we will have the whole of the ala together again."

"True Salvius but it is a shadow of its former self. When this campaign is done it will take a whole winter to train the Decurions and troopers for the spring wards against the Caledonii."

"Will they come again then sir?"

"Yes Livius. Until we put something up to stop them they will flood the land like locusts. They had too much success last year not to return. Why raise cattle yourselves when you can steal them from the Brigante? Why till the fields yourself when you can capture slaves to do it for you? No they will return and I want more than two hundred troopers to stop them."

They drank the dismal beer in silence until Decurion Princeps Cilo asked, "Decurion Macro? What of him?"

Thoughtfully Julius rubbed the side of his head. "A good question Salvius and one, I assume, that the men have been asking?"

"Well they have discussed it sir as men would."

"I know and I am not criticising you for that Salvius. What would you do were you Prefect? And don't give me the answer 'I wouldn't have locked him up in the first place'."

"All of us can understand his desertion. We might not agree with it but we can understand it. Macro is probably the finest warrior any of us have ever seen. He is certainly the best trainer we have ever had but most importantly, sir, he is the heart of the ala. He is the beat which drives the men on. You have said yourself on many occasions he is worth an extra turma on the battlefield."

"You have said much about his attributes I asked what would you do?

"Punish him and then reinstate him."

"As simple as that."
"As simple as that sir."
Finishing his beer he said, "I thank you for your advice which I will consider for, in truth, I have not yet decided what I am going to do. When I see him before me then I will know for I want to look into his heart and see what he wants me to do."

The next morning as the settlement woke up Morwenna and Aodh were already peering through the trees. As the gates swung open they saw the red crests of the Roman cavalry. "It seems that Colla, perhaps could not come to your aid."
"That has decided me. We head for the land of your birth. We head for Caledonia."
The sun had barely broken the eastern sky as the band headed north west towards the lumpy rise which formed the northern hills. Aodh was less than happy with their route for, although hidden for a while they would easily be seen on the treeless hillsides. The three survivors of the ambush had told them that they were still being pursued and Aodh knew how tenacious the cavalry could be. His only hope was that he could put many miles between them and get to his homeland before they caught him.

"Which way then sir?"
"Let us assume she would not use the road for fear of observation. She has two other options, the high hills to the north or the valleys to the south. The valleys take her to the land of the lakes and the high hills take her to Caledonia. You take your turma and head north, try to find her trail. They have over fifty warriors so they should be obvious. I will head south with Livius. Send messengers back to the settlement if you see anything and when we have discovered her direction we can join forces. And keep your eyes open for Cassius. The Allfather knows where he has got to."
Cassius was but three miles away still watching the elusive Ownie. He had been loath to send a message back to Morbium for

he felt he had not done what the Prefect would have expected of him and, as the newest Decurion he was eager to please. Ownie had left his camp early and was making his way with his weary warriors along the valley to the south of Brocauum. If Cassius had had more men he would have attacked but, as it was, he could only watch and try to pick off the odd straggler. So far they were not obliging and kept a tight little group.

The valley was a difficult one in which to maintain contact for there were dips and hollows and sudden copses which could hide ambushers or sentries. It also meant he had to keep a distance and follow the trail.

Ownie turned to the bearded warrior next to him as they lay in the small wood drinking from the bubbling mountain stream. "Are our friends still with us?"

"Yes . They are half a mile back."

"I think I have been followed long enough."

The bearded warrior's face broke into a grin. "Do we attack them?"

"No an ambush would be difficult and pointless. They would run away for we are too many. No we will walk down this stream and then head for Brocauum. Colla should be there and if not we still have many friends there. We will attack them when they follow us there."

"Will they be able to follow us if we are going down the stream?"

"They have managed so far. Let us assume they will do so again. I just want to get a distance away from them so that we can prepare inside the stronghold for when they attack."

Ownie was very familiar with this part of the land and he had his warriors moved easily through the craggy valley sides. As they moved over a small ridge into another valley they suddenly heard the neigh of a horse. Immediately they all froze. The scrubby elder bushes and hawthorn hid them from both sides but it also prevented their view of whoever was there. Ownie and his lieutenants whispered, “They cannot have got around us.”

“It may be a second patrol.”

Ownie made the decision. “We wait here but prepare your weapons.”

On the ridge Julius and Livius were viewing the valley. “We have seen no hoof marks this way sir. “

“I know Livius. I suspect she may have headed north.”

“Is that a bad thing? I mean won’t she be out of the way there and harmless?”

Julius flashed a harsh stare at the young Decurion. “Have you forgotten what she did last time? And this time she has caused even more problems. A third time might be the time she wins. No we need to rid ourselves of her. Besides Lulach is difficult enough on his own; with Morwenna by his side he might be unbeatable. We must stop them joining forces.”

“Sir!” One of the troopers pointed down the slope.

“What is it?”

“Over there on the top of the next ridge I am sure I saw a horse.”

“Stand to!” Immediately all the troopers drew their weapons and peered at the skyline. The worst thing they could do was to move for it would attract attention but it was infuriating to have to wait for the horses to appear again. The tension was palpable and every eye was fixed on the ridge. Livius’ horse snorted and was answered by a neigh from the ridge. Slowly a horse appeared from behind a tree.

“It’s Lucius sir. I recognise the horse.”

The lost turma emerged on to the ridge and Julius waved. He was relieved when Cassius waved back. “Well that answers one question. The Queen is not over there but it begs the question what is Cassius doing there? We will find out in a moment when he arrives.”

What none of the Romans could know was that Ownie and his men were crouched in the shallow valley half a mile below Julius and Cassius' route would take him straight through them. Livius touched Julius' arm. "What is he doing sir? He keeps looking at the ground, they all do."

"He's tracking."

"But there are no tracks up here."

"If he heads down the valley we will follow him. Perhaps the Queen went that way."

They both realised that Cassius and his turma, spread out in a wide line were heading directly for Julius and Livius. When they were less than thirty paces from the hidden warriors Ownie could wait no longer. A flurry of missiles was hurled at Cassius and his men hitting the Decurion and his leading scout and then, like flushing pheasant from the gorse, the whole warband erupted out of the elder copse. There was joint shock when they saw the two turmae on the ridge and Julius had not expected a warband. Both sides reacted quickly. The Brigante tried to escape down the valley while the three turmae converged on them. It became a series of individual battles as auxiliaries tried to slash down on the retreating warriors and warriors tried to maim and kill the horses and riders.

Ownie lay on the ground pretending to be dead. When he thought they had all passed him he stood and ran back up the slope from whence Julius and Livius had come. Most of the turmae were focussed on the men before them but Cassius had picked himself up and removed the arrow from his leg and in doing so saw the lone warrior running the other way. He sprang on his horse and picked his javelin from its sheath. Ownie was a powerful runner and making good time up the ridge. Cassius' horse laboured up the steep slope its wounded foreleg slowing it up but inevitably the Decurion caught up. Cassius realised, at the last minute, that he was being pursued and, as he turned around, Cassius thrust the javelin's razor sharp head into Ownie's throat. The look of surprise was forever etched upon his face.

By the time Cassius and the dead Ownie rejoined the turmae the warband were either dead or tied up. “Well Cassius I see that you were not pursuing the Queen then?”

“No sir sorry sir. Saw this lot leave and followed them.”

“Don’t worry you did the right thing. I managed to lose the Queen. Seems I am losing my touch. We’ll take this lot back to Brocauum and find the Decurion Princeps. Hopefully he will have had more luck with the Queen’s trail than we.”

When they arrived at the settlement there was a messenger from Cilo. “Sir , we found the trail heading north by west. “

“Good. Trooper. Shackle these with the other prisoners. When the Legate arrives, I would imagine that it would be some time later today, inform him where we have gone. I suspect it is towards Caledonia but now that I have what remains of the ala I will try to prevent that and drive her south.”

Less than fifty miles away Gaelwyn was climbing up the steep narrow pass carrying Young Decius. They had started calling Macro’s son Young Decius when Ailis tired of saying Decius come here and two of them arrived. The children had tired quite quickly on the long climb up the pass into the land of the lakes. The pass itself was foreboding with high crags and cliffs lining a very narrow pass. He turned and looked down the twisting trail and decided to wait for the others to struggle up. The path had widened a little and there was a flat rock on which Gaelwyn and Young Decius could sit.

“Are we there yet?”

Growling Gaelwyn said, “You have asked that every thirty paces. We are there when we are there.”

Young Decius looked around him. “When will that be?”

“Ask Ailis!”

Ailis sat down as soon as she reached the rock. Of the four adults she was finding the trek the hardest. She was not used to the hardships of the campaign trail as were the other three and while they soon got back into the routine to Ailis it was an alien experience. In addition she was worrying constantly about the three boys. Every sniffle and cough became magnified out here in the wild, away from her remedies and comforts. She longed for her own kitchen but realised, ruefully, that she no long had a kitchen and when they finally returned home they would have to rebuild that home.

Gaius looked at his wife with the concerned and trouble look of a husband who feels he has failed his wife. His dreams were nightmares and were the same every night; getting to his burnt home and finding his family slaughtered. He vowed each morning that they would never be left alone again.

"This would make a good site for a fort Gaius."

"Ever the Tribune eh Marcus? But you are right. The trail we are using must be used by the Irish when they raid."

"Poor Macro had a dream of serving the Irish. I wonder how that would have turned out?"

"He would have been a great success. The tribes value the qualities which Macro has, had. The Parcae had other ideas."

Ailis massaged her feet which were heavily blistered and bleeding. "How far Gaelwyn?"

Snorting in derision the scout pointed east. "You are worse than the children! I do not know in miles but it will take us almost a day to get to Glanibanta if we do not have these debates every few miles."

Marcus could see Gaius becoming angry and he put his hand on his arm. "Gaelwyn they are tired. They do not complain. Remember they are neither warriors nor soldiers as we are."

Gaelwyn's anger subsided quickly. "I am sorry niece. You and the boys have done well ignore an old man's temper."

Ailis stood and kissed him on the cheek. "Uncle, lose your temper as often as you like for I know we would still be prisoners in Caledonia but for you. Right boys shall we walk for a while and show these old men what fine soldiers we can be?"

The rested boys were eager to show off and stood proudly in a line. When they were all together Decius lead them up the path which sloped less severely and Ailis followed, a maternal smile creasing her face. “There you are Gaelwyn. That is how a mother deals with moans, she makes a game of it.”

Chapter 18

The Prefect soon caught up with the Decurion Princeps. “It feels good to have the whole ala together again. We may be few in number but at least we are a force now, not just a patrol. Which way Salvius?”

“They have taken the valley to the south of the road. They must be worried about our patrols.”

“Well let us use that to our advantage. If she is heading towards Caledonia we can use the road to get ahead of her and block her route.”

Livius spoke up. “Why do you not want her to go to Caledonia? At least there she is out of our way.”

“True Livius but when her mother went to the north she caused us many problems and remember Morwenna also created problems for us.”

“Yes sir, but, with respect, that was when she was a spy and Macro’s woman.”

“True but something in my water tells me that an alliance of the Brigante Queen and the heir to the Caledonii would be a bad thing. Besides which she would be harder to find in the north. At least here we know that her army is gone and she will have to build a new one. No we keep on her trail like a dog chasing a fox. It will twist turn and hide, but while it is being chased it cannot do ill.”

“Should I send out scouts then sir?”

“Yes Salvius. Ahead of us and to the north and south. I would like to flush her out. I take it you commandeered enough supplies from our hosts before you left.”

Grinning Cilo said, “Oh yes indeed. They were in a real dilemma for they wanted rid of us but begrudged us the food.”

“Does the option in charge of the legionary cavalry know who the suspected rebels are?”

"Oh yes sir. We spent some time yesterday walking around the settlement identifying them. When the Legate arrives they will be in for a shock for they believe we did not recognise them."

Morwenna was happier now that they had passed Brocauum for the only other fort they had to avoid was Luguvalium and it was easy to ride around that one. As it only had infantry they would soon be beyond the Roman reach. "Seven days and we should be back in my homeland."

"Do not sound so despondent Aodh. It is a good thing that we return. You will be bringing Lulach a great prize for the Queen of the Brigante gives him a lever with which to pry the Romans loose."

"It is still many miles to safety and there is still that cavalry turma pursuing us."

"There are not many of them. We only saw fifty."

"Yes my queen but fifty of those troopers have damaged our attacks before."

"Which is why we do not use their road. They do not know where we are going. Our only danger is when we cross the road to head north and I plan on using the night as our ally."

Aodh summoned the two Brigante scouts who lived locally and sent them towards the road. "Keep out of sight. We just need to know if they are on the road. Return as soon as you can confirm that the road is clear." Morwenna looked at him, a question written across her face. "If the road is clear we get across when we can. We have but twenty horses and we need to get north sooner rather later."

"You are the warrior. I bow to your knowledge." Aodh could not tell if she was being sarcastic or not. There were too many things about women which confused him. What made it worse was the permanently knowing, smug looks on the faces of the acolytes. He shook his head, men were so much easier to understand. What they said they meant. He glanced around to check that they were keeping the trail they left as narrow as possible. Although that increased the length of the small column it made it more difficult for those following. Apart from the three women all the remaining horses were being led, partly to save their strength and partly to avoid observation. He had been tempted to suggest walking to the three witches but thought better of it.

The two scouts came quickly scurrying back. "On the road there are many Romans and three of them are heading this way."

"Quickly down into this valley and away from the road. Romans!"

Even Morwenna obeyed and they spread quickly in a line down the gentle slope. With horror Aodh saw that the trail they had left, with so many foot and hoof prints could have been followed by a half blind old woman. They would have to fight the Romans and soon. He turned to his lieutenant. "Look for somewhere to lay an ambush or we will all be killed."

On the road there was an equal amount of consternation. "Sir the scouts to the south have found a trail it looks like they have headed south."

"Any idea how long ago?"

"Not long for the droppings from their horses and ponies were still warm."

"They must have seen us then sir."

"Yes Livius which means they could keep going south or double back north. Cassius. Pick up the other scouts and keep along the road to Luguvalium. Tell the Prefect, assuming there is still a garrison there, about the battle and Morwenna then come back down the road. If she doubles back she will not expect to meet you."

"And if I don't find her sir?"

"Then follow the trail. If she doesn't double back then there is only one place left for her to go, the land of the lakes and we know that the valleys there all run north to south. If they try to cross a ridge we will see them. Right Salvius let us see if we can end this now."

Aodh was picturing, in his head, the land into which they were descending. He had known it well when he and Morwenna had wintered there. There was one steep sided and barren valley with a long narrow lake and a high mountain. To the west, heading back towards Brocauum there was a much wider valley and a narrow pass and further west there was a narrow pass leading to the valley of the two lakes. He was tempted to go towards the two lakes for that was where the secret cave of Morwenna was located. The supplies which it contained meant they could hide there for a while. It all depended upon Morwenna. He rode his horse until he was alongside her. "I think Caledonia is not an option. The scouts say it was well over a hundred troopers. They have reinforcements."

She looked at him, her ice green eyes boring into him. "Your plan. Tell me."

He started! 'How did she know what he was thinking?' "I am thinking of the cave near to the land of the two lakes. Winter is coming and we could spend the winter there and travel to Caledonia when the snows melt. We can also ambush them for there are two places where they can be halted easily although it will cost us warriors."

She coldly dismissed the loss with a wave of her elegant hand. "That does not matter. Our survival does for only with our survival will the Brigante be free. We will go to the cave. As we can travel faster than those on foot we will leave the unmounted men to make mischief."

Aodh was a warrior and the thought of dismissing the lives of so many men without a thought terrified him but, in his heart he knew she was right. "You ride my love and I will follow." He gestured to the mounted men. "Follow the queen and protect her." He waved over Pol the Brigante chief. "We will take the queen to a place of safety nearby." While he hated lying to the warriors for the place was many miles hence, he needed them to buy them some time. "Ahead is a wood, lay some traps there to slow them up and then ambush the remainder at the col at the northern end of the valley of the two lakes. We will meet you at the old Roman fort of Glanibanta." Having decided to lie, Aodh gave enough information to his men so that, in the unlikely event that they survived he would be able to use them again. "Do not waste your lives but they must be slowed up."

The squat warrior nodded. "The horsemen will be stopped. Protect our queen Caledoni."

Grasping his arm he said truthfully, "I will give my life to protect her." As he galloped off he looked over his shoulder and saw them trotting quickly after him to the woods. Aodh made sure that his horse followed the trail left by the others knowing that Pol would use that bait to trap their pursuers. He soon caught up with the Queen and he quickly led them the four miles to the col. As soon as he arrived he knew he had made the right decision. On the northern side the cliffs rose vertically and could only be traversed by goats. The southern side fell away to a fast flowing stream with banks of pine growing thickly. No horse could use that route. The only way forwards was the ten paces wide path chiselled out of the slate. Here a few men could hold off a mighty force. He detached eight of the riders. "Prepare an ambush here and wait for Pol. When you have slowed the enemy down enough follow the valley and we will meet you at Glanibanta" Morwenna gave a quick smile; her lover was becoming devious. She had never heard him lie to a brother before. Leaving the eight the remaining nine warriors trotted off down the valley of the two lakes watching the thin light darken behind the steep mountain sides which enclosed them.

Gaius knew they could not go much further. The huge lake spread out below them to their right. The old fort was but two miles away and yet, looking at Ailis and the children that would be at least a mile too far. "We'll have to camp Marcus."

Gaelwyn looked up at the sky. "We'd be better off pushing on. The sky is full of snow and this hillside is a little exposed."
"Gaelwyn is right you know Gaius."
"It will do us no good if they collapse."
"I can carry on Gaius. Women are tougher than they look."
"There must be somewhere lower down."
Marcus suddenly slapped his head. "What a fool I am! Of course there is. The watch tower near to the lake."
"You are right and it is less than a mile from here. There is water nearby and we should be able to hunt some food." They quickly made their way down and crossed the swiftly flowing stream at the ford pausing only to fill their water skins from the icy, brown tinged water. They could see the tower rising in the distance. It had lost some of its wooden boards but it was above ground and would give them security. It was growing dark as they crossed the open space to the rickety ladder.
"I will see to the food. You two had better repair the ladder and the tower. Ailis, get the boys to collect some sticks and wood for a fire." Gaelwyn took his bow and slipped off up the trail to the woods which drifted south towards the fort at Glanibanta. When Ailis and the boys had found enough wood and returned to the tower the first flurry of winter snowflakes whipped around their heads; not yet settling but promising a white morning.
"That will have to do for tonight. It is getting too dark and too cold to mess around any more. Let's get a fire going and hope that old man has actually caught something."
"Even if it is a hare it will fill a small hole."
With the three boys huddled for warmth around Ailis the two men used flint and the dried autumn pine cones they had found to get a cheery blaze going. Soon the boys' faces were glowing in the warmth. They saw movement from the woods and the two men immediately reached for their weapons.
Decius keen young eyes picked him out quickly. "It is uncle Gaelwyn and he is wearing a fur."

The closer he came the more they realised that the boy was right. Gaelwyn had shot a badger and he had the old brock around his neck. He nodded approvingly. "The Allfather smiles on us tonight. He gives us dried wood and an old badger keen to get the last food before the snow. We eat well and the boys will be warm." He immediately set to skinning the animal.

"Will the fire not be seen?"

Gaelwyn shrugged. "It will be seen if anyone is foolish enough to be out on a night like this but remember Gaius there are few people in this part of the land." He threw the fur to Ailis who began scraping it ready to use. "Your sword Gaius." Taking the sword of Cartimandua, which was the sharpest one they had, the old scout chopped the mighty beast into manageable chunks and he threaded a thin branch through one. Soon the smell of roasting meat permeated the air and set everyone's juices salivating. He kept turning the juicy haunch until he decided it was ready to eat. Cutting thick slabs of the pink meat they all ate their first hot meal since leaving Stanwyck all those long weeks before. While they were still eating Gaelwyn walked over to a pine tree and cut off pieces of bark which he wrapped around the rest of the meat. Using water from the water skins he soaked the bark and then threw the remaining pieces of meat around the outside of the fire which was now burning steadily and not quite as fiercely. "Well Ailis if you take the bairns to the tower we will decide who watches first."

"I thought you said no one in his right mind would be out on a night like this?"

"True which means that anyone who is out tonight is not in his right mind. I think we should watch for someone like that eh Gaius?"

The ala had no difficulty following the wide trail left by the refugees even though the light was fading quickly. As they dropped down from the ridge they scanned the horizon for movement but could see none. “I think they must be in that heavily wooded area ahead.”

“I agree Salvius. You take your turma to the right and Livius take yours to the left. I will keep on the trail; just in case they split up once they are in the woods.”

Pol had been a hunter and knew all about deadfall traps and pit traps. He had stayed long enough to build a circle of them around the edge of the wood. His aim had been to slow the Romans up not to spend so long building them that he would be caught. Even as they were entering the wood he and the rest were running the four miles to the col. The snow began to flutter down, not heavy enough to lie but heavy enough to mask movements.

“The Allfather watches over us tonight. Perhaps we will not need to fight them at the col.” Pol had a healthy respect for these Roman cavalrymen and, while he would give his life for his queen, he was enough of a pragmatist to prefer to live for his queen and fight again.

Unfortunately for the Brigante, Julius had suspected traps and, once they found the first few, which only caused a couple of minor injuries, he brought in the flanking scouts and followed the trail which, because of the snow was easy to follow. “Are we stopping for the night? This could be dangerous. They could be leading us into an ambush>”

“Possibly Salvius but they are trying to delay us and I wonder why. Are they trying to head north again?”

“Not in this valley. They would have to pass us. But at the other end they can double back up either of the other valleys.”

“Or Salvius, head to the coast. This snow is inopportune for it will hide their tracks if it lies. We will push on a while longer.”

Fortunately for the Romans the snow did not begin to fall heavily and they were able to see the muddy line through the whitening snow as it wound and twisted through the thinning trees inexorably towards the land they knew so well. “Where you think they are heading sir? I can see by our speed that you anticipate their route I can discern nothing. Is this another lesson I must take from Macro when he returns to duty?"

"No Livius. This is not obvious but this valley leads to the land of two lakes and the fort, if it is still there, of Glanibanta. We caught Modius not far to the east and, many years ago hunted Aed and his warriors in this very land. They are heading for Glanibanta of that much I am now sure but after that is anyone's guess for she is a cunning opponent."

"If we know where we are going can we not travel faster?"

"We could but there are dangerous warriors ahead and, in the dark, they have the advantage. I fancy they will either try to ambush us at the col or where the second lake narrows the path. We still have a little way to go."

When Pol arrived at the ambush site the eight warriors left by Aodh greeted him. "Have you lost the Romans?"

"No curse them. They have stuck to us like a hunting hound on the trail of a wolf. They will be here soon, we should prepare. Take the horses down the trail and tether them to a tree for they will give warning and the Romans may believe we are further away than we are." He looked at the rocks at the side of the trail. "Build two walls, one behind the other across the trail."

"Why two?"

"They have horses and they could jump one. It is a pity we do not have their caltrops for that would slow them up mightily. You men with the bows split yourselves on two sides of the trail behind the wall. The rest of us will wait behind the first wall. Now let us work brothers. The higher the wall the better chance that we will survive this night's battle." He stopped and spoke quietly. "When we are but eight we run to the horses and ride to Aodh at Glanibanta."

One of the warriors said, half under his breath, "If there are eight of us."

While another added, "Aye and if Aodh has waited for us."

"Sir this is madness we can see nothing."

Livius was right the blizzard was whipping the snow into their faces and was now beginning to lie on the ground. Julius shielded his eyes with his hand and peered into the darkness. "I think the col is ahead. Either they wait there and we fight or they wait further on and we can rest in the less of the walls which run along the trail."

Decurion Princeps Cilo smiled as he heard Livius murmur, "Thank the Allfather." The boy was keen but even he was weary as the wild winds whipped the snow into arrows to pierce their skin and clothes. Suddenly he heard a whinny up the trail and he held up his hand. The others had heard it and they all drew out their javelins ready for the ambush they knew lay ahead. He slipped off his horse and gestured for the next two troopers to join him. Leaving his horse with the horse holder the three of them slipped to the side of the trail where an icy stream struggled through a small gorge. The three of them began to make their way up the stream.

Julius saw what the Decurion Princeps was doing and he led the rest of the troopers forward. Each man now knew that the first they knew of the ambush would be when it was launched and the first man died. The Prefect unstrapped his shield and held it so that it covered his body and his face apart from his eyes. The troopers all copied their leader. Livius had never felt such tension; it was like walking into a room blindfolded and knowing that someone was going to jump out on you except that this was a deadlier version of that childhood game. Their only advantage was that they were as difficult to see as the ambushers. Julius took it as slowly as he dared to enable Salvius to outflank them.

The first arrows thudded into shields; one unlucky trooper had his horse's neck pierced by a fortuitous shot. Realising that the time for caution was over he urged his mount forward to cover the ground to the ambush quickly. With a shock he came up against the wall and suddenly spears were stabbing at him. The trooper next to him thrust his javelin blindly at the spear heads and had the satisfaction of hearing a scream. Julius did the same but although he heard a grunt the spears still continued. More troopers arrived but four was the maximum which could use their weapons. One of the troopers fell as an axe sliced into his horse's neck. Over his shoulder he shouted, "Throw your javelins behind the wall!"

The effect was immediate; lacking helmets and armour the javelins, if they connected caused a wound and enough of them struck to lessen their resistance. Suddenly there was a cry of alarm from the Brigante ambush's right as Decurion Cilo and his two companions surprised the archers on the right. Julius drew his legs up so that he was standing on his horse's back and stepped on to the wall. He threw his javelin into the bearded white face closest to him and then leapt down, his sword slicing as he jumped. Livius and the other troopers copied their leader and, with the flank attack, the ambushers fled. When Cassius joined them they were busy killing the survivors. "Get these walls down!"

"Well done Salvius!"

"I tell you what sir, that water is as cold as a witch's tit!"

Shaking his head Julius said, "Bearing in mind who we are pursuing you might have chosen a better comparison."

"Sorry sir, it was just an accurate one and for the record I can no longer feel my feet."

By the time they had demolished the wall the ambushers had gone but they had left most of their companions lying dead behind the remains of the barricade. "We will camp here tonight and carryon the pursuit in the morning. I just hope that the snow doesn't totally destroy their trail."

Far ahead Aodh halted the small column. The snow was helping them and the remaining nine warriors were now even more impressed with the sorceress who could conjure snow to hide their trail. "It is not far to Glanibanta now. We will be there soon."

"Look there!" The warrior furthest ahead, scouting, pointed up the narrow valley. There they could see a fire and its light was reflecting on a roman sentry tower.

"That has spoiled our plans my queen."

"It is but a fire."

"A fire near a Roman tower which guards the valley to the fort. It means there will be some Romans there."

"Can we not just slip by them?"

"It is not worth taking the chance. If they are alert they will see us and challenge us and even if they are not it means that Glanibanta is probably occupied and we would be trapped between the fort, these Romans and those who are following us."

"We cannot stay here."

He rode next to her and spoke so quietly that no-one, not even Maban and Anchorat could hear him. "No we will have to go to your cave."

Reluctantly Morwenna had to agree. As much as she wished to keep it a secret, even the sorceress was suffering in the cold. Aodh pointed at three of the warriors. "You three go to Glanibanta, follow the river and they should not see but if they do then retreat back to Pol and his men. Spy out the fort and await Pol. In the morning I will send for you and bring you to the place we are hiding if the fort is occupied."

As the three men made their way cautiously down the icy, fast flowing stream, Aodh led the ever smaller party west across the stream to the hidden cave on the other side of the valley.

Pol came down the snowy valley with the last six warriors. They had one spare horse and he was keen to get to Glanibanta. By the time he had seen the fire he was already level with it for it had died down somewhat. Instead of halting he just moved quickly on. As the horses stepped into the ice cold water one of them whinnied and its rider hit it savagely on the side of the head.

"What is that?"

"I heard nothing Gaelwyn and I am on guard not you."

“I know Gaius but I am sure I heard a horse.”

“Well I cannot see anything so either watch instead of me or go back to sleep.”

“Fine guard you are. I cannot sleep knowing that there may be enemies out there. You sleep and I will watch.”

“They could be Roman horses.”

“When have you known Romans ride at night?”

For the rest of the night Gaelwyn peered into the blizzard which raged along the valley. He watched as the snow grew higher uncia by uncia. Once the first rays of daylight hesitantly peered over the ridge he could see that the snow was unspoilt. It was still virgin snow. He went to the fire and blew it into life. Removing the badger meat he went to the stream to relieve himself. When he looked into the water he saw that he had been right for there, still steaming in the snow was a small pile of horse droppings and in one of them was a hoof print, a print of a horse shoe. It had not been a wild horse it was shod. There were enemies about.

Chapter 19

Julius had the ala on the trail as soon as it was light enough to see. The snow covered the trail but it was obvious which way their enemies had gone. When they came to the neck of land between the two lakes he stopped. "They could have gone that way Salvius. If they were heading for the sea and a ship to Mona or Ireland they would go there. Well I have cast the dice and said Glanibanta, Glanibanta it must be."

Cilo gestured up the trail. "That was where you said the next ambush might be."

"Yes we travel cautiously from now on. Fortunately we are not flailing about in the dark."

One of the troopers muttered, "No just flailing around in snow cold enough to freeze your bollocks off."

Salvius shouted, "You won't need them out here anyway."

As the ala laughed Julius nodded his satisfaction. If they could joke in their adversity then they were getting over Macro's desertion and when he returned they would be twice the ala they had been before. They could see quite a way ahead and Livius, who had the youngest eyes shouted, "Smoke sir. I can see smoke."

"Well done Livius. This may be our chance Salvius. They may have thought they lost us and are camped up ahead. Let's throw caution to the wind and get there as quickly as possible."

The snow was deeper than the previous night but the horses made good time as they pounded through the freshly fallen flakes. The closer they got to the smoke the more familiar it became to Salvius and Julius. It was close to the tower. Did that mean there were Romans there or had they caught the Brigante taking advantage of the shelter? Julius was not taking chances and he drew his sword. "Column of four!"

In an almost seamless move the ala went into a column of four troopers behind the Prefect. If the enemy were occupying the tower then he wanted to be able to deploy into line as quickly as possible. They galloped up the low rise towards the tower and, seeing no Roman insignia Julius raised his sword and prepared to to give the order to charge. Suddenly, and to his everlasting surprise, Gaius and Ailis stepped out from behind the tower. "Julius what are you doing here?"

Gaelwyn appeared, spear in hand from the top of the tower and the three boys peered over the top their faces a mixture of shock and sheer joy at seeing the familiar figures of Marcus' Horse before them. Julius was the first to react. He sprang from his horse and embraced Ailis. Clasping Gaius forearm he said in a voice choked with emotion. "It is good to see you. We will talk." Turning to the ala he shouted. "Livius, Cassius send out scouts and rest the remainder of the men."

Salvius had also dismounted and embraced both Ailis and Gaius. Livius, watching from the back of his horse felt excluded from this family which had such a close bond between them. The three boys ran up to Julius and threw their arms around him while Gaelwyn watched on. "Marcus!"

Julius asked, "He is here too?"

"Aye. He went to check for hoof prints."

"Hoof prints?"

"Yes. Gaelwyn heard horses in the night. It was not yours I take it?" Julius shook his head. "I thought not. We found signs by the river and Marcus wanted to check the path that runs along the hillside in case whoever it was had used that trail as well."

"It is Morwenna. We were pursuing her."

"Let us eat while we talk. I know the bairns are hungry and I have yet to see a soldier who would refuse food." Ailis threw more wood on to the fire and then unwrapped some of the badger meat. Salvius looked over his shoulder at the dismounted troopers who were watching the reunion. "Don't worry Salvius we have enough for your men. Enough to take the edge off their appetite anyway."

"Livius."

The young Decurion came over and bowed to Ailis. “It is good to see you Ailis. I am pleased that you were rescued.” Ailis kissed him on the cheek and then handed him one of the larger haunches of badger. “Thank you for the meat the men will be happy.” He walked back to the troopers the still warm meat giving off steaming the early morning chill.

A sudden movement from the woods made everyone go for their weapons until they saw that it was Marcus who began to run when he saw the troopers. He grabbed Julius in a bear hug. “You cannot know how glad we are to see you.”

As Marcus clasped arms with Salvius Gaius said, “The horses this morning. It was Morwenna!”

“Eat then talk!” Ailis was happier than any that the ala had arrived for she now knew they were safe but she wanted to avoid anyone mentioning Macro’s death for by not talking about it they could believe that he was still alive. She knew that once they talked of their escape and Macro’s death their world would be changed forever.

Marcus chewed on a slice of badger meat. “So Morwenna is back.”

Julius said, “More than back. She has claimed to be the Queen of the Brigante and raised the Brigante in rebellion.”

Gaelwyn paused mid-chew. “The Brigante! Who was stupid enough to lead that fool’s revolt?”

The names we had were Parthalan, he died near Lindum, Ownie and Coll. We are still looking for those two.

“Colla,” Gaelwyn spat into the fire, making it sizzle, “he was always a pompous jumped up self-important little toad.”

“You didn’t like him then?” joked Salvius.

“I just can’t believe that anyone would follow him.”

“They didn’t. Morwenna used her mother’s tricks and had the support of the women.”

There were a few moments when they all contemplated the fire and remembered Fainch and her evil and ruing the return of her daughter. “And I didn’t help by chasing over these hills after Modius.”

“Yes Macro told us about that.”

Suddenly Salvius and Julius stopped mid chew and looked at each other. Ailis threw Gaius a look which spoke volumes. Gaelwyn shook his head. “We couldn’t not talk about it could we.” He took a deep breath. “Macro met us in Caledonia and helped us to rescue Ailis and the boys from Lulach and his men.”

“But where is he?” Even as he spoke Julius knew the answer.

“He died saving us.” Ailis put her arms around Young Decius who had been hanging on every word. His eyes were large with tears.

“He took many warriors with him and he had a brave death. He had a warrior’s death.”

“I can’t believe that there was anyone who could defeat the big man.”

“If your enemies stand off and fill you full of arrows there is nought any warrior, even a great one like Macro can do.”

Salvus looked over at the troopers. “The men will take it hard.”

“We will not tell them until we are back in Morbium. We have to finish this. Gaelwyn the tracks you found, they headed to Glanibanta?”

“Aye.”

“And Marcus, were there any tracks on the path.”

“No Prefect. And yes you are correct. The only place they could have gone last night is Glanibanta. There would be shelter there.”

Gaius threw his gnawed bone into the fire. “What do you think her plans are?”

“I believe she was trying to get to Caledonia. She has a Caledonii warrior by her side. She served Lulach before and she will do so again for it serves both their purposes. We prevented that and drove her down here. I think the snow, while it aided her may have changed her plans. She could go back to Mona.”

“And you would follow her there?”

"I would follow her beyond the seas to the ends of the world if needs be. But first I will take most of the men to Glanibanta and see if she remains there. Hopefully this chase ends today and we can return with you to Brocauum and the Legate. Cassius."

The Decurion had been standing with Livius about thirty paces away and was there almost instantly. "Yes Prefect?"

"Detail ten troopers to stay here and guard the Tribune and prepare to move out later today."

"We don't need that Julius."

"Marcus I do not intend to lose you again. This is as close to a family as I have outside of Rome and each one of you, even the old man, is dear to me. Livius mount. We ride and end this today."

On the ridge to the east Aodh and his scout watched as they saw the cavalry mount and ride to Glanibanta. "I fear we will not be meeting Pol today."

"No Tadgh, and it also poses a problem for us. We will return to the cave and the Queen for we have much to discuss." Aodh took the two men back over the rocks which were bare of snow. It was even more important for them to hide their presence from the hunters. They walked up the stream which led from their cave and waved the signal to the hidden sentry.

"We are all that remains of your army." Aodh made the bald, cold statement for he wanted the young Queen to be under no illusions about their predicament."

"Could we still get to Caledonia?" There was still calmness about her and Aodh noticed that when she spoke the acolytes, Maban and Anchorat, closed their eyes as though they were communicating with their mentor.

"It would be difficult. The snow is not yet deep here but the road is a long one to Caledonia. A boat might be found but we would need to travel to somewhere where they have boats capable of such a voyage and they, I fear, would be Roman."

"As ever Aodh I know that you have already come up with a solution have you not?"

Tadgh and the other warriors looked in amazement at the Queen who seemed to be able to read minds. Aodh merely smiled, he had seen this trick many times before. "I suggest we stay here. The cave is warm and we have supplies. There is water and wood nearby and, once the Romans have gone, when they can no longer find us we will be able to hunt. In the spring, when they think we are dead we will travel north and meet with Lulach."

"That is the wisest suggestion and I concur with one amendment. When the Romans have gone I want you to go to Lulach and inform him of our deeds and our plans. I would send Tadgh or one of the others but Lulach will know that you come from me as my emissary. When you go I will give you my raven to protect you and to ensure that he believes you."

"I would prefer to stay here my love."

"I know but this is more important. You trust these warriors?"

"Of course and they are sworn to protect you."

"Then there is not a problem. I agree that the journey for a large group would be fraught with danger but one determined warrior such as you should have no difficulty and, as I am sure that during the winter we will end up having to eat some of these beasts you can bring more horses and warriors when you return after the snows."

Pol and his remaining few warriors had spent a more comfortable night than they had expected for there were still some shelters left from the time of the fort. The camp and the fort had been dismantled but the shelters and huts erected for the slaves had been left. They had even had warm food for one of their number was a fine fisherman and able to catch their meal. Pol would have been happy but for the fire and the watchtower. When they had approached the old fort in the darkness they had seen immediately that it had been abandoned but who was in the tower? As dawn had broken they had seen the thin spiral of smoke dark against the snowy hillside. It worried Pol for it made no sense. If the Romans had returned in numbers then they would have fortified the fort. He regretted not investigating the previous night; he made a decision. Aodh would have to come down the trail to meet them and it would make sense if they could eliminate whoever was at the tower. He shouted, "Mount up we will ride back up the trail and meet with Aodh. But be on your guard for I intend to see just who is there at the tower."

The seventeen men quickly mounted their tired mounts. Pol knew that many of the horses would have to be killed soon for they were almost lame. He glanced at the warriors; they were in a poor state too. A lack of food, constant combat and some wounds meant that they were not the fine fighting force they had been in the heady, successful days of summer and the destruction of Cataractonium.

As he led the ala from the tower Julius detailed Cassius and his turma to follow the river to the old fort. "We will travel down the trail. These are the only two routes that she can have taken. I know the snow will have hidden tracks which is why we need to be careful."

The snow helped their stealth for the soft snow, which was quite deep in places, masked the noise of their hooves. Cassius, in the river, had no such problem for the river was so fast flowing that it made a crashing sound as the fresh water tumbled over rocks and stones. In his heart Julius was convinced that, having established a lead, the wily Queen would have hastened south as soon as the dawn broke. It was with some surprise that he saw the scout in the river, some way ahead, raise his arm, and Cassius draw his sword. He waved the turma into a line and, drawing his own sword, moved forward slowly all his senses alert to danger.

The Brigante scout was tired and he was worried about his horse which seemed to be favouring its foreleg. He was watching for danger to his horse rather than the Romans as Pol had suggested. He paid for his error with his life as the Javelin plucked him from his saddle. Suddenly the small group of warriors found themselves assaulted on all sides by the Roman cavalry. They fought bravely enough but they were outnumbered by troopers, who were refreshed and rested, who had eaten and were eager to revenge themselves upon the hated sorceress.

Julius shouted, “I want prisoners. Do not kill them all!”

Pol was a wily warrior and had placed himself in the middle just in case they were ambushed. In the event there was little he could do to avoid the ambush but he was determined to save himself. He saw the turma in the river which ruled out an escape west and so he headed his horse east, towards the trees and the ridge. There was one luckless trooper in his way and he made the mistake of slicing with his spatha at Pol’s head. A small man anyway he was able to duck beneath the blade and he jabbed the spear into the trooper’s chest. The head went deeply in and was ripped from Pol’s hand. When he saw the gap he kicked his horse on and he found himself free of the fray.

Livius had despatched his opponent and, seeing the warrior fleeing, raced after him. Livius was proud of his horse, Night star, for he had trained it, under Sergeant Cato’s tuition, to respond to his body without the need for reins. Kicking forward he released the reins and took his javelin from its scabbard. Night Star loved to run and he was soon catching the horse which was tiring. Drawing back his arm he threw the javelin at the horse. Pol looked over his shoulder as he saw Livius and he jinked his horse to the right. The javelin carried on its course but instead of hitting the horse it plunged into Pol’s leg and carried on into the tired mount. The beast reared in pain and Pol was thrown to the ground. Livius was upon him in a moment and he quickly disarmed the wounded man.

One of Livius’ troopers rode up. “You alright sir?”

“Yes Aulus, fetch the horse and we’ll take our prisoner back.”

When they rode up Livius saw that the only prison they had was his own and that only six horses had survived. Even as he approached the turmae he could see that they had only lost one man, the trooper killed by Pol, in the encounter.

"Well done Julius. Will he live?"

"Just a spear to the leg."

"Capsarius. Bandage the warrior's leg. Salvius take your turma to the fort and find the Queen." Turning to the wounded warrior he said, "Where is the Queen?"

In answer the wounded warrior spat. "Do you want me to loosen his tongue Prefect?"

"No Livius. We will wait for Salvius and then return to Gaelwyn. He is far more persuasive than we." At the mention of Gaelwyn's name Pol showed fear for the first time and Julius smiled. "You know Gaelwyn eh? Well he is here and he hates traitorous rebels and more than that he hates your Queen. You can talk now or talk later but talk you will." The Brigante paused and then shook his head but Julius noted that he did not look as confident.

By the time Salvius returned the turmae were ready to ride. "No sign of her sir. It looks like these were the only ones who were there. No tracks, apart from theirs could be seen." He saw the disappointment on Julius' face. "She may have slipped away in the night sir. There was no way we could watch everywhere."

"I know Salvius. We will take this one back to the tower and find out."

The closer they were to the tower the more apprehensive Pol became. He could smell the wood smoke and he knew that soon he would be interrogated by a Brigante. He prayed to the Allfather that he would not betray his Queen and his comrades who he knew were somewhere nearby. He suddenly had the thought that Aodh had deliberately not told him of the secret place for just such an occasion. It, strangely, made him feel better for it meant that Aodh knew that any warrior has a breaking point.

Julius threw the wounded man to the ground in front of Gaelwyn, Gaius and Marcus. "He will not tell us where the Queen is to be found."

Without looking up Gaelwyn said, "Ailis take the boys to the river to collect some water. Gaius will come for you when we leave."

Ailis looked sympathetically at the wounded warrior and the icy look on Gaelwyn's face and was about to object when she remembered how Decius had died and the fate that they had nearly suffered. "Come on boys we have a job to do."

Gaelwyn did not say a word. He just placed the spear head in the embers of the fire. Pol's eyes were wide with fear. The ala had dismounted and were standing around in a circle, intrigued about the methods Gaelwyn would employ. When the head was glowing bright red he said to the capsarius, "Take off his bandage." Everyone seemed to be holding his breath. The capsarius looked for a moment as though he was going to object but a quick look at the Prefect ensured that he performed the task.

"I am not going to ask a question yet I am going to help you. Capsarius hold his shoulders. Livius hold his legs." When the man could not struggle Gaelwyn threw a piece of wood at the Prefect. "If you would put this between his teeth Prefect we wouldn't want him biting his tongue off would we?" When Pol had the wood between his teeth, his eyes wide with terror wondering what Gaelwyn was going to do, Gaelwyn took the spear from the fire. "Your leg is bleeding, quite badly and the capsarius there will have to keep tightening the bandage. It might become infected and you might lose the leg and we don't want that so I will help you. I will seal the wound with this red hot blade and save your leg. Had I wine I could give you that for the pain but I have not and so my friend you will have to suffer this." He suddenly put the flat head of the spear on to the wound. Immediately there was the smell of burning hair and flesh. Pol tried to lift himself against the weight of the three men and his eyes rolled back into his head with the pain. "You can thank me later for saving your leg. Livius remove his breeks." Livius pulled the soiled and bloodied breeks revealing the warrior's genitals.

"Prefect you may remove the wood now for we need him to speak."

The Prefect was impressed by the calm quality of Gaelwyn's voice which seemed to make it more chilling. There was no threat and no anger just a quiet cold determination.

Pol suddenly pleaded, "Please, please."

"Please what? Stop? But all I have done is to save your leg."

"Do not hurt me. Please."

"In saving your leg I had to cause some pain. Isn't that better, to suffer a little pain and survive than suffer with great pain? Now I will put the blade back into the fire because it is not hot enough and I will tell you what I will do next." The blade hissed into the fire. "The leg has been repaired but I notice that you have two testicles there which I am sure you do not need but I don't want the wound to become infected therefore I will cut them off with the hot blade. It will seal the wound and prevent the wound from becoming poisoned. Am I not a kind man, Brigante?"

"Please! No!"

Gaelwyn withdrew the spear and slowly moved it up the healthy leg of the warrior. Pol could feel the heat from the blade and, when he looked at Gaelwyn, he could see that the Brigante scout was being careful not to touch the leg, almost as though he was being kind. The closer it came to his testicles the more he struggled but he was firmly held. "I would not struggle for I am an old man and my hands are stiffer these days than they were. If I slip then you may lose more than your testicles. Now do hold still for I am almost there."

Pol could feel the heat and he could suddenly smell the burning as the blade touched and singed the hairs. "I will tell all! Please stop! I will tell all that I know!"

Plunging the spear head hissing into the stained snow between Pol's legs, Gaelwyn stood up. "He's all yours Prefect."

Looking at the scout with even greater respect Julius said, "Livius give the man his breeks and you speak."

Pol could not get the words out quickly enough. "The Queen and Aodh sent us ahead last night to the fort. They were to join us today and meet us at the fort. They had somewhere they were going to hide but I do not know where it is. Believe me!"

"Who is with the queen?"

"There is Aodh and her two servants and eight warriors. The rest are dead." His sobs and the puddle of urine told Julius that he was probably telling the truth.

"Sounds right to me Prefect. And with this snow they could be anywhere."

"You are right Marcus. She is a cunning opponent. Tie his arms and mount him on his horse." Julius idly kicked snow into the fire and looked around at the hills. Suddenly he roared, "Morwenna this is not over! We will find you! I swear by all that I hold dear! Gaelwyn, go with Livius and scout around the lake. See if you can find tracks. We will head back to Brocauum. Do not waste time looking for her but join us. I hope to be with the Legate by dark."

"Aye. I will look but the snow makes tracking almost impossible. She could be anywhere."

"The bitch is probably watching us even now."

"In that case Gaius she heard my oath and she knows I will find her."

Chapter 20

The Legate had been at Brocauum for three days when the snows which had fallen with such force on the ala unleashed their power on the Carvetii stronghold. There were no deep valleys and high mountains to channel the snow and it swept across the moor land unchecked driving the snow into banks as high as a man. "I hope the Prefect has found some shelter from this storm Titus."

"He struck me sir, as a resourceful man."

"Indeed and so young too." He warmed his hands on the glowing brazier and became more business like. "We have how many captives?"

"There are twenty here and almost two hundred at Morbium."

"They will fetch a fine price." Titus looked askance at the legate. "No not here. Prices are far too low. No I shall send them to Rome. Some of these warriors will make gladiators and the rest all have strong backs. The Emperor prefers Celts to Dacians. Those from Dacia have to be constantly chained and watched. The Celts soon accept our ways. Now about the leaders. The Prefect said that there were leaders here. Do you recognise any?"

Titus became embarrassed; it was only in the battle around Morbium that he had bothered to look at the enemy. Until then he had been safely ensconced behind walls. "No sir."

He was relieved to hear the Legate agree, "No me neither. The Prefect and his men were the closest to them we will await his return."

"If he does return sir. There may be more rebels in the hills."

"I daresay these auxiliaries know the land and the people. They have, after all, been here a lot longer than we have."

"The settlement is a little crowded sir."

"I know and the cohort from the Ninth feels a trifle superfluous, after all it is the Tungrians I shall be leaving here as a garrison."

"You have decided then sir?"

“Yes Morbium is all very well for the eastern side of the north of this land but we need something in the middle. Luguvalium can be supplied and reinforced by sea as can Morbium but here it is exposed. We need a whole cohort here, perhaps more. It may be that I station the Prefect’s cavalry here.”
“They are much depleted sir. Has Rome mentioned reinforcements and replacements?”
“I think the Emperor is still busy with the funeral games for the Emperor Domitian but the slaves should encourage the Imperial book-keepers to be a little more generous eh? And now we await the return of our horse.”

The next evening the Legate heard the shout from the main gates. “Cavalry approaching!”
By the time the Legate and Tribune had arrived at the entrance the weary, snow driven travellers were dismounting, their exhaustion evident. “Children and a woman!”
“Is that the Queen, Legate?”
Laughing at the awe in Titus’ voice Appius said, “No I remember seeing her on the field at Eboracum, she was a red head. I believe this is the family which was abducted by the Caledonii. We may have an interesting and diverting tale this evening. Welcome Prefect.”
“Sir!”
“No Queen then?”
“No sir, sorry sir.”
“I am sorry that was not a criticism. Come to the headman’s home I have commandeered it and bring the er well the rest.”
Once they were in the warmth Julius introduced everyone. “The is the Legate, Appius Mocius Camillus. This is the former Prefect Marcus Aurelius Maximunius, the Brigante scout Gaelwyn, Former Decurion Princeps Gaius Metellus Aurelius and his wife Ailis. The three boys are their children and the son of Decurion Macro.”

"Sit sit. Annius bring some blankets and warm drinks we cannot have people freezing to death in this forsaken piece of the Empire." Soon they were all warmer and the children lay, asleep at their mother's feet. The Legate smiled; he had never had time for a family but the sight of the boys and the mother made him wish that, perhaps he had done so. "So Tribune," Marcus started at the use of his former title. "Yes Tribune I recognised the name. There are not many leaders who are so renowned that they have an ala named after them. I am indeed honoured to meet you. So you managed to rescue the family," his sweeping arm expansively took in the family.

"Yes sir. We had to travel all the way to Caledonia but we succeeded. There are still many Brigante captives there."

"I know. I know. I am afraid that a reprisal raid to rescue them is out of the question for the moment. All we can do is to hold on to what we have and hold on by our fingertips at that."

"We could not have managed it without the heroic sacrifice of Decurion Macro," Marcus gestured at the sleeping Young Decius, "the boy's father. I believe he deserves an honour for his action."

The Legate put his fingers together and held them under his chin. "Uhm. Would this be the same Decurion who assaulted a sentry and broke out of Cataractonium by any chance?"

"Sir, Decurion Macro was not arrested. He was placed in the cells for his own protection. He was upset because his son had been kidnapped. I don't think the sentry actually complained."

"A little lame Prefect but… so this Decurion Macro did not desert then?"

"No sir."

"Was he on some sort of mission? Perhaps ordered by his Prefect?"

"That is it exactly sir."

"Good well in that case we can arrange for a decoration which will, of course, mean a small stipend for his son. Now about the Queen."

“We, that is the Tribune and myself, believe that she is hiding somewhere in the land of the lakes and will go, in the spring to either Mona or to Caledonia.”
“Why those places?”
“Mona is her spiritual home sir and she is an ally of Calgathus and Lulach.”
“Any chance of finding her?”
“In the winter? No sir. In the spring? Probably.”
“Well we will have to leave that. Now a more pressing matter. You have brought one prisoner back? Is he one of the leaders of the rebellion?”
“No sir, just a warrior.”
“Tomorrow, when you are rested we will need to find the leaders and punish them.”

The following day the snow had abated and the day was clear and blue. The Legate had ordered the cohort of the Ninth to gather all the males in the stronghold and bring them to the headman’s house. There were over a hundred of them and they looked in terror at the hardened faces of the legionaries who were lined up around them. When Gaelwyn and Julius emerged some of them paled.
The legate stood on the steps. “We have been awaiting the return of the Prefect and his Brigante associate, Gaelwyn”; the Brigante looked in puzzlement at Julius who shrugged, “I will ask you once and once only which of the men before me are your leaders. I wish them to step forward.”
No-one moved. Julius and Gaelwyn had spotted Colla trying to hide amongst the others, towards the back. Their eyes bored into him, letting him know that they had recognised him.
“Obviously your leaders have not got the courage to reveal themselves, a pity. I now ask you to identify them for me.” Again there was silence and shuffling of feet. “Oh what I forgot to mention was that if I do not receive cooperation from you then the

Prefect and, er, Gaelwyn will identify the leaders for me and I will decimate the male population."

This time there was confused silence until Gaelwyn coughed and said, "That means one in every ten men will be crucified. Sorry sir."

Smiling behind his hand Appius said, "Thank you Gaelwyn, clarity is all important." Turning back to the crowd who were now visibly rattled, he continued, "One out of every ten men will be crucified and their families sold into slavery."

There was a collective scream from the women and a murmur of outraged anger from the men. "Well Prefect."

Colla stepped forward. "I am the one you want. I am Colla chief of these people."

The Prefect said, "You are one of the ones we want. Should I identify the others?" Six men reluctantly stepped forward. "Where is the leader Ownie?"

One of the leaders spat out, "Look in the valley you will see his head on a spear!"

The legate looked at the Prefect. "We had a small skirmish before we pursued the Queen he must have been of those we killed."

"Any more Prefect?"

"No sir, that looks to be it."

"You are very lucky people of the Carvetii and Brigante for it is in my power to sell into slavery everyone who participated in the rebellion whether leader or just warrior or even a woman who made some arrows but I am disposed, after talking to those who know you," he gestured towards Marcus and Gaelwyn, "to leniency. However, as you have demonstrated that I cannot trust you, yet. I am leaving a cohort of Tungrians here. You will assist them to build a fort and they will ensure that you are all the good citizens I know you to be. First Spear take these men away."

The next day the snows had started to melt a little and the people of Brocauum awoke to the sound of hammering. By the time the sun had fully risen and the blue sky was filled with thin wispy clouds, they could see on the hillside above the town eight crosses moving up the hill, carried by legionaries. The prisoners marched along the road which traversed the hill for the Legate wanted everyone who used the road to see the power of Rome. Even as they watched they saw the seven leaders taken there and one by one held down on the crosses. As soon as the first nail was hammered into Colla's ankles they heard the scream which echoed through the empty chilly hills. Women hid their faces in husband's shoulders and children crouched fearfully behind their parents. When the last scream had stopped they heard more hammering but this time no scream. One by one the crosses were lifted in to their holes and the soil and stones packed around them. When the eighth one was erected they peered to see who it was for only seven leaders had been taken. A young woman with sharper eyes than the rest screamed as she saw the headless corpse of Ownie nailed to the cross.

"Carvetii and Brigante look upon this hill. This is a warning of the danger of rebellion and, as you can see, death does not prevent punishment. As well as my soldiers let this serve as a reminder as you go about your daily work. Rome is here to stay and all rebellion and rebels will be treated in this way."

Epilogue

In the cave, sheltered from the harsh winds buffeting the land, Morwenna and her acolytes sat naked around the fire burning the secret herbs and fungi. Their guards were banished to the entrance as they dreamed their dream and communed with the Mother. Despite the cold the hot perfumed sweat dripping from their bodies spoke of the powerful spell they were creating. The three distended bellies all showed the first sings of new life and the spell would ensure that the three new life forms would be part of the circle, they would be part of the mother.

At the cave entrance none of the Brigante guards would have dared to turn around and witness the mystery. They would all stand there until summoned back to the warmth or die frozen. Tadgh, the new leader, had had his instructions clearly laid out by Aodh before he departed.

Aodh, for his part was leading his two horses through the pass which led north from the land of the Carvetii. He had performed his duties to Morwenna and her acolytes and when they were sure he had planted his seed in all of them he was dismissed to perform his next task and lay the groundwork for the spring offensive which would see Caledonii, Votadini and Selgovae join forces with the Brigante for a new uprising to destroy the Romans.

Decius Lucullus was hiding. He was cursing this new legate who had sent his men to look for him and his gold. There had been no chance to find a ship of any description in Deva and he and his small band of warriors and their mules, laden with gold, were looking for a safe place in which to winter. The mountains around Wyddfa were ringed with soldiers seeking the gold and the mines from whence they had come. He suspected that his uncle had left some written clue which the new legate had discovered; whatever the reason his future lay not in the land of the Ordovices. Further south there were just too many Romans and he and his small group of mercenaries had been forced to take a decision they did not wish to take, they were heading north where there were fewer Romans and more barbarians! Decius just prayed to the Allfather for a ship somewhere on the west coast, a ship which could outrun the Classis Britannica.

"Julius you cannot resign! What would we do without you?"

"Kind words, Salvius, but think of the deaths I caused this year and the misery I brought to these lands because of my selfish and unjustified pursuit of Modius. No it is the right and the honourable thing to do. Besides my father is getting old and seeing Ailis and the boys with Gaius I am mindful of my family obligations. I ought to be there for him."

"But the ala."

"The ala will go on, as it did after Marcus left. Besides there will be so many new recruits that it will take a new leader to bring out the best of them."

"We will miss you sir. You have been a good leader."

"I don't know about that Salvius if I were a good leader then the best soldier in the ala would be alive today and not lying in the back of beyond. But I will miss the country and the ala but most of all I shall miss my friends like you and Marcus, Gaius and Gaelwyn. I will miss the keen officers like Livius and Cassius. I will even miss those who have cursed me like Sergeant Cato but I will do the honourable thing and I will go. I leave for Eboracum in the morning."

"You will stay with me until we have rebuilt your home and this time it will be even stronger."

"Thank you Marcus. I will not argue with you. I am just grateful that we have a home in which to winter."

“Aye many Brigante will die this winter for the Caledonii stole their cattle and many men died. Families will suffer because they have no food.”

“I know Gaelwyn but that is the price rebels pay.”

“Not true Marcus. The rebels are dead. It is the price their families pay. And it is a high one.”

“What I do know Marcus, and Gaelwyn, is that I will ensure that my family will never again suffer.” Drawing the Sword of Cartimandua from its scabbard he added, “I thought I had finished with this but I can see that it still needs to be wielded and, until Decius comes of an age to own it I will continue to use the Sword of Cartimandua.”

The End

Author's note

The Brigante did rebel in the mid to late 90s but the reason was not necessarily the Caledonii. Much of Agricola's gains were lost in the six years following his departure, mainly due to the withdrawal of legions from Britannia. Coriosopitum was burned in the mid nineties and shortly after a horde buried beneath the fort (the fort was rebuilt in 108). It was considered the best way to look after money- no banker's bonuses then!

Morwenna is, of course, like her mother Fainch, fictitious but the religion which she is part of was not and Druids, male and female were powerful figures.

Seton is based upon the submerged village off the north east coast between Hartlepool and Seton Carew. There is a submerged forest and it would have been one of the larger settlements upon that coast.

As always in my books, and by the way thanks for reading them, they are works of fiction. I know that they are not necessarily totally accurate but that is not by intention, more by incompetence!

Griff Hosker December 2014

Other books by Griff Hosker

If you enjoyed reading this book, then why not read another one by the author?

Ancient History

The Sword of Cartimandua Series (Germania and Britannia 50A.D. – 130 A.D.)

Ulpius Felix- Roman Warrior (prequel)
Book 1 The Sword of Cartimandua
Book 2 The Horse Warriors
Book 3 Invasion Caledonia
Book 4 Roman Retreat
Book 5 Revolt of the Red Witch
Book 6 Druid's Gold
Book 7 Trajan's Hunters
Book 8 The Last Frontier
Book 9 Hero of Rome
Book 10 Roman Hawk
Book 11 Roman Treachery
Book 12 Roman Wall
Book 13 Roman Courage

The Aelfraed Series (Britain and Byzantium 1050 A.D. - 1085 A.D.

Book 1 Housecarl
Book 2 Outlaw
Book 3 Varangian

The Wolf Warrior series (Britain in the late 6th Century)
Book 1 Saxon Dawn
Book 2 Saxon Revenge

Book 3 Saxon England
Book 4 Saxon Blood
Book 5 Saxon Slayer
Book 6 Saxon Slaughter
Book 7 Saxon Bane
Book 8 Saxon Fall: Rise of the Warlord
Book 9 Saxon Throne
Book 10 Saxon Sword

The Dragon Heart Series
Book 1 Viking Slave
Book 2 Viking Warrior
Book 3 Viking Jarl
Book 4 Viking Kingdom
Book 5 Viking Wolf
Book 6 Viking War
Book 7 Viking Sword
Book 8 Viking Wrath
Book 9 Viking Raid
Book 10 Viking Legend
Book 11 Viking Vengeance
Book 12 Viking Dragon
Book 13 Viking Treasure
Book 14 Viking Enemy
Book 15 Viking Witch
Bool 16 Viking Blood
Book 17 Viking Weregeld
Book 18 Viking Storm
Book 19 Viking Warband
Book 20 Viking Shadow
Book 21 Viking Legacy

The Norman Genesis Series
Hrolf the Viking
Horseman

The Battle for a Home
Revenge of the Franks
The Land of the Northmen
Ragnvald Hrolfsson
Brothers in Blood
Lord of Rouen
Drekar in the Seine
Duke of Normandy

The Anarchy Series England 1120-1180
English Knight
Knight of the Empress
Northern Knight
Baron of the North
Earl
King Henry's Champion
The King is Dead
Warlord of the North
Enemy at the Gate
The Fallen Crown
Warlord's War
Kingmaker
Henry II
Crusader
The Welsh Marches
Irish War
Poisonous Plots
Princes' Revolt
Earl Marshal

Border Knight 1190-1300
Sword for Hire
Return of the Knight
Baron's War
Magna Carta

Welsh War
Henry III

Modern History
The Napoleonic Horseman Series
Book 1 Chasseur a Cheval
Book 2 Napoleon's Guard
Book 3 British Light Dragoon
Book 4 Soldier Spy
Book 5 1808: The Road to Corunna
Waterloo

The Lucky Jack American Civil War series
Rebel Raiders
Confederate Rangers
The Road to Gettysburg

The British Ace Series
1914
1915 Fokker Scourge
1916 Angels over the Somme
1917 Eagles Fall
1918 We will remember them
From Arctic Snow to Desert Sand
Wings over Persia

Combined Operations series 1940-1945
Commando
Raider
Behind Enemy Lines
Dieppe
Toehold in Europe
Sword Beach
Breakout
The Battle for Antwerp

King Tiger
Beyond the Rhine

Other Books
Carnage at Cannes (a thriller)
Great Granny's Ghost (Aimed at 9-14-year-old young people)
Adventure at 63-Backpacking to Istanbul

For more information on all of the books then please visit the author's web site at http://www.griffhosker.com where there is a link to contact him or you can Tweet me at @HoskerGriff

Printed in Great Britain
by Amazon

66171421R00151